THEIVES PROFIT

Profit Logbook Series
Book Two

Bruce C. Davis

Brick Cave Media
brickcavebooks.com

2018

Brick Cave Media
brickcavebooks.com
2018

Acknowledgements

Thanks to Al Kalar, for giving the books their first life, and Brick Cave, especially Bob, for seeing their potential and giving them a second incarnation.

THEIVES PROFIT

Profit Logbook Series
Book Two

Bruce C. Davis

Brick Cave Media
brickcavebooks.com

CHAPTER 1

"Place your bets, ladies and gentlemen, place your bets please," said the croupier in his singsong patter. "Nobody wins if nobody bets!"

He was far too pretty. His hair was perfectly combed and static sprayed in place, and his nails were buffed to a high sheen. His cologne suggested sandalwood and spice; it clashed with the stale sweat and machine oil that wafted from the freighter mechanic sitting next to me. He was losing badly, and turned to glare at me between plays. My head ached and felt heavy in the Earth-standard gravity maintained by the casino's field generators. The constant din didn't help matters; a pulsating blend of bells and buzzing half-heard conversations, overlaid with syncopated music. The air was thick with the smells of too many people in too little space.

"Bets, please, ladies and gentlemen. Last call!" sang the croupier, as his hand hovered over the roulette wheel. My own hand twitched toward the large pile of chips I'd collected over the past few hours.

Sylvia's voice whispered "Wait for it," in my ear through the datalink implanted in my right mastoid bone. Easy for her to say. She was aboard our ship, the *Profit*, and artificial intelligences never got headaches anyway. My fingertips tingled as the nanofibers in them picked up tiny surges of current passing through the table to small electromagnets embedded in the wheel.

"Black," whispered Sylvia.

I slid a handful of fifty New Yuan chips onto the black bar just as the croupier spun the wheel and dropped the ball in one smooth motion.

"No more bets; the ball is in play. Round and round it goes, where it stops nobody knows but the Lord, and he won't tell," said the croupier. He glanced at me and licked his lips nervously. I allowed myself a faint smile. This had been a bad day for the Golden Moon Casino, and his employers would not be happy with him, even if it wasn't his fault.

Instead of watching the ball, I rubbed my aching temples. I already knew where the damned thing would drop anyway. I was dead tired and less than halfway to our goal of a hundred thousand New Yuan. The money no longer excited me. Even the satisfaction of cheating a cheater had lost its charm. This was too much like work.

"Seven, black," chirped the croupier. "Winner!"

I reached out to rake in the pile of chips as the stickman shoved it in my direction. I glanced up at the croupier, but he was no longer looking at me; his eyes were focused on something behind me. Just as I began to turn around, a massive hand clamped down on my left shoulder.

The hand was attached to a mountain of muscle in a dark Cheoy Lee suit. If the guy wasn't genetically augmented, he must have spent most of his waking hours in the gym. His head was shaved fashionably smooth and his face had the bland, bored look of a professional doing his job.

"Mr. Mbele." His voice was surprisingly soft and mellow.

"I'm with casino security. My employers would like a word with you."

"Not now," I said, hauling in chips with my free arm. "I'm busy." The grip on my shoulder tightened. Pain shot down my arm to my fingertips, and I lost all movement below the shoulder. *Oh, well,* I thought, *It was worth a try.*

"I'm afraid I must insist, sir," said the muscle in the expensive suit.

"Okay, okay," I gasped. "But this is going in my report to the Hospitality Commission. Not good for Lunar tourism." If that worried him, he hid it well.

I flipped a fifty yuan chip to the croupier. I'd seen that in the realies, and always wanted to do it. In the realies, the croupier caught it in the air and made some witty remark. This guy bobbled it, and the chip rattled off the roulette wheel.

The security man eased his grip, and I could feel my fingers again. The nanofibers retracted into the pores of my fingertips, none the worse for wear. Mr. Security gestured away from the table. I followed his lead, leaving my chips to the stickman. They'd be tallied and credited to me if I got the chance to collect. Cheoy Lee Suit stayed at my elbow, guiding me unobtrusively across the casino floor toward the back wall. A second goon in a dark suit fell in behind us, just out of reach.

We crossed the great rotunda of the gaming area. The crowd swirled around us, parting before my intimidating escort. It was a mid-week crowd: hard-core, low-stakes players from the Lunar working class. The high-stakes tables lay silent, behind golden velvet ropes. The high rollers they catered to were still in bed, sleeping off the previous night's action.

We passed off-duty spacers in worn flight suits, water miners and tunnel riggers in heavy work pants, night traders jabbering on their datalinks as they fed credits into hologame consoles. Here and there we brushed aside a little knot of tourists from Earth or the LaGrange arcologies, mostly older matrons wearing the latest style of synthofur wraps and cultured glowgems.

The Golden Moon Casino took its name seriously. Gold gleamed from every surface. Overhead, the shade was open and the nighttime lunar sky filled the domed skylight. A full Earth hung like a shiny blue bauble in the dark black of space. My escorts seemed unmoved by the sight. We reached the edge of the gaming floor and the second security man pushed forward. We paused as he opened a concealed door in a decorative cornice near one of the cashier's cages. He stepped back, allowed us to pass and then followed, closing the door behind him—smooth and efficient, no wasted motion, and no chance for me to get a grip on him.

These guys were good. Casino security usually meant greasy little men in synthetic fiber jumpsuits. Professional muscle in thousand-yuan suits meant that we'd attracted the wrong kind of attention. We'd figured on some fallout from the casino, but by staying at a crowded, low-stakes table and spreading our winnings over several hours, we'd hoped that they would absorb the loss as a cost of doing business. Besides, to bust us, they'd have to admit that their tables were rigged.

"Zack!" Sylvia whispered in my ear. "What's going on? Who are these guys?"

"I don't know," I said subvocally, the nanos picking up subtle movements of my vocal cords and transmitting the words through my link. I glanced at the goon on my left. There was no indication he'd heard anything. "Have Deuce bring the scooter around to the casino's service entrance in case I need a quick exit. Tell him to come armed, but keep the hardware out of sight. How's your visual?"

"Sharp and clear," she responded, after checking the image picked up by the contact lens camera in my right eye. Everything I saw was transmitted over my link. Sylvia could also download video to me if necessary.

"Good," I said. "Start recording, encrypted file, my voiceprint only, just in case we need some evidence."

"You got it, Boss."

The passageway had rough walls, an old construction tunnel blasted out of solid moon rock, the gravity grid exposed in the floor. The security cams were plainly visible, slung from the ceiling instead of concealed behind decorative geegaws. The walls weren't even painted, a sharp contrast to the opulence of the casino floor. Neither of my escorts spoke.

A small blinking light in the lower corner of my right visual field confirmed that Sylvia was recording. I turned my head to give her a good look at Mr. Security's face. I didn't ask him to smile for the camera. The passageway took a sharp turn to the right and ended at a large door. It was real wood, highly polished, and carved in intricate Chinese symbols invoking good fortune and long life. I glanced back as the man behind me muttered into his sleeve. The door unlocked with a clunk that echoed down the passage. The second goon pushed it open and waved me through.

The small room beyond was crowded by an oversized security console. Three high-resolution holomatrices showed views of the casino. Behind the console, slouched in a padded desk chair, sat the most beautiful man I had ever seen. He was Chinese, with the classic features and flawless skin that could only come from high-priced genetic augmentation. His jet-black hair was drawn back in a long queue. He was dressed in a traditional robe, heavily embroidered with gold and silver thread. Matching slippers encased his small feet. He stood as we entered, facing me. His movements were graceful, like a dancer, or trained fighter.

"Mr. Mbele," he said, and bowed almost imperceptibly— just enough to convey greeting while emphasizing his superiority. "So good of you to come. My name is Wu."

"As in Kwai Chang Wu," Sylvia whispered in my ear. "Youngest son of Kwai Hong, founder and CEO of Kwai Hong Holdings. This isn't good, Zack."

"Not good" was an understatement. People to whom Kwai Hong took a dislike had a habit of dying in particularly gaudy ways.

"Does your father approve of manhandling guests at his casino, Mr. Kwai?" I asked. *What the hell. If we're busted, I might as well go for broke.*

He nodded slightly. "Your reputation is well deserved, Mr. Mbele. I should have known." He waved a well-manicured hand at one of the holomatrices. It filled with lines of text. "Zachariah Mbele," he read. "Born: New Pretoria, United Colonies, Mars. Your forebears were Zulu, I believe."

"My parents were Martians," I said coldly. Ethnic identity was a luxury available only to the Earthbound or the very rich. Out in the deep black, people were scarce and what you could do counted for more than where you came from.

Wu smiled indulgently. "Of course," he said, and continued, "You served in the Third Directorate Special Forces, trained by Metternich himself. And yet, after the Martian Revolution you disappeared for nearly two years, only to be liberated from Bruneault prison after the Reunification." He paused and smiled in my direction, a gesture that reminded me of a Komodo dragon I'd once seen in the New Pretoria zoo. I suppressed a shiver.

"By all appearances, you were one of Hans Metternich's golden boys. You should have been in the forefront of his Glorious Revolution. What did you do to fall from grace?"

I said nothing, my body remembering the biotank and the searing heat as the nanofibers bonded to my nervous system. I'd joined the Special Ops Corps as a true believer in truth, justice and the Martian Way, but left my ideals in that biotank as Metternich drove the Corps into madness and suspicion. I looked out for myself now.

Wu turned back to the holomatrix. "Currently, owner

and captain of the high-speed freighter *Profit*. I see you owe quite a lot of money to the New Houston Federated Bank, the lien holder on your ship."

"One hundred thousand yuan," I said.

"One hundred two thousand, four hundred and twenty seven New Yuan, to be exact," he said. He settled into the desk chair, tenting his fingers and tapping them against his upper lip. "You see, Mr. Mbele, I know a lot about you. For instance, I know you have found a way to defeat our roulette wheels and have cost this casino over thirty thousand New Yuan today." He raised a hand as I opened my mouth to speak. "Don't deny it, Mr. Mbele. Your winning percentage is sixty eight point seven over the past four hours. Even without our modifications to the wheels, it would be enough to attract attention."

"If you bust me, I'll have to tell the Gaming Commission about your modifications. I'm sure they'd be interested in looking at the inner workings of your wheels," I said, trying to sound confident.

He laughed, "You misunderstand the purpose of our chat. I don't plan to have you arrested. I want to hire you. I need someone with your talent for doing unconventional jobs."

My initial relief was replaced by cold anger. I knew that the smart thing to do was to thank him and to jump at the offer to work for Kwai Hong Holdings, or at least to listen to his proposal. But then, no one has ever accused me of doing the smart thing. Instead I said, "Sorry, the *Profit* is in for refit and I'm on sabbatical. Find someone else."

"Zack! Are you crazy?" Sylvia's voice was so loud that I almost winced. I damped her volume with a grind of my molars. Maybe she was right, but I hate being pushed around, especially by rich slime like Wu.

Wu sighed. "That's too bad. I hope your winnings will be enough to pay the balance of the loan on your ship. You won't be permitted to return to the gaming floor, of course. And we'll be informing the other casinos that you are barred from our floor." Which meant that I'd never be allowed in their doors, either. "You can expect to hear from the lien holder on your ship soon."

"What's he talking about, Sylvia?" I asked subvocally.

"Checking," she said. "Shit! New Houston Bank was bought out last week by Sang Wu Financial Group, a subsidiary of—"

"Kwai Hong Holdings," I completed the sentence out loud. Wu smiled broadly. He knew I was in communication with the *Profit* and clearly didn't care. "It seems that the lien on my ship has changed hands."

"Indeed."

"And if I accept your job?" I asked.

"The lien will be paid in full, with a bonus equal to the amount of the lien if the job is completed on time." His smug smile deepened the chill in the pit of my stomach.

"Sylvia," I said subvocally. "Any chance we can use the thirty thousand to refinance the loan?"

"Not a chance, Zack. Your credit is tanked. The lender put a freeze on you because of late payments. No one else will touch us."

"So what do I have to do?" I asked Wu through clenched teeth.

I hate it even more when the slime wins.

Wu's smile evaporated as he shifted in the chair, gesturing toward the holomatrix. More lines of text appeared. "In twelve standard days, the *Ulysses S. Grant,* a heavy freighter of the American Presidents Line, will arrive inbound from Ceres. She's carrying a shipping container. I will provide you with its lading number and access codes. I want you to obtain that container by any means necessary. Once you have it, you will place it in a sealed business container and transport it to our research facility on Kwai Hong One. Payment will be made on delivery. Get it there before the seventh of next month and the bonus will be paid as well.

Needless to say, this must be done discretely."

"No cops," I said.

"As you say." Wu looked away and made a dismissive gesture with his hand. "If you should fail, this meeting never took place."

"And then what? What if I change my mind and go to the *Federales*?" I knew better, but I had to ask. "Will you send Mr. Casino Security here to take care of me?"

Wu laughed at that, a chilly sound that sent another shiver through me. "Vincent? No, Vincent wouldn't hurt a fly. There are other ways of guaranteeing your cooperation. Aside from repossessing your precious ship, that is."

I believed him.

There wasn't much more to be said, unless we were going to threaten each other for the rest of the night. Vincent stepped forward and pressed a data stick and a casino voucher for my winnings into my hand. Wu turned his back and began studying the holomatrices. I'd been dismissed.

Vincent steered me out the door and down another side passage to the kitchen area. The cook staff studiously ignored us as we passed through swirling clouds of fragrant steam, a heavy door at the back, and then out to the service entrance. Deuce was there, big and broad, his blonde beard twisted into two braids that hung down to his chest. His head was bare, and shaved fashionably clean. He sat casually on the scooter, our three-wheeled all-purpose hauler. His pulse rifle was slung across the handlebars, covered by a scrap of tarp but still clearly visible—Deuce's idea of a concealed weapon.

Vincent came up on the balls of his feet and fingered the lapel of his jacket

Deuce gave him a hard look. I stepped between them before they incinerated each other. "Down boy."

"Everything Jake, LT?" Deuce pronounced each letter, El Tee, a holdover from the old days. Deuce had been with me since Special Forces Basic. He'd managed to avoid the

Black Ops squad that swept me up during the purges and was the first friendly face I saw as I walked out of Bruneault prison.

"We're golden here, Deuce. Let's get back to the ship."

I climbed aboard the scooter and he gunned the engine, keeping a wary eye on Vincent as we pulled away. A few tight turns through service passageways brought us out on Armstrong Boulevard, Tycho City's main drag. Deuce merged into the traffic pattern, dodging in and out. He said nothing. That was Deuce, all business. He knew I'd tell him what he needed to know.

I just didn't feel like talking. Somehow, Kwai Chang Wu would pay for this.

CHAPTER 2

Overhead, the main city dome was three hundred meters high and holosimmed to look like the lunar sky. The effect was disconcerting, like driving Outside without a suit. Traffic was heavy, but Deuce made good time, dodging nimbly between larger and slower vehicles. The sounds and colors of Tycho City's main shopping district whirled around us. I'd long ago learned to set my datalink to privacy mode to keep from being swamped by the targeted spam that poured out of the stores and shopping arcos lining both sides of the broad street. High above the center of the Boulevard gleamed the silver arch of the Promenade, Tycho's enclave for the super rich. A single hour up there could cost more than the average Lunatic earned in a year.

The Boulevard ran straight to the spaceport, ending at the passenger terminal. Deuce swung right and slowed the scooter to a stop in front of the checkpoint for the commercial terminal. He flashed our registration number at the AI controlling the gate, and it let us pass. We sped past the rows of berthed ships, large and small, until we got to number VC-334, home sweet home—the *Profit.*

She was long and slim, a flattened cylinder with a pronounced bulge amidships where the gravity drive and reactor were housed. Her atmosphere wings were retracted to narrow stubs just aft of the bulge, the impulse engines used for fine maneuvering and landing folded into their recesses in the undercarriage. Her hull was flat black, with gold trim outlining the sally ports and cockpit. A trim, deadly looking ship. She took my breath away, as always.

She'd started her life as a fast interceptor in the Martian navy. I'd come by her the way that most war surplus is obtained; I stole her in the aftermath of the Reunification War. Fitting her out as a freighter and getting forged registration and commissioning documents for her had been expensive, to the tune of two hundred thousand yuan. I'd paid about half of the debt over the past four years, but decent jobs were few and far between lately, and I'd fallen behind on the loans.

Wu's offer stank like week-old vat meat, but the prospect of paying off the bank was too good to pass up. Besides, I didn't seem to have any other choice.

The ship's forward ramp was down, and Deuce drove straight up it. He parked the scooter in its stall and the recharge cable snaked out automatically, plugging into the hanger's main bus.

I jumped off the back, still seething.

"Sylvia!" I shouted. "Where's Cleo?"

"Cleo is in her quarters, Zack. And you needn't shout. My audio pickups are functioning perfectly." Sylvia sounded peeved. For the thousandth time, I wondered if it had been a good idea to program her with a female personality.

"Tell her to meet me in the salon right away. And burn a copy of the Wu recording for the cops, just in case."

"Sorry, Zack," she said. "He must have been wearing a personal scrambler. All I got was your end of the conversation. His face is a blur and the audio is gibberish."

I wasn't surprised. He obviously hadn't cared that I was in contact with Sylvia during the meeting. "Can you clean it up?" I asked.

"I doubt it. First glance, it looks like high quality gear. I may be able to tease out a few words."

Deuce stowed his rifle in the weapons locker and looked at me. He leaned casually against the bulkhead, his thick arms folded across his chest. He wouldn't ask, but I could see he was curious.

"Salon, ten minutes," I said to him. I still didn't feel like talking.

I turned and went aft to the ladder at the rear of the hold. The salon was one deck up. I ran up the ladder two steps at a time, paused at the top and looked to the right, along the catwalk that ran above the hold to the cockpit. I considered going that way to talk with Sylvia and download the data stick to her, but changed my mind and ducked through the hatch into the salon. I knew that Sylvia didn't really 'live' in the main computer up in the cockpit. Instead, she duplicated herself many times in independent data nodes all over the ship. But I still thought of the cockpit as her home, and preferred to have private conversations with her from the command seat.

I slapped the data stick into an input port next to the salon hatch and slumped down on the curved couch in the main seating area. The salon décor was Sylvia's doing, an elegant confection of pastel blue and sea green, with accents of wood tone browns and ochre. Textured fabric tapestries softened the curved metal bulkheads. A complex glass wall sculpture, a Diego Salazar original, hung on the bulkhead across from the couch. It had been a wedding gift from Eddie the Rabbit, who warned me later that I shouldn't try to have it appraised. Two active contour chairs faced the couch across a polished burl-wood table. The overhead and bulkhead lighting softened as the couch sensed my posture and assumed I wanted to rest.

"Full daylight," I ordered. The damned thing was keyed to Cleo's profile. I hardly spent any time in the salon anyway. The lights brightened. "Sylvia, see what you can find out about this container we're supposed to snatch. I want to know what's so damned important about it. And where's Cleo?"

"I'm right here." Her voice sang a contralto melody to turn a man's head. Her body then demanded his full attention. She must have been in the shower when Sylvia called her; she stepped into the salon wearing only a thin towel, her long black hair wet and clinging to her back. The towel barely reached to the tops of her perfect thighs. Her skin was cinnamon and velvet, and her eyes shone like moonlight on the ocean, the slight Oriental lift at the corners hinting at exotic mysteries beneath. She shifted around, tucking in the top of the towel to free her hands. For a brief second I felt an old familiar pang of longing and lust—then the sharper pain as I remembered why she was my ex-wife. There was a fine line between ecstasy and despair when a man got involved with Cleopatra Lee.

For all of her exotic beauty, Cleo was a dangerous woman. She'd never told me who trained her, but trained she was. An expert in weapons, both projectile and edged, she was also the best unarmed fighter I'd ever seen—better than the instructors who'd taught me a dozen different ways to kill a man. She bent forward to pick up a bottle of water from the tabletop, giving me a peek down the front of her towel.

"Jeez, Cleo," I said, looking away. "Put some clothes on, would you? Deuce won't be able to think straight if he sees you like that."

"But, darling, you said right away," she pouted and sipped her water.

My anger boiled over and I reached out to grab her wrist. I pulled her down onto the couch next to me—a reckless move, since she could have broken my hand without dropping her water, but I was on the edge of losing it

"Where were you tonight, 'darling'?" I snapped. "You were supposed to be at the casino, watching my back. Instead, I got snatched away from the tables by a couple of security goons and spent an enlightening half hour with the owner's son."

"I had a date. Besides, what was I supposed to do, hold them off while you took the money and ran?" She elbowed me in the chest. "Let go of me, damn it!"

I let go of her wrist, but shoved her back down on the couch when she tried to stand. I was mildly surprised that she allowed it. "You were supposed to let me know if I was attracting too much attention. I'd have backed off for a while," I said, then: "A date? I'm counting on you for backup in a big score, and you've got a date?"

"You wouldn't know a big score if it bit you in the ass," she said. "I was lining up a score of my own; a charter job at twice the usual rate."

"With you as the sweetener, I suppose," I spat back.

"Now you're just being crude and insulting," she said coldly. "He's a big shot with TransAstral. He'd throw a lot of business our way. It's called networking, Zack. You should try it sometime, instead of pissing off every passenger we've ever taken on."

"This is a freighter, not a damned pleasure liner." I slumped lower into the couch and rested a foot on the table. I knew she hated people putting their feet on the expensive salon furniture. "I needed your eyes tonight. As long as you're a member of this crew, you'll stick to the mission as planned."

"I'm not Deuce, Zack," she said, frowning at my foot. "I don't follow your orders like a bloody lapdog. And I'm not a crewmember. I'm part owner of this boat, and I've got a divorce decree to prove it." She couldn't resist rubbing that in. "I'll look out for my share as I see fit." She stood up. I didn't fight her. "I'm going to get dressed. If you can be civil after that, I may listen to the rest of your story." She walked toward the hatch leading aft. I almost let her have the last word, but I couldn't let it go.

"Kwai Hong Holdings bought the lien on the *Profit*," I said. "They've offered us a job that'll cancel the loan if we take it."

That stopped her. She turned to face me, hands on her hips. "All right, I'm listening."

"So am I, LT," Deuce said from the forward hatchway. "Hey, Cleo." He nodded in her direction. "Nice towel. So, what's the job?"

Cleo reddened slightly with anger. I felt sure it wasn't a blush.

I filled them in on my conversation with Kwai Chang Wu, and the offer of a bonus if we delivered the package before the seventh. Deuce whistled softly. Cleo sat in the chair across from me and lit a cigarette, but said nothing. I hadn't mentioned that the bonus would be enough for me to buy out her share of the *Profit*. The divorce decree included that option as well.

"How do you figure to snatch the goods?" Deuce asked as he sat on the arm of the other chair. "Those freighters are tough enough to thumb their noses at Fed cruisers."

"We can't hijack them in space, you dolt," said Cleo. "They'd have the *Federales* down on us before we got within a thousand kilometers of them." She glared at Deuce until he shrugged and sat properly in the chair.

"Cleo's right," I said. "We can't take them in space and we can't wait for the goods to be picked up. Too much risk of local law getting involved. Our best bet is to hijack the container after it's offloaded from the *Grant* but before it clears customs."

"Right." Cleo's voice dripped scorn. "It'll be so much easier to break into a Federal Customs installation. Get real, Zack."

"The customs holding yard is all torn up with construction on the new terminal." Deuce leaned forward and outlined an imaginary grid on the tabletop. "Might offer an opportunity."

"Sylvia?"

"On it, Boss," she answered. A second later she said, "Deuce is right. The yard is part of a major revamp of the freight terminal. Contracts to three big construction firms. This is interesting: customs hired a bunch of temporary security recently, and one of the subcontractors on the job is a specialist in security grid installation."

"Looks like the security grid's gonna be off-line while they upgrade the yard," said Deuce.

"When's that due to happen, Sylvia?" I asked.

"I don't know, Zack. That's top secret. Only the Station Chief would know for sure."

"I'll bet Wu's people know," I said. "And I'd stake my last can of air that it's the same time the *Grant* is in port." I rubbed my temples. I felt sure I was being set up, but didn't know why or what to do about it—yet. "Sylvia, what have you got on this container we're supposed to snatch?"

"Just a lading number and hold location on the *Grant*," answered Sylvia. "The actual bill of lading, shipper's identity, and recipient are encrypted. I've got a subroutine trying to crack it now."

"Any clues?" I asked.

"The point of origin is definitely Ceres. That narrows the possible shippers to four: TransAstral Parcel Service, Nucor, Ceres Mining and Manufacturing, and Zeneca-Hong Pharmaceuticals. They're the only operations on Ceres. There's no other commercial activity, and the only people living there are employees."

"We should concentrate on TransAstral and Nucor," said Cleo.

"Why?" asked Deuce.

"Kwai Hong owns ZHP and Ceres M&M," said Sylvia. "If Wu wanted something they carried, he wouldn't need us to get it."

"Maybe," I said. "Or maybe Wu wants to keep something

17

from Kwai Senior. We don't know anything for sure." I turned to Cleo. "How tight are you with your sugar daddy from TransAstral?"

"He's an acquaintance," she said.

"Whatever. Can you find out if they're expecting anything big in the next few days?"

She looked away for a moment, inhaling smoke and letting it out slowly. "I suppose so," she said finally. "But I don't like this."

"Neither do I. Just find out if the container is theirs. Deuce, see if you can learn when the security grid will be offline. Try the Guild Hall. Out-of-work spacers always seem to be tapped into the latest rumors."

Deuce nodded. "I'll ask around down at the Blue Booby, too. Maybe the new security guys drink there."

I grinned. "Don't get drunk. I need you sharp."

"No fear, LT."

"Never, Deuce."

"Have you figured out how you're going to get into a secure customs yard and back out again with a shipping container?" asked Cleo. "It's not like you can stuff the thing in your pocket."

"Misdirection, darling," I said as an idea began to take shape in my head. "We make them look at something else while we drive it right out the front gate."

Cleo snubbed out her cigarette in the ashtray that popped up from the arm of her chair. She stood and gave me a look I knew well, the one that said, 'You haven't got a clue.' She cinched up her towel and stalked from the salon.

Deuce watched her go, then turned to me. "So what's the plan?"

I shook my head. "I don't know yet, Deuce. Just see what you can find out about the security downtime."

"Right." He nodded, stood and started to walk off, but paused for a second as he stepped through the forward hatch. "Don't let her get to you, LT. She's still a shipmate.

She'll come through in a pinch."

I didn't answer, just nodded. That was the simple calculus by which Deuce lived: duty, honor, loyalty to his friends and shipmates. That and all the beer he could drink.

"Sylvia," I said after he was gone. "What would it take to change the lading number of a shipping container?"

"You mean reroute the shipment while it's still aboard the *Grant*?" She made a sound suspiciously like Cleo's sarcastic laugh. I made a mental note to delete that bit of programming."Forget it, Zack. Even if I could slice the *Grant's* security at this distance, the cargo manifest is encrypted separately."

"No," I said. "I mean once we have the container. What would it take to change the shipping label and lading number?"

"Get your nanos in contact with the label and I can make it read whatever you like," she said, sounding smug. "But what good will that do? You still have to get it by the customs inspectors. For that you'll need a copy of the shipping manifest that matches the bill of lading from the *Grant*, which we haven't got. And even if we did, it would still be encrypted."

"Yeah, I'm still working on that one," I sighed. Truth be told, I did have a plan of sorts, or at least a jumble of ideas that might be worked into a plan. I didn't want to say much to Sylvia yet. If everything went to hell, I didn't want too much information in her memory where a federal warrant could compel her to spill it. AI's might be smart, even loyal, but they were still property under the law and didn't have the right to remain silent if a magistrate ordered them to talk.

"What have you got on Kwai Chang Wu?" I asked, changing the subject.

"Do you want the whole bio, or just the high points?"

"Just the last few years," I said. "I don't care where he went to grammar school or who wiped his ass as a baby."

She laughed. "For the past couple of years he's been running a big chunk of his Daddy's company. He's head of Kwai Hong's operations on Ceres, C.O.O. of ZHP and Ceres M&M. Doing a good job of it, too. Profits are up, stock through the roof; nothing but happy times for Kwai Hong and its shareholders. There have been a few rumors of shady accounting and under-the-table deals, but nothing that stuck and less than you might expect after such a dramatic turnaround."

"How's that?" I asked.

"When Wu took over on Ceres, Kwai Hong's operations there were in the crapper. ZHP had lost a big patent fight and the mines were just about played out. CM&M was near bankruptcy. A few months later, the mines were producing again; a big new strike of high-grade ore and a proprietary extraction method that boosts recovery from old deposits. And ZHP bought out the same rival that had beaten it in patent court—at a bargain price, I might add."

"Interesting," I said. ""Any dirt on the buyout?"

"Nothing firm," Sylvia answered. "Officially, they ran into a cash-flow problem and ZHP bought up their debt. Unofficially, the rumors of under-the-table financial manipulation by Wu start at the same time."

"What about his personal life?" I asked.

"Nada. He spends most of his time on Ceres. Lives like a monk by all accounts. Occasional female companions, nothing long-term. No other known vices. He's all business and totally ruthless. There was a big scandal in his younger days; he used to be quite the party boy until he got mixed up in some sort of trouble in Kuala Lumpur about ten years ago. Almost went to jail but bought his way out of it with daddy's money. He was whisked away to Kwai Hong One, the company's LaGrange station. He dropped out of sight for a few years, then reemerged as the current boss on Ceres."

I grunted. "Nothing there we can use unless you can find

out what happened in KL. Otherwise it's ancient history."
A wave of fatigue washed over me and I stifled a yawn. My
head throbbed and my fingertips burned like fire. "Anything
else?"

"You're tired, Zack," said Sylvia, her voice modulating
from a crisp business tone to mother hen. "You've been
up for twenty-six hours. I'll keep searching the public
databases and flag anything of interest. You can look it over
after you've had some sleep. We have twelve days before the
Grant arrives. There's plenty of time."

"I guess you're right." My anger had burned out, leaving
only a dry husk of weariness. "Wake me in six hours, or if
Wu or any of his people try to get in touch."

"Yes, Boss," said Sylvia. "Good night."

I dialed down the salon lights as I left the compartment,
and walked aft toward my stateroom. As I passed Cleo's
door, I could hear her speaking to someone. Probably on
the comm to her 'acquaintance.' I almost knocked but then
remembered the last time she'd torn into me for interfering
with her life. I was too exhausted to fight, or even apologize
for twisting her wrist. I sighed. My relationships with women
other than Sylvia, the AI, were always self-destructive. I
stepped through the hatch to my room and collapsed on
the bunk.

CHAPTER THREE

Sylvia disobeyed orders and let me sleep for twelve hours. It was afternoon, ship's time, when I awoke, but still late morning Lunar time. I grumbled about uppity AIs as I shaved and dressed, knowing she could hear me. Inwardly, I had to admit that I felt better. And I didn't miss the pounding headache.

I stopped by the galley and ordered an egg-substitute omelet. Chickens were a rare commodity on the Moon. At least the mushrooms were fresh. I was feeding the dishes into the recycler when Sylvia called.

"Good afternoon, Zack," she said. "How was breakfast? Are you feeling better?"

"I'm still debating whether to have you reprogrammed," I teased her as I wiped my hands. "But yeah, I feel better. Headache's gone."

"I'm worried about your headaches, Zack. Every time you use the nanos, they get worse."

I leaned against the table. "I can handle it. Besides, how else could we have read the tables last night?"

"Maybe it wasn't such a good plan after all," said Sylvia. "You don't know what those things are doing to you."

"I said I could handle it," I snapped. "I can control the nanofibers."

"Sure, Zack, sure," she replied. "But still, there were only a few stable bonds created in over a thousand prisoners who went into the tanks. Only one in ten even survived. Most of them had their nerves shredded as the nanos bonded to the nerve sheaths. You're almost unique."

"What's your point, Sylvia?" I sighed. "I can't rip them out. They're part of me now."

"I know," she answered. "But try not to use them so much. I'm certain the pain means those things are damaging your nervous system."

I grinned. "No fear, Sylvia. I know what I'm doing." *Yeah, sure I do.* I changed the subject. "What more did you find out about Wu?"

Sylvia hesitated a second. "It may be nothing, but there's something fishy about CM&M's production numbers. According to the original ore surveys from a hundred years ago, the mines should have played out just about when they seemed to, a year before Wu took over. And yet, under Wu, the mines and processors are working around the clock turning out top quality steel, iridium, nickel, even rare earths. The company claims they have some new proprietary extraction method that allows them to work the old deposits. And the original survey has been updated with a new one showing reserves for another twenty years."

"When was the survey updated?"

"A few months after our boy took over. He commissioned an analysis of the old data by an outfit called McAllen Engineering. They've since gone out of business and the Federal Resources Management Agency's records are limited to the final report. The details are proprietary work-product and were kept by McAllen."

"So for all we know, the new survey is legit," I said.

"Yeah, I suppose. It just looked funny to me."

I thought about it for a moment. If Wu was involved in rigging the analysis, it might be relevant to our job, but I didn't see an obvious connection. Besides, CM&M was producing in line with the new survey. "Well," I said to Sylvia, "it does seem odd. See if you can track down anyone who worked for McAllen. Maybe we can talk to them directly. Anything else?"

"About Wu, no. But I do have three messages for you from Edward Conejo. He wants to talk to you."

I groaned. Edward Conejo—Eddie the Rabbit, or just Rabbit to his friends—called me every couple of weeks to rant about his latest conspiracy theory. I humored him. He might be annoying, but he was the best data slicer this side of the Belt and he knew everything about every operating system on three worlds. Besides, he saw me as his protector because I'd looked out for him in Bruneault Prison during the Revolution. Still, that didn't mean I wanted the job permanently. But it was a job I couldn't seem to quit.

"Play back the latest message," I sighed. Might as well get it over with.

"Yes, Boss. Time index 11:35 Zulu, about ninety minutes ago."

"Zack, this is the third message I've left for you." Rabbit's voice was pinched and breathless as always. "I need to see you right away at my place. I can't stall them much longer. They want the cheat code today, but I can't give it to them— not with *him* in the loop. I found him, Zack! I know where he's been all these years. Come quick. I really need some help with this one."

"He sounds scared," said Sylvia. "Who is he talking about?"

"How should I know? Rabbit always sounds scared. He sees spies in every shadow and checks his room for bugs three times a day."

"So you're not going to see him?" she asked, making it

sound like an accusation.

"Does he say anything more in the other messages?" I asked.

"No, just 'call me.' That last one is the longest."

"I'll go. He won't stop calling until I do."

"Good." Sylvia sounded satisfied.

I grumbled some more about her forgetting her place and then left the galley. Across the passageway, the door to Cleo's stateroom was half open and I could hear her moving around. I knocked and pushed the door open.

She looked up from her dressing table. She wore a cream-colored suit, tailored to emphasize her figure without looking tight. The jacket was cut low in the front, hinting at a world of possibilities. She twisted her hair into a soft bun at the back of her head and secured it with a long wooden pin.

"What do you want, Zack? I have a lunch date with my friend from TransAstral. I'll ask him about your container if the time seems right."

"I thought he was just an 'acquaintance.'"

She frowned. "If you're going to be crude again, you can leave now."

"Sorry," I said. "Look, Cleo, about last night..."

She shook her head. "Forget it, Zack. I just passed on some information about the tables. You and Sylvia cooked up the scheme to take the casino for a small fortune. I never liked the idea. It wasn't worth the risk." She stood and picked up her small purse and beaded shawl from the dressing table.

"It would have been if we'd won enough to pay off the loan," I grumbled.

"No, Zack," she said sharply. "It wouldn't—because we wouldn't be moving ahead, building a business like real grown-up people." She draped the shawl over her shoulders and looked away. "You were just playing a score, a one-time hit so you, and Deuce, and Eddie could keep playing pirate."

"The *Profit* would be ours, free and clear," I said. "What's so bad about that?"

"But we're not free and clear, Zack. Admit it. Eddie called again and you're running off to see him, like all the other times. You're always running. From prison or the Revolution or God knows what other demons. I'm through with it! I can't live that way." She wiped a tear from her left eye, as close as I'd seen her come to crying in a long time.

"I'm sorry about last night, Cleo," I said. It sounded lame, even to me.

She shook her head, dismissing my apology. "Let's just get this job done, pay off the loan and divide our shares. Then we can go our own ways."

I nodded. She brushed past me and out into the passageway. My gut tightened again as her scent filled my head.

I stood in her stateroom for a minute. The same scent, lavender with a hint of musk, lingered in the air. Her dressing gown was draped over the chair. I ran my hand over the satin, remembering its soft promise. I followed her out into the passageway.

She was already gone.

"Smooth," said Sylvia.

"Shut up."

"Shutting up, Boss. But you might want to head down to the forward hold. We have company."

"Who?"

"Lieutenant Henri Boucher of the Federal Bureau of Public Security," she intoned, imitating the officious accent of a Fed AI. "Shall I let him in?"

"Let him stew a while. I'll go down."

I took my time crossing the cargo deck. The forward ramp was up and locked, but the starboard sally port was open. Hank stood in the hatchway, leaning against the bulkhead. He wore the dark suit, white shirt and dark glasses that were high fashion for federal plainclothes cops. The suit covered the shoulder holster with only the slightest bulge, and I knew the glasses concealed a datalink with a heads-up display and automatic targeting sensor. He raised a hand as I approached.

"Hey Zack," he said. "May I come aboard?"

"Hey yourself, Hank." I quickened my pace across the deck in case he decided to come in anyway. "Have you got a warrant?"

"Aw, Zack." He frowned as he rubbed a hand over his shaved scalp and removed the dark glasses." You know I don't. Don't be a hard ass; I just want to talk to you."

"Sure, Hank, anytime. Outside."

He sighed, shaking his head. "Whatever you say, Zack, but I don't know why you're so touchy. I've seen your Salazar sculpture. The BPS doesn't care where you got it."

"If you want to come up and have a beer and talk about the girls down at the Blue Booby, I'll invite you in. If you want to talk as a cop, we talk out here. Principles."

"Principles." Hank said the word like a curse. We descended the short stairway from the sally port to the ground. "Two years in the Bear, and you still stand on principle?"

"Let's not go there, *Sergeant*," I said quietly.

An uncomfortable silence fell between us. Bruneault, aka Bruno 'The Bear.' These days, every Martian defined himself through the lens of that place. Ex-prisoners like me and Rabbit, former guards like Hank, informers, patriots, soldiers, and resistance fighters; all caught in the web that spun out of Bruneault Prison. As a guard, then-Sergeant Boucher had been one of a few professionals who scrupulously observed the rules. He'd done me several kindnesses that had probably saved my life. But our time in the Bear was on opposite sides of a sharply drawn line, one that could not be crossed if we were to remain on speaking terms.

"What'd you want to talk about?" I asked.

Hank took a deep breath and let it out slowly. "I hear you had some trouble at the Golden Moon last night."

I shrugged. "Who, me? No trouble at all."

Hank laughed. "Don't bullshit me, Zack. You were pulled away from the tables by a couple of goons in high-priced suits, and an hour later you're on the ban list at every casino from here to Tharsis. What did you do, crap in Kwai Hong's rice bowl?"

I smiled. "Something like that. You know their roulette tables are rigged?"

Hank nodded. "We suspected as much. You want to file a complaint?"

"Hell, no." I shook my head. I figured Hank didn't know about the Wu job, or this chat would have involved handcuffs. "I found a way to beat them. They've junked the crooked tables by now anyway. Leave it alone."

"And that's all?" Hank asked. He looked me in the eye, rubbing his head again. "Because our AI's identified Vincent Talafofo as one of the guys who stopped your play. He's freelance muscle for hire; expensive and good enough to back it up. Not someone I'd expect to see on a casino security gig."

"What can I say, Hank?" I said, hoping it was casual enough. "I get nothing but the best."

"Kwai Chang Wu is on the moon," said Hank, looking closely at me again. "He's Kwai Hong's number-two son and the head honcho on Ceres. Ever meet him?"

Okay, so maybe Hank did know something. I tried to keep my tone light. "Come on, Hank. I'm just a poor ship driver. I don't run in those circles."

Hank shook his head. "All right, Zack. Have it your way. But someone is holding Talafofo's leash, and it isn't the local casino manager." He lowered his voice. "Seriously, the Kwais are bad news. Don't get in over your head."

"And if I do, should I expect the *Federales* to throw me a

line?"

Hank shrugged. "Maybe, at least here on the moon or on Mars. Out in the black, especially in the Belt, you're on your own. We don't have much juice with the independent miners these days. Too many of Metternich's old boys out there."

"The Revolution's dead. Nothing left but a bunch of badass wannabes."

"Maybe," Hank said, looking away. "Lots of rumors still going around. Some high-level people escaped just before Reunification."

"You should know," I said, knowing I shouldn't. The bitterness came through anyway.

Hank frowned. "Look, Zack, we both had choices to make, but I don't have a damn thing to apologize for. I did my best to look out for everyone on that cellblock, guard or prisoner. And my testimony put a lot of people away for a long time. If that's not enough for you, then to hell with you."

He was right. I knew it, but it didn't change anything. I was sick of people seeing Metternich hiding under every rock. I just wanted to move on. Still, Hank was a decent guy, for a cop. He deserved better from me. "Sorry, Hank," I said finally. "You did right by me and Rabbit in the Bear. I shouldn't have said that."

"Yeah, well, just be careful," he said. He turned and walked toward the police cruiser that waited a discreet distance away. I watched until he drove off.

"Sylvia," I called as I climbed up to the sally port. "Where's Deuce?"

"In the aft cargo hold, Zack. Shall I open a link to him?"

"Never mind," I said. "I'll find him. Could you get the scooter ready for me, please?"

"Sure, Boss."

I ducked as I passed under the ladder at the back of the hold. A narrow passageway ran toward the stern from

29

there. I walked past the engine room and threaded my way around the bulge of the gravity generator. The hatch to Deuce's workshop was open. I stuck my head in, but he wasn't there. Tools and spare parts covered every flat surface, including the bunk he slept in. I walked on, into the aft hold. He was there, all right, with half of the *Profit's* main drive spread out on the deck in front of him.

He looked up as I stepped through the hatch. "Hey, LT. What's up?"

"Not much," I said. "How much longer on the refit?"

"Two, maybe three days—if the shipyard can get me a new induction coil. Old one's shot. Parts guy said he might have one coming on the next run from L4. We in a hurry?"

"Not yet." I told him about my conversation with Hank. "We may need to move as soon as we snatch the goods," I concluded.

Deuce nodded. "You think he knows anything?"

I shook my head. "No, just fishing. But we should stay light on our feet, just in case. I'm going across town to see Rabbit. Want me to check on parts at the salvage yard?"

Deuce grunted and stood up. "I'll get my pulse rifle."

"Stay," I said, waving him back. "Rabbit's just having another anxiety attack. I'll let him rant for a while, check the closets for bogeymen and chill him out. Then I'll grab a coil from the salvage yard and be back by chow time."

Deuce stood with his hands on his hips. "I should go with you. Conejo is trouble, and that cave he lives in ain't safe."

"Stand down. I'll take a pneumatic and be careful."

"I should go with you," he said, crossing his arms and thrusting out his jaw.

It was my turn to get stubborn. Deuce meant well, but I needed a change of scenery. Some days are just like that. A fragment of conversation, a scent of ammonia, the sound of a door slamming, and I was back in the belly of the Bear. Cleo had been right about that; I was still a prisoner. The *Profit* meant freedom, but it was the freedom to run farther and faster. The Bear was still in my head, waiting. Rabbit often brought it back with his rants, but we shared a bond, Rabbit and I; a bond sealed in a biotank.

I stopped by the weapons locker and pulled out a squat Huang pneumatic pistol in a clip-on holster. I slipped it onto my belt in the small of my back, and climbed aboard the scooter.

Rabbit was luckier than most 'tank survivors. He had no use of the muscles below his waist but had kept his mind and what passed for his sanity. He could even use the nanos to control a walker or power chair. I knew of only two other victims of Metternich's biotanks who had come out with anything approaching the stability of my own bond, and both of them were dead, eaten by the Bear.

Rabbit lived clear across town, out past the industrial sector in a warren of abandoned tunnels left over from the old days. Most were off the power grid, outside the gravity field, full of nothing but cold hard moon rock. Some weren't even mapped.

I parked the scooter near a recycling plant at the edge of the grid and walked the last hundred meters. Tycho City ended at the mouth of a rough tunnel sloping upward toward the surface. Yellow-and-black striped warning barriers crisscrossed the opening. A slight shimmer in the air marked the edge of the gravity field.

As I ducked under the lowest barrier, a recorded voice blared, "Caution! The area beyond this point is not safe. Citizens are warned that they enter at their own risk. The Tycho City Authority accepts no responsibility for any personal injury or property loss."

I'd heard it all before. Anybody who'd come out here wouldn't care about the City Authority's liability.

Walking in low gravity takes practice. The skill comes back after a dozen or so steps, but at first I bounced and slid like a newbie. By the time I got the hang of it, I was halfway to the turn for Rabbit's place. I glided past several side tunnels. Off to my left, I heard a rustle of movement in the dark, probably a jolt-head or a juicer hiding out with his stash. The really dangerous monsters lived deeper in the warren. Even Deuce was afraid to go in there.

I bounced to a stop at the entrance to Rabbit's tunnel. Heaps of scrap metal, tangles of wire, and the crumpled hulk of an old cargo loader nearly blocked the opening. The junk looked random, but it forced anyone entering to walk along a specific path. I slid over to the cargo loader, flipped open an access port to the engine compartment, and reached up inside to pull down a palm scanner. The second I saw the scanner, I felt a chill in the pit of my stomach. The security system was deactivated. I drew the Huang from my belt and dropped to a crouch.

Rabbit took his security seriously. Even when friends came to call, he didn't shut the system down, but allowed them to pass unchallenged. Anyone else would be targeted by some rather nasty weapons concealed in the tunnel walls. I suddenly regretted leaving Deuce and his pulse rifle at home.

I moved forward slowly, keeping low and inching up to each bend in the junkyard path as it meandered through piles of scrap and salvaged components. I went to one knee to look around a corner. The hard stone of the floor felt cold through the thin fabric of my trousers. There was little dust on the floor. Either Rabbit had been seized by an uncharacteristic fit of cleanliness, or several people had passed through here recently. Rabbit almost never went out. Sweat trickled down my back in spite of the cool air.

I heard the lookout cough before I saw him. He stood in a dark spot, just outside the airlock to Rabbit's front door. He held a needler, a high-end Steinbauer with a pneumatic booster, in that casual grip that comes from familiarity. It was an assassin's weapon, nearly silent. His expression said boredom but his eyes were alert. A professional, then. But working for whom? I doubted he'd let me get close enough to ask.

I raised the Huang, but then thought better of it. Pneumatics were noisy, and in the rocky confines of the tunnel the sound would be amplified. Whoever was inside Rabbit's place would hear the shots, and I'd lose any chance of surprise.

I slipped back up the tunnel. I needed help, and I needed a silent way past that lookout. More than that, I needed to know what Rabbit was into and why he'd involved me.

CHAPTER FOUR

"Sylvia! Sylvia, can you read me?"

No response. I was too far off the grid for my datalink to log on. So much for calling the cavalry. I activated my eye camera and set it to record.

I rooted through the pile of scrap by the tunnel entrance, wincing at each sound. *Damn*, I cursed silently, Rabbit had already salvaged everything of real use. This junk was just for show. Finally I came up with a piece of polycast pipe, about a centimeter and a half in diameter and almost as long as my forearm. One end had been cut on a bias. A few seconds of scraping against the rough stone of the floor rubbed away the loose shreds of plastic and gave me a decent point. I took it over to the old cargo loader and opened the engine compartment. The insulation that lined the access panel was frayed and ragged. I tore off several strips and used them to wrap the blunt end of the pipe. It made a poor shiv, but at least it was pointed and sturdy.

I took out the Huang and hefted it, considering. One shot would put the sentry down. I shook my head and tucked the pistol back in its holster.

I knew what I had to do next, but I didn't like it. I closed my eyes and exhaled, clearing my head and allowing the nanofibers to extend themselves into my inner ear and retina. I'd pay for it later with another blinding headache, but I needed an advantage before I went up against that Steinbauer.

I opened my eyes and let them adjust to the dim light in the tunnel. The overhead lights shimmered in my augmented vision. The fixtures radiated a red glow of waste heat and the light itself was blue with ultraviolet overtones. My breath sounded as loud as a hurricane, and my footsteps echoed in my hyper-acute ears. I slipped off my shoes. Barefoot was better for silence. I slid down the tunnel, quiet as mist.

The lookout had moved. He stood closer to Rabbit's front door now—in the light, with his back to the passageway. His head was cocked toward the open airlock. I stilled my breathing and listened. I could hear two voices, but couldn't make out what they were saying. One was low and coarse, like gravel; the other louder and more refined, almost lyrical. Both sounded angry. Rabbit wasn't entertaining friends. Still, I didn't want to do anything stupid, especially if it turned out that these guys were Feds.

I crept forward, hugging the wall. The nanos amplified the light as I picked my way around a tangle of loose wire and scrap, stepping over the remains of an old holoset. I was in deep shadow now, almost straight across from the airlock, five meters away. The lookout shifted closer to the opening, leaning toward it, straining to hear. I crouched, motionless, gauging the distance as I debated my next move.

The cultured voice rose again, shouting questions. Rabbit answered, his voice more plaintive than defiant. A shout cut him off. I tensed, waiting. Rabbit's shriek of pain decided the issue. These definitely weren't the good guys.

Everything shifted into slow motion as the nanofibers

pushed my muscles into overdrive. I leaped forward off of my right foot, covering half the distance to the airlock in a single step. The lookout must have sensed me, because his head snapped around as soon as I left the ground. His face registered surprise even as he swung the needler toward me. I dove forward, twisting onto my right shoulder as the Steinbauer spat needles. They pinged off of the floor behind me. One tugged at the loose fabric of my jacket. Another whizzed past my ear like a gold-colored wasp. I rolled across my right shoulder, driving to my feet directly in front of him and lashed out with my left arm, knocking the needler from his right hand. It spun upward in slow motion.

He was quick. He aimed a roundhouse left at my head before the gun reached the top of its arc. I barely ducked his fist, and it grazed the top of my head. Momentum carried his arm across his chest, exposing his left flank. I thrust upward with my right, driving the shiv under his ribcage into his chest. He gasped as a gush of warm blood flooded over my hand. He deflated like a balloon, collapsing across my shoulder. I eased him to the ground. He stared at my face for a second, and then his eyes went dark. I shuddered, struggling to control the rush of relief that swept through me. I pulled the shiv from his chest tossed it away into the darkness.

I scooped up the Steinbauer and crouched near the door, listening for the sound of approaching footsteps. I could hear Rabbit sobbing. The pleasing voice was speaking softly, soothingly. The needler had been almost silent and the fight hadn't made enough noise to interrupt the interrogation. My hands shook slightly as I struggled to slow my breathing. The gravelly voice said something that made Rabbit squeal again.

I crept back to the man I'd just killed. I wiped the blood from my hand on the corner of his jacket and looked carefully at his face. Pale skin; short, light brown hair; high cheekbones; firm chin; no scars or distinguishing marks.

Thoroughly bland and nondescript, even in death. A face you could pass in a crowd and never really see.

I checked his pockets, laying the contents on the ground next to him. He carried a twenty yuan gold piece, two fifteen-shot magazines for the Steinbauer, a transit pass for the Tharsis to Tycho City shuttle, and an identity card for one Thomas Brody of Ward Eight, Upper Beta, Tharsis, United Mars. The dead man's face stared back at me from the holographic image on the card. All of which told me exactly nothing.

Stuffing Brody's things into my pocket, I stood and grabbed his wrists to haul him away from the door and into the shadow. Then I saw the tattoo on the palm of his left hand, the one nearest his heart: a green shield with a white diagonal stripe bearing a stylized red dragon, rearing on its hind legs. I dropped his wrist and squatted next to the body.

Shit, Rabbit! I thought. *What have you gotten me into?* Brody here was a soldier for the Red Dragons. I shook my head. *Of course, dummy. Tharsis.* The Dragons ran half the casinos and all of the brothels there. Everyone else paid them protection money. And those were their more savory businesses, sidelines to drug running, piracy, and slave trafficking. They controlled a whole sector out in the Belt, where even the *Federales* left them alone.

I flipped open the magazine of the Steinbauer—six needles, all yellow. I checked the spare mags. Yellow as well. Anectine. A scratch would drop a man in a heartbeat, muscles twitching uncontrollably, paralysis and death followed in a few minutes, with the target awake and aware the whole time. Nasty way to go. No non-lethal sleeper needles for this Dragon; he played for keeps. It made me feel better about killing him.

I dragged Brody into the shadows. Holding the needler ready, I slipped through the airlock and into Rabbit's den. I smelled ozone and burnt plastic. Off to the left, the ruins of the security panel explained why the system was offline. The airlock's inner door was ajar. I peeked around the edge.

Rabbit's cave was just that, an old mined-out ice cavern. All of the ice had been used up before Tycho City had been dug. The ceiling was 10 meters high, the cave itself twice that across. Four giant flat-screen monitors covered the rear wall, and a two-meter holomatrix dominated the room's center. Rabbit stayed plugged into the Lunar net through his own hardwired datalink. Now, the monitors and the matrix were dark. Rabbit's private network was also offline. Next to the matrix was a workbench covered with dismembered components. A corner of the bench held an antique monitor, its screen glowing with lines of code.

Rabbit sat in a straight-backed chair near the middle of the room, his arms bound behind his back. A metal contraption was wedged into his mouth, forcing his jaws open. Blood and spit trickled down his chin and onto his shirt. His chest heaved with wet sobs.

In front of him stood a tall, thin man wearing a tailored black jacket and gray cashmere slacks that would have looked good on the Promenade in Upper Armstrong. He wore plastic gloves, and a clear plastic apron protected his expensive clothes. He lifted a stainless steel dental hook from the bench and held it to the light, as if checking the point. He hefted it lightly in his right hand before turning to Rabbit.

"Mr. James, if you please," he said, his voice soft and melodious.

The second man, broad-shouldered and thick-limbed, and wearing a limegreen silk shirt, stepped in behind Rabbit and seized his ears, forcing his head back. The Tall Man leaned over and drove the sharp point of the hook into the space between Rabbit's front teeth, pushing it deep into the gum. Rabbit screamed. Green Shirt held his head in a vise grip. Rabbit's chest bucked and heaved. His screams merged into a single undulating shriek of pain and terror.

Then, as quickly as he'd struck, the Tall Man straightened and pulled the hook from Rabbit's mouth.

"Mr. James," he said casually, as he wiped the hook on a clean white cloth," I think Mr. Conejo is ready to talk to us now. The bite-block, please."

Green Shirt, or James, or whatever his name was, let go of Rabbit's ears and jerked the metal bite-block out of his mouth. Rabbit cried out again as one of his teeth flew out of his mouth and landed on the floor.

"Gently, Mr. James," the Tall Man said in that soothing voice. "I'm sure Edward is convinced that we're serious. Aren't you, Edward?"

Rabbit sobbed some more, nodding his head vigorously.

"Good. Now, where are the codes?"

Rabbit shook his head. The Tall Man gestured slightly. Green Shirt cuffed Rabbit's right ear with an open palm, making him cry out again.

That was enough for me. I stepped out from behind the inner door with the needler leveled. "That's enough. Nobody move."

Green Shirt didn't listen. His kind never does. He barely hesitated before reaching behind his back and drew a black pneumatic pistol. My needle caught him in the neck before he could bring his gun to bear. He dropped, twitching and writhing as the gun clattered to the stone floor beside him. Rabbit stared at him, wide-eyed.

The Tall Man didn't hesitate at all. He stepped behind Rabbit as he pulled a short-barreled 7mm from his jacket and held it to Rabbit's head. I swung the needler in his direction, but even with my augmented reflexes, I was too slow.

"Drop your weapon," the Tall Man said, tightening his grip on Rabbit's neck. "Or I'll shoot your friend."

"I don't think so," I said taking a two-handed stance and aiming the needler at his head. "You'd better see to your man there. He's stopped twitching, which means he has about two minutes to get the antidote."

"He's not important," the Tall Man said casually. "You don't think I'll kill this man?" He pressed the gun harder into Rabbit's temple.

"You all right, Rabbit?"

"Yeah," Rabbit's voice shook. "I think so."

"You won't kill him," I said to the Tall Man. "Whatever Rabbit has, you want it pretty bad. Bad enough to break in here and torture him. Kill him and you get nothing."

"Except, maybe, an example to others." He tightened his grip on Rabbit.

"Perhaps. But if you shoot Rabbit, you'll be dead before you can make another move. Or, you could try to shoot me. You might get a shot off, but you'll eat a needle and join your friend on the floor. Either way, you're dead and the Dragons get nothing." I paused. "The way I figure it, you're a consultant, hired to do a job. Dying isn't part of your game plan."

"It's not." He smiled. "But it seems my options are limited."

"There is a third option," I said. "Let Rabbit go. Lay down your gun and walk out of here. Who knows? Maybe you can convince Colin Jones to give you another chance. I hear he's an understanding kind of guy."

He shook his head, still smiling. "That hasn't been my impression of Mr. Jones. How do I know you won't just kill me if I drop my gun?"

"You don't."

He looked hard into my eyes. His were light blue, cold as ice. I don't know what he saw in mine. After a couple of seconds, he let go of Rabbit and stood straight and tall, both hands above his shoulders. The gun dangled by the trigger guard from his right forefinger. He stretched out his hand and let it fall to the floor. Rabbit slumped forward in the chair, gasping.

The Tall Man stepped around Rabbit and walked toward

me, holding my eyes. I edged to one side, covering him with the Steinbauer, staying out of his reach. He paused as he passed me.

"May I know your name?" he asked.

"Santa Claus," I answered. "And you're gettin' nothin' for Christmas."

He smiled again, but there was no mirth in his eyes. He pulled off the apron and tossed it aside. Then he walked calmly up the tunnel and out of sight.

I lowered the needler and took a deep shuddering breath. The headache had already started and I could feel my calf muscles beginning to twitch with fatigue. Playing superman sucks.

I flicked on the Steinbauer's safety and stuffed the weapon into the waistband of my trousers. Stepping behind Rabbit, I cut him loose with a blade from the workbench. He clutched at my arm, eyes closed, tears streaming down his cheeks. I held his head, and let him cry. I was burning with questions, but we'd been here before, Rabbit and I, and I knew what he needed just now. He'd come around in a few minutes.

* * *

Finally, Rabbit straightened. "I knew you'd come, Zack," he said. His eyes were red and there was blood on his chin, just below his buck teeth. One of his lower teeth was missing, leaving a bloody hole in the gum that accentuated his slight lisp. "I told myself, 'If I can just hold out for a little while, Zack will be here,' and you came. They thought I'd break, but I showed them. That tall guy is scary, but not half as scary as the biotanks—right, Zack? Nothing compared to the 'tanks. They tried to scare me, but I wasn't scared. Even when they smashed my power walker and tied me up and stuck that thing in my mouth. But they got nothing from me. Nothing." He ran out of breath and stopped. He looked up at me. "What kept you?"

I didn't answer right away, but bent down to check on the man in the green shirt. He was dead. The anectine had paralyzed his muscles, suffocating him. I felt a pang of regret at letting him die that way, even though he'd have killed me without a second thought. His boss had left me no other choice.

"How the hell did those goons get in here, Rabbit?" I asked, checking the body for ID and weapons.

"They came with Mikey," he said. "Had his code. Mikey still owes me for a data worm I built for him, so I let him in. Then this tall freak kicks in my door and blows away the alarm panel and, pop, pop, shoots Mikey, too, and then these other guys come rushing in..."

"Wait, slow down," I said. "Mike Finney? Mikey's here?"

Rabbit pointed toward the rear of the cavern. I saw a crumpled form in the shadows, under the big monitors on the back wall. I rushed over, but knew the instant I saw him there was nothing I could do. Mike lay on his back, arms stretched above his head. There was a round hole surrounded by scorch marks in the center of his blood-soaked shirt, and another in his forehead. I squatted beside his body, and closed his eyes.

Mikey was a freelance surveyor and part time prospector. He was Deuce's step brother; the two of them shared a lot of history before Deuce and I teamed up. Sitting next to him, I felt empty and ashamed. I should never have let that tall bastard go. But why Mikey? Just to get past Rabbit's security?

"Is he really—" Rabbit asked softly.

"He's dead, Rabbit," I said, standing. Rabbit sat staring at the other body on the floor. Any regret I might have felt at killing Green Shirt vanished.

"What the hell is going on here?" I demanded. "Please tell me you didn't welsh on a deal with the Dragons."

"Well, I did do a job for them," Rabbit whined. "But it

wasn't like they paid me anything in advance. I just said I'd do some slicing for them in return for a cut of the take. And I did the work, too. Can't say I didn't do it. But see, when the time came to deliver and I found out that *he* was involved, I just couldn't give them the code. Not if *he* was in the loop. I told them so. Sent a message to Jones that he'd have to dump *him* before I'd give them the code.

"Can you believe he never even sent me a reply? Then these guys show up and ruin my door and... Aw, shit, Zack, what are we gonna tell Mikey's wife? What are we gonna tell Deuce? Oh, Deuce is gonna kill me when he finds out."

"Damn it, Rabbit, you're babbling. Who the hell are you talking about? Who does Jones have to get rid of?"

"His security man. I recognized him. I wasn't looking for him—well, of course I was looking for him; I'm always looking for him. But I wasn't looking for him at the meeting. Jones insisted I come in person to make the final deal. You know how I hate that kind of thing, but I went. I never expected it, but there he was, out of the blue, sitting next to Jones at the restaurant like a normal person. He's changed, had surgery or genetic mods or something. He's heavier, too. But the eyes gave him away. The eyes didn't change! I see those eyes every night before I fall asleep. I knew right away it was *him*."

I shook my head, trying to make sense of the verbal salad Rabbit was spouting. "Stop, Rabbit! What the hell are you talking about?"

Rabbit looked around, as if there might be someone else in the room. He leaned toward me, his voice a hoarse whisper. "Metternich! He's here, Zack. On the moon. He's working for Colin Jones! Running security for the Red Dragons."

CHAPTER FIVE

Before I could say anything, an amplified voice boomed from the tunnel outside the airlock. "This is the Bureau of Public Security. Lay down your weapons and come out with your hands in plain sight."

Damn, could this day get any worse? My head started to pound. The last thing I wanted to do was explain a room full of stiffs to the *Federales*. Rabbit cringed, almost as afraid of the Feds as he had been of the Tall Man. What hadn't he told me?

"Edward Conejo! I'm an officer of the Bureau of Public Security. Please respond if you are able," the amplifier boomed again.

"Is that you, Hank?" I shouted, recognizing his voice. "It's Zack! I'm in here with Eddie! We're coming out. Tell your guys to cool their jets"

"I can't move, Zack," whined Rabbit, refusing to meet my gaze. "They wrecked my walker."

"No fear, Rabbit. It'll be just like the Bear. I'll be your legs." I squatted down, and Rabbit wrapped his arms around my shoulders. I stood and swung him up onto my back, pulling his useless legs up so that he rode piggyback, like a child. The movement felt comfortably familiar, like slipping on an old jacket. Whatever he was worried about could wait until we dealt with Hank.

"Two coming out," I shouted as we approached the lock. "We need a medic." I turned my head to whisper to Rabbit. Nothing about Metternich. We'll handle that ourselves." I wasn't sure I believed him, but dealing with Hank and the Feds would be touchy enough without wild conspiracy theories.

I stepped slowly through the outer door. Bright light flooded the tunnel outside, making me squint. Three yellow-green spots painted my chest—laser sights. Several guys in black uniforms rushed us out of the blinding floodlights. More covered them with leveled pulse rifles. Hank stood off to one side, arms folded, face blank. Someone lifted Rabbit from my shoulders and placed him on a stretcher. One of the men in black handcuffed him to the frame while a second searched him.

A third stepped behind me and said, "Hands where I can see them."

I knew the drill. I clasped my hands behind my neck and spread my legs. He frisked me quickly and thoroughly. He took the Steinbauer and the spare mags. My own Huang, too. I heard the rattle of handcuffs behind me, but Hank waved a hand. The man put the cuffs away and stepped back.

"Put your hands down, Zack," Hank said. "You look ridiculous." He turned his head to shout back up the tunnel. "Medic! See to the man on the stretcher! And Wilson, take those cuffs off. He's the victim."

The Medic brushed past me as I walked toward Hank. One of the black uniforms stepped up as if to stop me. Hank shook his head, then put his hands in his pockets and inclined his head toward the corpse in the shadows.

"Want to tell me what went down here?"

"Not particularly," I said.

"Then we'll need those cuffs."

"No need for that. I'll fill you in." I looked back at Rabbit, talking excitedly to the Medic. What the hell, I thought. Rabbit couldn't keep his mouth shut. I might as well try to control what damage I could by talking to Hank. I considered turning over the recording in my datalink, but decided that would be a bad idea. It might not help my case that much, and I wanted a chance to review it before I gave the Feds a peek.

"I'm waiting, Zack," said Hank, following my gaze toward Rabbit.

"Just before I talked to you back at the *Profit*, Rabbit called me in a panic." I went on to outline the fight with Brody, Rabbit's torture and my encounter with the Tall Man. I didn't mention Rabbit's obsession with Metternich. "The guy over there," I concluded, "Is named Thomas Brody, at least that's what his ID says. He's from Tharsis. He's also a soldier for the Red Dragons."

Hank whistled softly." And you killed him?"

"Yeah," I answered." The Steinbauer was his. The Huang pneumatic is mine, by the way. I'll be wanting it back. There are two more bodies inside. One is Mike Finney; he was a freelance surveyor, and Deuce's stepbrother. The other is a goon named James Hvalsa." I handed Hank the identity card I had taken from Green Shirt's pocket. "Aside from having terrible taste in clothes, he has a Dragon tattoo on his palm."

Hank signaled to two of the BPS guys standing over Rabbit, and motioned them inside. "Did you kill them, too?"

I shrugged. "Only Hvalsa. Finney was already dead. Either Hvalsa or the tall guy killed him before I got here."

"What can you tell me about this Tall Man?" Hank asked as one of the BPS troopers handed him a datapad. He glanced over it, clicking through screens.

I chose my words carefully. "Height, 185 to 190 centimeters. Slim, maybe 85 kilos. Well dressed; gray slacks, real cashmere, not synthetic, and a black tailored jacket. Black hair, cut short but not shaved, light blue eyes." I suppressed a shudder. "Dead eyes. His accent was Earth, or maybe high-class LaGrange arcology. The real thing, too. Not affected. He comes from money. He's cold. No regrets, no wasted motion."

"Dragon?" asked Hank.

I shook my head. "I don't think so. He's too slick. He's an independent contractor, a ghost. You won't find him unless he wants you to. And he was packing a 7 millimeter Ruger pistol." Hank looked up from the datapad. I nodded. "Yeah, he has the juice to get a gun past security." On the Moon, projectile weapons that might punch through a pressure dome were strictly forbidden. Needlers, pulse rifles, pneumatics, blades, all things deadly to flesh and blood were fine, so long as they couldn't damage the domes that kept us all alive. Hank said nothing, digesting the implications, until one of his troopers approached.

"Lieutenant?" said the trooper tentatively. "We've got two DB's inside. One has a needle in his neck." The trooper gave me a sidelong look. "The other has two bullet wounds; one dead center in the chest, the other in the head. Chest wound would have killed him. There are some bloody dental tools on the workbench and tape on the chair. It's consistent with his story." He jerked a thumb toward Rabbit.

"Right. Thanks. Get the images to the data techs, and seal the room. The crime scene unit will be here soon." The trooper nodded and turned away. Hank tucked the datapad under his arm and turned to me. "Ready to talk to the magistrate?"

"Magistrate?" I said. "Come on, Hank, this was self-defense. What do we need with a magistrate?"

"We do this by the book."

I gave an exasperated sigh.

He glared at me. "Damn it, Zack, this isn't Tharsis. You can't leave dead bodies lying around and expect the City Authority to look the other way. All those pampered tourists who spend their money in the casinos and on the Promenade will disappear if there's even a hint of gang trouble here."

"We're off the grid, Hank. What they don't know won't hurt them."

"Too late for that. This became official the moment my guys got here."

I realized then what bothered me. *Why the hell was he there in the first place?* "Yeah, about that. How did you know there was anything going on here?"

Hank looked uncomfortable. "An anonymous tip over the public net. Voice only. The caller said there was a firefight in progress and that people were dead. Dispatch took it seriously and rolled a full team on it."

"Doesn't that seem a bit odd?" I asked. "A full combat team on an anonymous tip? Off grid at that?"

"Maybe." He nodded toward Rabbit. "But the tip was right."

"There's no way anyone could have known that unless they were here in the tunnel. I killed Brody with a shiv. The needler is practically silent. The only shooting took place before I got here, and you couldn't have rolled that early unless the BPS is slower than it used to be."

Hank checked his datapad. "Call came in about 30 minutes ago."

"I was in the tunnel by then," I said. "If someone else was here, I'd have seen them. This was a setup."

"Who was set up?" Hank said, irritated. "You? This tall guy you say was torturing Conejo? Or does this have something to do with your little adventure at the roulette tables yesterday? You want to tell me what went on between you and Kwai Chang Wu?"

I shook my head. I couldn't see any connection between

Wu and the Dragons. Besides, what could I tell him that wouldn't either land me in jail or cost me my ship?

Hank went on. "Set up or not, all I know is that we were ordered to roll on this, and found you here with three dead bodies. Now, are you ready to talk to the magistrate?"

I didn't answer. Ready or not, I wasn't going to talk him out of this. Hank took my silence as agreement and waved a technician over. Despite being off the grid, the tech set up a hololink to the magistrate in a matter of minutes. The BPS has its resources.

The magistrate was an AI, of course. Flesh and blood justices were too busy to handle day-to-day cases. Not for them the messy vagaries of petty crime. I could always appeal the assignment of an AI. It was my right as a citizen of the Republic. And then I could wait in custody until a human was available in, say, six to eight weeks. Not an option.

This particular AI had chosen an avatar that looked like a nineteenth century British hanging judge, complete with the black crepe square atop his powdered wig. I should have seen that as a warning but was too angry to notice.

I stood by, only half listening while Hank spoke officiously to the magistrate about case numbers and time indices and his badge number. This whole situation stank. I couldn't decide if it was more paranoid to think that someone was following me, or that Wu and the Dragons were somehow connected. Or maybe one of the jolt-addicts or juicers who hung out in the tunnels heard the shots that killed Mikey, and called the cops because it was the civic-minded thing to do. *Yeah, right.*

I glanced over at Rabbit. One of the sergeants was taking his statement with a portable holorecorder. The medic hovered nearby. I hoped Rabbit's story would at least be close to the version Hank was outlining for the magistrate.

I perked up as Hank said, "In summary, your honor, the needle pattern and the position of the body outside the residence correspond to Mr. Mbele's statement. Further, there is corroborating evidence of Mr. Conejo's torture and the presence of two bodies inside the residence, which facts also bear witness to Mr. Mbele's statement. I therefore believe that Mr. Mbele acted in defense of Mr. Conejo and of himself. I recommend release O.R. pending a formal inquest."

"Mr. Mbele," the magistrate addressed me for the first time. "Do you have anything to add?"

I had plenty to add, but wasn't about to tell him about Wu or Metternich. "No, your honor," I said. As soon as I said it, I felt as if I'd missed something important, something that might help my case. I shrugged. *Too late for regrets.* It had been too late the minute I'd shoved the shiv under Brody's ribs.

"Lieutenant Boucher, were there any corroborating witnesses to the killing of Thomas Brody?"

"No, your honor. But the position of the expended needles..."

"May have reflected Brody's attempt to defend himself," interrupted the magistrate. "Conejo's rather convoluted version of events inside the residence matches Mr. Mbele's. I see no such corroboration for events outside the residence. Why did Mr. Mbele not simply await the arrival of your team?"

"Rabbit was being tortured!" I protested. "How could I know...?"

"Silence, Mr. Mbele." The faux Brit shook his gavel at me, suddenly red in the face. "You had your chance to speak. You may make a further statement at the official inquest. I am revoking your port clearance and placing a launch hold on your ship. The inquest will be set for the seventh of next month at 09:00 Lunar Standard Time."

"But your honor—"

"That is enough, Mr. Mbele," he roared. "With your record, you should consider yourself lucky that I don't remand you to custody until the date of the inquest. This proceeding is ended." And with that, he broke the connection.

"Thanks a lot, Hank."

"Hey, at least you're not in the lock-up. I didn't have any choice here."

"Saying it's your job doesn't make it right."

"What? A few more days on the moon are gonna kill you? I've got three dead bodies to account for and a Captain who wants to be Director of Security. One screw-up and I'll be running a substation down in Freetown. Sorry, Zack, no favors on this one."

What could I say? We've all got our problems, and Hank's by-the-book attitude was making mine worse. Even if I could steal Wu's container, I'd have trouble delivering it on the seventh if I was tied up by a federal inquest. Then again, telling the magistrate, "I'm sorry, your honor, but I can't appear on the seventh because I have to deliver some stolen goods off-world on that day" didn't seem like an alternative.

"Never mind," I sighed. "Like you said, just doing your job."

I left Hank to his officialdom and walked over to Rabbit. I waited for the medic to finish clucking over him, then squatted next to the stretcher and checked Rabbit over myself. Seeing no obvious bugs or listening devices, I leaned close. "Did you mention Metternich?"

"Oh no, Zack. You told me not to, so I didn't tell them anything. They were awful curious about the tall guy, and why the Dragons had it in for me, but I didn't mention Metternich at all."

"Shhh. That's fine Rabbit." I held up my hand when he looked like he was going to start babbling again. "Let's get out of here."

"But my walker is smashed. I've got a power chair in a locker just inside the grid. The walker's too slow in standard G, anyway. You'll have to carry me that far."

"No sweat. Let me check with the Law." I stood and shouted, "Yo, Hank! Are we free to go?"

Hank glanced at the sergeant who'd interrogated Rabbit, then waved us toward the tunnel. Lifting Rabbit, I slung him onto my back and held out my hand to the trooper who'd taken my pneumatic. Hank gave him an OK sign, and he handed it over with a pained look.

By the time we reached the main tunnel and started toward town, my calves were in knots and my head pounded with each heartbeat. Rabbit felt heavy, even in one-sixth G. Every time I used them, the aftereffects of the nanos seemed to get worse.

I eased Rabbit down onto an old packing carton and bent over to massage my legs. Off to my right was the opening to a secondary tunnel. Something about it nagged at me as I rubbed the kinks out of my calves. Then I remembered— the faint rustle of movement as I'd passed by here on my way to Rabbit's place.

"Wait here a sec," I said. "I need to check something out."

I hobbled a short way into the other tunnel, just far enough into the shadows to be invisible from the main passageway. I leaned against the wall, rubbing my legs, until my eyes adjusted to the dim light. The floor was strewn with trash and rubble, the walls rough and stained with brownish rust-streaks. There was nothing else to see. I'm not sure what I'd expected, but it wasn't here.

As I turned to head back, I caught a faint scent in the air, like day-old sweat. I scanned the area, looking at everything more carefully. Shoulder high on the wall I found a handprint, faintly outlined in the rust stained rock. I placed my hand near it. The print was larger than my own, the fingers massive. Whoever had made it was taller and heavier than I was.

I walked the short distance back to Rabbit. Anyone could have made that print. It was newer than the rust, but could have been days old. Any derelict from the warren could have leaned there. But I knew they hadn't.

Rabbit sat where I'd left him, scanning the tunnel in each direction. His pinched expression eased as he saw me approaching. I didn't say anything, just bent down and helped him climb up onto my back. By the time I felt the familiar walking-downhill sensation of approaching a gravity field, I was loping along with smooth, easy strides. I hardly noticed Rabbit's weight, and my legs had recovered except for the warm afterburn of hard exercise.

My datalink started squawking at me before we reached the barriers.

"Zack! Where the hell have you been?" Sylvia fussed once I opened my link. "I've been calling you for almost twenty minutes."

"I'm with Rabbit. I'm bringing him home with me. We had a bit of trouble at his place."

"No shit! It's all over the Net. Three dead and you under arrest, according to the news services. There's a launch hold on my pilot program, and our port clearance has been revoked. We're grounded, Boss. What the hell did you do out there?"

"I'll explain when I get home. Have you heard from Cleo?"

"Not exactly. She's on the grid but has her link set to 'ignore.' Do you want me to override?"

I thought for a minute. Even if the Dragons tried to get at me through Cleo, I doubted they would move this soon. And if anyone less capable than their hired ghost tried to snatch her, they'd be in for a nasty surprise. Cleo could take care of herself.

"No," I said." She's already pissed at me. It can wait until she comes home. Patch me through to Deuce, please. Rabbit and I will be there as soon as we pick up his power chair."

"Hey, LT." Deuce answered a second after Sylvia broke off. "What's up?"

"I ran into trouble at Rabbit's place." I could hear him

curse under his breath but couldn't make out what he said. "I mixed it up with some guys who turned out to be Red Dragons."

"Are you OK?"

"Yeah, I'm fine. Rabbit's okay, too. But Deuce, Mike Finney is dead. I found him at Rabbit's place. I'm sorry, partner, I know he was your brother. He was dead before I got there. I couldn't help him."

"How?" Deuce's voice was flat and cold.

"Shot. Clean, no pain. He got mixed up with the Red Dragons somehow. They were after Rabbit, too. They used Mikey to get past Rabbit's security." I didn't want to say more, especially if Mikey was an innocent bystander, grabbed only because he could get to Rabbit.

"I don't give a shit about Conejo," growled Deuce. "What was Mikey doing with the Dragons?"

"I don't know, Deuce."

He was silent for a long moment, and then he sighed, "Has anyone told Mariko?"

Damn! I'd forgotten about Mikey's wife. She and Mikey had been at my wedding, and had visited the *Profit* several times. I felt like a jerk for forgetting her.

"No. Do you want me to go by there on the way?"

"No," Deuce said quietly. "I'll go. She should hear it from me."

"Wait for us. I'll go with you. I owe her that."

"Okay, LT, but keep Conejo away from her. Away from me, too."

"Sure, Deuce. Anything you say." There was already bad blood between them. If Mikey was dead because of his connection to Rabbit, I'd have to keep Deuce from killing him. I wasn't sure I could.

The scooter was still parked near the perimeter fence of the recycling plant. I loaded Rabbit onto the back. We drove through dim tunnels that stank of organics, to the public storage where Rabbit kept his chair. The AI that ran the gate had a glitch in its voice recognition program. Rabbit had to recite his pass code three times before it opened the security door. If I'd had Deuce's pulse rifle, it would have taken a lot less time.

We found Rabbit's locker and opened it. I helped him into the power chair. His eyes glazed over for a second as his nanofibers linked up with the chair's systems. The gyros spun up with a whine and the chair rose on two wheels, lifting Rabbit to eye level with me.

"Like it, Zack?" he asked. "It's an old DeCastro gyro-chair that I found in a scrap heap. I fixed the stabilizers. The originals were fried, but I found a couple of gyroscopic thruster-servos on a wrecked shuttle and adapted their interface to fit the chair. Then I added..." Rabbit rattled on. I tuned it out. At least he was babbling technogeek, not obsessing about Metternich.

Whatever Rabbit had done to his chair, it worked. He had no trouble keeping up with the scooter.

CHAPTER SIX

I brooded all the way home. It had been such a simple plan: a one-time score on a crooked casino, a little poetic justice. Now I was plotting grand theft for one criminal syndicate while a second wanted my head. All because Rabbit had sucked me into another of his delusions. Metternich was dead, damn him! I'd seen the air strike on the Presidential Palace from the roof of the Bear.

* * *

We rolled up the ramp into *Profit's* forward hold. Deuce was waiting for us, murder in his eyes. Standing in the middle of the bay with his meaty fists at his sides, he said nothing as I pulled the scooter into its stall. Rabbit stayed near the portside bulkhead, as far from Deuce as he could get.

"Can you climb the aft ladder with that fancy chair of yours?" I asked Rabbit as I shut the scooter down and checked the charging plug.

"Sure, Zack," he said. "The top wheels rotate around the bottom ones like a Ferris wheel. I can climb a vertical ladder if I need to. I even have—"

"Stop." I held up my hand. To my surprise he shut up. He never took his eyes off of Deuce. "Just go up to the salon and wait there. I'll come for you as soon as we get back from Mariko's"

"Okay, Zack." Rabbit started for the aft ladder, carefully avoiding Deuce's gaze.

"Sylvia," I called as Rabbit rolled away.

"Yes, Boss?"

"Make sure Rabbit is bedded down in the charter cabin."

"Will do."

"And download from my datalink the video from Rabbit's place. Secure file, voiceprint access. Go over it and make sure we can use it as evidence if this magistrate wants to push a criminal charge at the inquest." That last got me a hard look from Deuce. "See if you can find out anything about our ghost assassin. Check law enforcement, military, immigration. Get me an ID. I want to know who this guy is."

"What about the launch hold, Boss? We're grounded without a port clearance."

"Get Rabbit to work on it." I glanced at him and he nodded. "Maybe he can slice us a clearance."

"If you say so," she said doubtfully.

"Just do it," I ordered, not in the mood to argue with a collection of overclocked microprocessors.

Deuce stared after Rabbit, clenching and unclenching his fists. The tips of his forked beard shook slightly as he ground his teeth together.

"Stand down, buddy. We don't know what happened with Mikey. We'll sort it out after we see Mariko." I reached out and touched his shoulder. The muscles were hard as hull metal. "Deuce! Look at me!"

He turned his eyes my way. He relaxed slightly and unclenched his fists.

"Do Mike and Mariko still have their place down in Freetown?" I asked.

"Yeah," he said.

"Then bring your pulse rifle. I don't want to go to that part of town with just a pneumatic." He didn't move, just stared after Rabbit as the wheelchair slowly climbed the ladder. I squeezed his arm. "Deuce, get your pulse rifle. Then we'll go see Mariko."

"Why does Deuce need a pulse rifle to visit Mariko?" Cleo asked from behind us. I turned to see her stepping through the sally port. She still wore the crème color suit, the shawl draped over one arm. She caught sight of Rabbit, halfway up the aft ladder. "And why is Eddie here?"

"Because Mikey is dead and that rat bastard got him killed!" Deuce shouted, shaking off my hand and starting toward the ladder.

"It wasn't my fault, Deuce," Rabbit whined. "I didn't know they were gonna use Mikey. He was my friend too, you know."

"Shut up!"

"Stand down, Deuce!" I shouted back, trying to get a grip on his shoulder. I'd have had more luck trying to stop a rockslide.

"That's enough, Deuce," Cleo's calm voice cut through the tension. Deuce stopped, turning toward her. She threw the shawl over one shoulder and put a hand on her hip. "Eddie, go up to the salon. Deuce, Zack, somebody tell me what's going on here."

"Mike Finney's dead," I said.

Deuce opened his mouth to say something, but closed it again at a sharp gesture from Cleo. She looked at me expectantly.

"When I got to Rabbit's some high-priced enforcer was working him over, backed up by a couple of goons. They used Mikey to get past Rabbit's security system and then killed him when they got inside. I took out the goons, but the enforcer got away." I quickly outlined the fight at Rabbit's place, ending with Hank's timely appearance.

Cleo's face paled. "What does Mike have to do with the Wu job?"

"What?" I asked. "Who said anything about Wu? These guys were Red Dragons. The enforcer was working for Colin Jones. Rabbit tried to welsh on some deal with them and Jones hired this guy to make Rabbit turn over the work. As far as I know, they picked Mikey because he owed Rabbit money and could get them past the security system."

Cleo nodded as some color returned to her face. "Has anyone told Mariko?"

I shook my head, still trying to sort out her question about Kwai Chang Wu. "No. Deuce and I were just going to talk to her."

"I'm going, too," Cleo said. "Give me five minutes." She started for the aft ladder as Rabbit reached the top and rolled down the passageway toward the salon.

"The hell you are," I said. I stopped her with a hand on her shoulder. "That's down in Freetown, and the Dragons are probably looking for me. They've got deep contacts inside the *Federales*. As soon as Hank filed his report, you know Colin Jones got a copy. I'm not risking any more of us."

She whirled and faced me, eyes flashing.

"I'm going and that's the end of it! I'm not letting you two apes tell Mariko about Mikey all by yourselves." Her eyes softened. "She just lost her husband. She'll need to talk to a woman."

I started to say something else, but stopped myself. She was right. I was lousy at dealing with tearful women. "All right," I conceded, "we all go. Deuce, get your rifle."

Deuce looked at Cleo. She nodded. "Do as he says, Deuce. I'll change and be down in five minutes."

Deuce opened the weapons locker and lifted out his pulse rifle. He checked the power indicator on the stock, grunted, slid out the power pack, and exchanged it for a fresh one from the charging rack. I stood by with arms folded, waiting.

He looked up. "Something on your mind, LT?"

"Just wondering exactly when I lost command of this ship."

Deuce slung the pulse rifle over his shoulder and shook his head. "You're still the Boss, LT. It's just that Cleo understands about Mikey—about why I want to murder that bastard Conejo, if this was his fault." He held up his hand as I opened my mouth to speak. "I know, you won't let me. I wasn't there in the Bear with you. He was. Long as he stays your friend, I won't kill him." He leaned against the bulkhead, looking down at the deck, slowly moving the toe of his right boot back and forth. I'd never seen him look that way before. "You know, Mikey was my stepbrother," he said finally.

"I know," I answered softly, suddenly aware of how little I knew about Deuce's life outside of the ship and our time in Spec Ops. He'd latched onto me after I hauled him through the basic training swim test, and he'd watched my back ever since. Deuce was formidable on land, but he swam like a rock.

"You never asked about him."

"No, I didn't. But I guess Cleo did."

Deuce nodded. "Mikey's dad married my Ma after Pop died. Mikey was about fifteen then. I was already out on my own, working a mining claim in the Olympus highlands. Ma really took a shine to him. I guess with me grown and Pop gone, she missed having a kid in the house.

"A little while after the wedding, the family headed out to the Belt. Mikey grew up out there. By the time I saw him again he was twenty-three and finishing school at Mars Tech.

"Anyway, the mining claim didn't work out. I didn't have too many options—no tech school or skills—so I enlisted. Made the cut for Special Forces. You know the rest of that story."

Deuce shifted the rifle on his shoulder. "You remember when the Black Ops squad came to pick you up?"

"Nothing you could have done if you'd been there, except get yourself killed. You're lucky you were on leave, or we'd both have ended up in the Bear."

Deuce nodded. "I know. Doesn't make it any easier. What I meant was, did you know where I'd gone?"

"Home to see your Ma, you told me."

"Yeah, that's right. Ma was real sick. Bad heart. Out in the Belt, things are pretty primitive. No organ farms or transplants, except for them as can pay. She died a couple of days after I got there. Mikey said she hung on that long just to see me again." He must have seen the look on my face. "The last thing Ma asked me to do was look out for Mikey, be a big brother to him.

"Just after the funeral, we got word about the purges back on Mars. I packed to leave right away, but Mikey asked me not to go." Deuce smiled sadly. "He always was smarter than me, and he was more plugged in to the politics of the Revolution. Sure enough, a couple of days later, I heard from a staff sergeant I knew in Spec Ops HQ that you'd been taken and I was on a termination list."

Deuce gripped my shoulder, eyes filled with pain and regret. "Hardest thing I ever had to do, LT, leaving you in that hole."

I didn't say anything, just laid a hand on his arm. We'd been over this before.

"Anyway, Mikey and I kicked around the Belt for the better part of two years, doing freelance work with the independent miners until Reunification. I didn't know if you were still alive, but knew I had to be there if you got out of the Bear. Mikey didn't even ask. He just packed up and came with me."

"You did right by him, Deuce," I said. "From where I sit, you were a good brother. Mikey was all grown up. He had a wife and a home. If he'd been in trouble, he'd have handled it or called you."

Deuce slammed his fist into the side of the weapons locker. Blood spurted from his knuckles, but he didn't seem to notice. "That's just it, LT. He *did* call me. Yesterday, just before Sylvia asked me to break out the scooter and meet you at the casino. He wanted to meet me this morning. Said he had a problem he needed to talk to me about. I wanted to get that induction coil pulled from the drive, so I said I'd come over after supper instead. I should have been there this morning when those bastards grabbed him."

I didn't say anything right away. I let him stand there, head down, wrestling with his own demons. Nothing I could say would change his mind, at least not right away. He didn't protest when I took the first aid kit from the bulkhead and sprayed skin seal on his torn knuckles.

"You don't know what went down at Mikey's place," I said. "You may have been able to help. Or you may have ended up like Mikey. The best way for you to be a good brother to him is to make sure Mariko is taken care of. It's what Mikey would want from you now."

"He's right, Deuce," said Cleo, from the top of the aft ladder. I didn't know how long she'd been standing there, or how much she'd heard, but her voice seemed to settle Deuce.

She slid down the ladder, hands and feet riding the handrails, and walked toward us. She was dressed for action, in a one-piece black jumpsuit bloused over lightweight boots, her hair drawn up in a tight bun. Twin stun batons were tucked into her belt. She reached into the weapons locker to draw out a blue steel Smith and Wesson needler in a shoulder holster. She looked good. Dangerous, but damned good.

I pulled my own S&W needler from the locker and clipped the holster to my belt. For insurance, I strapped the Huang pneumatic to my ankle and slid my trousers down to cover it.

"Lockdown, Sylvia. Voice code: October second."

"Yes, Boss. How long will you be gone?"

"Don't know," I said. "Maintain until I release."

"Yes, Boss." Sylvia would button the *Profit* up tighter than a vacuum bottle until I gave her the release code. If I didn't come back, Rabbit would be stuck for a very long time.

"Our anniversary?" said Cleo. A sad smile crossed her face as we descended the sally port stairs.

I shrugged, but said nothing. Some dates are memorable no matter how painful the aftermath. Deuce followed us down the stairs. The hatch hissed shut behind us.

Cleo logged onto the public net and hailed us a cab. We'd be traceable, but there was safety in staying in plain sight of the cab's security cameras. Once we reached the dropshaft to Freetown, we'd be on foot; the tunnels there were too narrow for vehicles. If the Dragons were going to move on us, that would be the place.

The cab arrived and we climbed in, three seriously hard cases, armed to the teeth, more than a match for any Red Dragons.

Yeah, right.

CHAPTER SEVEN

The cab let us out near the Feng Liu Street dropshafts. The plaza was crowded with Lunatics from the deeper tunnels, going to and from work. Hawkers and food stalls sold everything from falafel to yakisoba. Panhandlers worked the crowd as a three-man band played Martian blues for no one in particular. It was nearly shift-change time at the casinos, and the crowds were thickest near the upshafts. We blended right in. On Armstrong, Deuce's pulse rifle would have stood out—although it was technically legal. Here, there were half a dozen private security types and bodyguards wandering around, even more heavily armed than Deuce.

We made our way to a downshaft and stepped onto a carrier. The car was empty except for a couple of older women in coveralls, who stood at the back and chatted in a mixture of Mandarin and Szechuanese. The doors hissed shut and the gravity field cut out. We dropped in free fall to the two hundred meter level before the generators whined again and slowed the car to a stop.

Freetown. The first thing you notice is the smells. Unwashed bodies mingled with cooking odors, garlic overlaid with boiled cabbage and vat meat, hints of spice and sour fish sauce, stale urine and fresh flowers. The scent of humanity huddled together in close quarters. For tunnel-rats like me, the smells of home.

Armstrong Boulevard, the Promenade, and the Domes were Tycho City's playgrounds for the tourists and the rich. Pressure domes and electromagnetic radiation shields were fine for them, but real spacers—Martians and Lunatics and 'Roid miners—preferred several tons of friendly rock over their heads. If all your fancy systems failed, you could still barricade yourself in with food and water and a few cans of air, and wait for help. And if help never came, at least you could die close to friends and family.

The lower plaza was just as crowded as Feng Liu Street had been, if a bit darker and seedier. Here the vendors were as likely to sell secondhand and salvaged goods as new, and the crowds did more looking than buying. We stepped from the dropshaft and headed for the wide tunnel directly across from it. Deuce swung his pulse rifle off his shoulder, checked the safety, and kept it cradled under his right arm, ready for use. Cleo and I fell in behind as we threaded our way through the crowd.

Deuce's size and grim face caused most folks to step aside. The tunnel mouth squeezed the flow of traffic even tighter for a few meters, jostling us and forcing us to walk single file.

Cleo flicked out with one of her stun batons when a hand groped her. There was a crackle of electricity and a loud yelp. No one got close enough to touch us after that.

Deeper into the warren that was Freetown, the crowds thinned. Tunnels branched away on all sides in a twisting maze. I called up a map from my datalink and displayed it on the heads-up of my contact camera, but most of the passages we followed weren't even marked. Deuce knew the way, though, so Cleo and I followed.

Deuce stopped at a branching intersection. A small food stall occupied a niche in the wall, beside the right-hand tunnel. Hanging baskets, filled with fresh dwarf oranges and star apples, hung from the roof on either side of the high counter separating the stall from the tunnel. Bright packages of taro chips and dried papaya littered the tunnel floor. I looked over the counter, but the niche was empty.

Deuce brought his pulse rifle up and clicked the safety off. "Something's not right," he said. "Mrs. Kuakini wouldn't leave her store open like this."

Cleo and I drew our needlers. "Which way?" I asked.

Deuce pointed toward the right fork and we eased our way into the opening. This was a residential warren, with apartments at regular intervals on each side of the main passageway. All of the doors were closed. No one passed us as we crept down the corridor toward Mike and Mariko's place. There was a sharp turn to the left, and Deuce stopped to peek around the corner. He pulled back and held up two fingers, then pointed them at his own eyes: *two lookouts.*

I nodded and motioned him back.

"Is there another door?" I whispered.

Deuce nodded. "Back to the store, left tunnel, then a hard right. There's a utility tunnel for all of the flats on this side of the corridor."

"Give us a few minutes. I'll call over the link when we're in position. Get their attention in front, and we'll go in from the rear."

Deuce nodded. I glanced at Cleo. Her face lit up in a savage smile.

"Just like old times," she said.

"Playing pirate?" I asked as we started up the passageway.

"This is different. Mariko's in trouble."

I wasn't sure I understood the difference, but was sure I'd never understand Cleo. We slipped back up the corridor to the fork, found the utility tunnel and popped the lock on its door. The passage was dark and barely shoulder width, lined with cables and power conduits. We padded swiftly along to a sharp bend that paralleled the main corridor. I dropped to a crouch and looked around the corner, my head at knee level. Cleo stood over me. I could feel her hand on my shoulder.

The back door was guarded. I wasn't surprised. Easy just didn't seem to be happening today. The guard leaned against the tunnel wall, arms crossed. No weapon was visible, not that it mattered; I'd have to cross eight meters to get to him. A needler would put him down, but if there was another sentry inside the door, we'd tip our hand too soon.

I pulled my head back, trying to decide what to do next. The flat spitting sound of Cleo's needler decided for me. I surged forward as the guard sank to his knees, holding his neck with a surprised look on his face. I caught him and eased him to the floor. The door stayed shut. The only sound was the pounding of the blood in my head.

"Damn it, Cleo," I whispered. "What the hell do you think you're doing?" I pulled a wicked folding knife from the guard's back pocket and a blunt nosed pneumatic from his shoulder holster.

"Taking action," she whispered.

"And what if there had been another one inside the door?" I grunted as I hauled the inert body out of the way. "What kind of ammo are you packing?"

"Sleepers. He'll be out for five or six hours."

I stepped up to the door, exhaled, and allowed the nanos to augment my hearing. There were muffled voices on the other side of the door, but I couldn't make out words or tell for sure how many there were. Three at least, maybe four. None seemed close to the door. I tried the wheel in the center of the door; it was unlocked.

I raised Deuce on the datalink. "We're in position, Deuce. Make some noise."

"Glad to," he answered.

I looked at Cleo, holding up fingers as I silently counted: *one, two, THREE!* I spun the wheel releasing the metal dogs, and shoved hard with my shoulder.

The heavy door swung inward. Cleo dove past me. Rolling left, needler ready, she swept the room. I stepped through in a crouch. Cleo's needler spat as a heavy-set man in black fatigues turned toward us, pointing a long-barreled pneumatic. He sagged to the floor, his gun pumping slugs into the overhead. I heard shouts from the next room and, beyond that, the sizzling twang of Deuce's pulse rifle.

We were in a small utility room. Two folding bicycles hung from hooks on the wall behind the door. Storage containers lined the other walls. A short hallway connected with the main room of the flat. I stepped over the body on the floor, my back pressed against the hallway's right wall. Cleo moved down the left side.

The flat consisted of a large main room, a small bedroom to the left and a smaller kitchen to the right. The main room was a wreck. Shattered furniture, broken glass and shredded clothing littered the floor. A chair lay on its side, the upholstery slashed and padding ripped out.

Directly across from us, the front door stood wide open, a body in the doorway. Deuce stuck his head around the edge of the doorjamb and snapped off two quick shots into the room. The shots went wide, sizzling and crackling along the walls as the pulses of coherent microwave energy dissipated.

Two other goons crouched behind a syntholeather couch. Scorch marks showed where Deuce's shots had come close. One of them lifted a short-barreled pistol and returned fire, but Deuce had already pulled back behind the jamb.

I looked to Cleo. She nodded to her left and raised her needler. I took the guy on the right, dropping him with my first round. I shifted aim to the second, but Cleo's needle had already found its mark. I stepped into the room, sweeping my aim around, but nothing else moved.

"Deuce!" I shouted. "Hold your fire. We're clear."

Deuce stepped into the door frame, pulse rifle leveled. "Where's Mariko?"

"Here," said Cleo, rushing into the small bedroom.

The door was open. Mariko was naked, bound spread-eagle to the bed frame. Blood stained the sheets around her head and between her legs. Her face was a mass of bruises, clotted blood and matted hair. Cleo sprang toward her. As she reached the bed, a foot lashed out from behind the door, kicking the needler out of her hand. I saw the flash of a blade as she whirled to face her attacker, then the door slammed shut.

"Deuce! Trouble!" I shouted, dashing for the bedroom. I leapt over the upturned chair and hit the door with a flying kick. It crashed inward and I jumped through, needler up.

Cleo crouched with her back to me, her stun batons weaving a complex defensive pattern. Facing her was a large man in black fatigues. He held a short *wakizaki* sword at low ready, shifting it back and forth, looking for an opening. He looked familiar somehow, but I pushed the thought away as I sighted along the needler, looking for a shot. Cleo kept weaving into my line of sight.

"Move, Cleo," I shouted.

She did, but not the way I expected.

She dropped her guard with her left arm, inviting an attack. The man took the bait, thrusting with his blade at her flank. She spun into him, slashing down with the stun baton, catching his arm just above the wrist. The electric charge jolted him, sending the thrust wide. Cleo grabbed his wrist and continued her turn, pulling him forward and bracing her back against his chest. She twisted his thumb and pried the *wakizaki* from his grip. With a flip of her wrist, she reversed the blade and thrust backward, driving the sword deep into his chest.

He sank to his knees, gripping the haft of the sword as

she stepped away. I brought the needler up, but before I could take the shot Cleo spun on her heel and delivered a roundhouse kick to the side of his head, slamming him into the wall.

She looked at me, as if noticing for the first time that I was there. "Thanks for the help," she said.

"Hey, I tried to take a shot. You kept getting in the way." I clicked the needler's safety on and slid it into the belt holster.

Cleo rushed to Mariko's side, touching her face and her neck. "She's still alive," she announced, and tugged at the tape binding Mariko's hands to the bed.

"Cleo. Here." I tossed her the knife I'd taken from the guard, and she went to work on Mariko's bonds.

I knelt next to the man she'd stabbed. He was dead. I checked his pockets for ID. The feeling that I knew him returned. He had no identification, but his face finally clicked in my head with a shock of recognition. I rocked back on my heels, certain I was wrong but, in the next instant, just as certain I was not.

He was the second security man from the Golden Moon, the one who'd been with Vincent when he pulled me away from the roulette tables.

CHAPTER EIGHT

I turned as Cleo cut the last of Mariko's bonds. She put her hand on Mariko's shoulder and shook her, gently at first and then more insistently. "Mariko? Come on, Baby, wake up."

Mariko's eyes flew open, and she gazed around the room in panic. Then she focused on Cleo. She reached out with a strangled cry. Cleo grabbed her in a fierce hug. Deuce slung his pulse rifle and moved to the other side of the bed.

"Hush, Mariko," Cleo said softly. "We're here. You're safe now."

Mariko struggled to speak, but her face and jaw were busted up and all she managed was a hoarse croak. She clung to Cleo with one bloody hand and reached out with the other toward Deuce. He grasped it, but she shook it free and croaked again, gesturing at something over his shoulder.

"What is it, Koko?" he asked, looking behind him.

She pointed to a hologram matrix on the bedside table. It lay on its side, Mikey and Mariko on their wedding day, smiling and feeding each other cake, the image looping over and over. The matrix frame was cracked and part of the image was out of synch with the rest.

Deuce picked it up and held it out to her. "Mikey?" he asked. "I'm sorry, 'Ko. I'm sorry. Mikey's dead." His voice broke as he said it.

Mariko covered her eyes and sobbed softly for a moment. She took a deep shuddering breath and shook her head. She reached out and took the hologram from Deuce and turned it over. She held it out to me, tapping a finger on the base.

There was a small slot in the base for the image chip and a battery. The cover bulged outward as if it had been forced down over something too large for the compartment. I pried it up with a fingernail. Wedged into the small opening, on top of the image chip, was a second loose datachip. I took it out and held it up on my fingertip.

"Is that what they were after?" asked Deuce.

Mariko lifted her hand, more weakly now and pointed to the tiny chip. She nodded and tried to speak, choked on her own blood and fell back on the bed.

"Koko!" Deuce cried out, clutching at her hand.

Cleo felt for her pulse. "She's still alive. We need to get her to a hospital. I'm calling the medics." I saw her clench her jaw, activating her datalink.

"Wait," I said. "We need to get her out of here first."

"Zack, look at her. She's half dead. We can't risk moving her."

"And we can't risk being here when the law shows up," I shot back. Cleo put on her stubborn face. "Think," I said. "We're already grounded by the launch hold. We may not be able to meet Wu's deadline even if we can snatch the container. And, there's an AI magistrate just itching to throw me in a BPS cell for the rest of my life. What do you think will happen if we get connected to another room full of dead bodies?"

"He's right, Cleo," Deuce chimed in, still holding Mariko's limp hand. "We can't afford any more heat. I'll take Koko up to Mrs. Kuakini's store. Send the medics there. It'll look like a robbery gone bad. Happens all the time in Freetown. Just another day."

Deuce lifted Mariko into his arms, cradling her head like an infant's. He started for the door and then looked back at me. "These guys ain't Dragons, LT. I checked the stiffs by the door. No tattoos."

"I know."

"Conejo might be right," Deuce conceded. "Maybe Mikey was grabbed because he could get them past the security system. Doesn't explain what these guys wanted with Mariko. Someone's behind all this. I aim to find out who. And then I aim to kill them."

"We'll find out," I assured him. "Right now, just take care of Mariko." He nodded and stepped through the door.

Cleo retrieved her needler and slid it into her shoulder holster. "I know that look," she said. "You know something you didn't tell Deuce."

"Deuce is right. These guys aren't Dragons. I think they were working for Kwai Chang Wu." I pointed to the man on the floor, skewered by his own *wakizaki*. "This one was at the Golden Moon yesterday. He's hired muscle, paid by Wu."

Cleo shook her head. "That doesn't make any more sense than the Dragons being behind this. What do Mike and Mariko have to do with Wu?"

"I don't know." I held up the datachip on my fingertip. "But I'll bet this will tell us something." I spoke into my datalink. "Sylvia, override lockdown. Voice command: 'September second.'"

"Here, Boss," she answered. "Is Mariko okay?"

"Deuce is getting her to the medics. We ran into trouble down here. I'll fill you in later. Right now I need to access a datachip and upload its contents to you."

"Half a second," she said. I got the impression she was conversing with Rabbit in the background. "All right, ready for upload."

I closed my eyes and concentrated on the tip of my finger. My sense of touch heightened as the nanofibers migrated into the sensory receptors of my skin. The nanos extended and linked to the datachip's input and output ports. My hand and arm tingled, muscles twitching, as the nanos used the electrical potentials from my own cells to power the chip. My fingertip began to feel hot. I knew it was an illusion, created by over stimulation of the pain fibers as the data streamed up my arm to the datalink, but that didn't make it hurt any less. I gritted my teeth and tried to ignore the pain.

"Upload complete," said Sylvia. I shifted the chip to my other hand and shook my fingertip until the heat subsided. "Sorry, Boss," Sylvia continued. "The files are encrypted. High quality algorithms. I'll put a subroutine to work on it, but I doubt I'll get anywhere without the encryption key."

"Thanks, Sylvia. We'll work on that from this end, too. Stay buttoned up until Cleo gets there." I handed the datachip to Cleo. "Make sure Mariko gets to the medics, and then take the chip back to the *Profit*. I'll meet you there. I don't want to be holding it if the law shows up. Maybe Rabbit and Sylvia can crack the encryption. Ask Deuce if he has any clues. The key is probably a word or date that was significant to Mikey."

"What about you?"

"I'll clean up here. Then I'm going to call Hank and beg a favor." I wasn't looking forward to that conversation, but didn't see any other way to buy the time we needed.

Cleo touched my cheek as she passed; an unexpected gesture of tenderness and concern.

"Be careful," she murmured, leaving me even more confused about women and their moods. I stood with my hand on the cheek where her fingers had brushed it.

I noticed that the nanos were still active, augmenting my hearing and touch. That alarmed me. They'd never stayed active for this long after I was done with them. I tried to make them retract, but nothing seemed to change. I thought about calling Sylvia, but there wasn't anything she could do except worry with me, and I didn't have time right now. There was work to do if I was going to stay out of the slammer.

I moved around the flat, collecting all of our needles. I wiped down the hilt of the *wakizaki* and collected the knife Cleo had used to cut Mariko free. The pieces of tape and the bloody sheet I rolled together and stuffed into the recycler. I started the burn sequence, and they were reduced to ash within a couple of seconds. There were other prints and DNA trace everywhere, but that could be explained. We were family friends, after all.

My cleaning job wouldn't stand up to a concerted crime scene analysis, but if I could get Hank to cooperate, it might not have to.

Any hope of that faded when I found the dead cop stuffed in the kitchen cupboard.

She was a young woman with pale skin and flaming red hair. She wore the blue and green uniform of a BPS beat cop. I knelt beside her, careful not to touch anything. A neat round hole in her right temple showed where the pneumatic round had entered through the red hair. There was no exit wound. Her blue eyes were open and empty. She was dead, and I was well and truly screwed.

I activated my datalink and called Hank's office. An AI answered.

"This is a priority call for Lieutenant Boucher," I told it. It tried to argue with me until I cut it off with the override pass code Hank had given me several months back. I hoped he hadn't changed it.

"Boucher," he said once the call went through.

"Hank, it's Zack Mbele. I need a favor."

"How did... Aw, shit! I knew I should have changed that pass code. What do you want, Zack? I can't do anything about the port clearance, so don't even ask." He sounded harried but not seriously pissed off. I hoped.

"No, it's not about the port clearance. It's about Mike Finney and his wife, Mariko."

"What about them?" asked Hank. "Mrs. Finney should be on her way to the Freetown substation by now."

"Yeah," I said. "That's what I need to talk to you about. Mariko's on her way to the hospital with Cleo and Deuce. The patrolwoman sent to collect her is dead."

He was silent for a moment. When he spoke again his voice was hard and cool. "I'm listening," he said.

"We came down to Freetown to tell Mariko about Mikey, to be there for her. She's family. Anyway, we ran into a bunch of thugs at Mike and Mariko's flat. There was a firefight. Three dead, four down with sleepers, and I found your patrolwoman stuffed in a cupboard with a pneumatic round in her head."

"You're in the flat now?" Hank interrupted.

"Yeah."

"Stay there. I'll have medics and a patrol unit there in ten minutes."

"Can't do that Hank," I said. "If I get tied to this, that AI magistrate will lock me up for sure."

"Damn it, Zack!" He was mad now. "That can't be helped. Everywhere you've gone in the last twenty-four hours, you've left a trail of bodies. The reports alone will tie me up for a week. If things happened the way you say, you'll get off after the inquest."

"I can't chance it," I said. "I'm working on a deadline. I can't find out what this is all about if I'm cooling my jets in a BPS holding cell."

"What deadline?"

I took a deep breath. No choices left. "You were right about Kwai Chang Wu banning me from the Golden Moon.

His hired muscle dragged me into the back room where Wu made me an offer I couldn't refuse. I'm doing a job for him. If I don't finish it on deadline, he'll take the *Profit.* He bought the lien on my debt, and will foreclose on me."

"What sort of job?" Hank asked.

"Can't tell you. Self incrimination and all that. Principles." I smiled in spite of myself. "I can tell you that Wu is mixed up with the Dragons who took Mikey and killed him. One of the dead guys here at Mikey's flat was the second security man with Vincent Talafofo yesterday, when he pulled me away from the roulette table."

"Yeah?" said Hank. "We ID'd him from the surveillance cameras. His name is...was, George Constantine. Local talent out to make a name. A real nasty piece of work. Nobody down in Freetown will cry at his funeral. But what does that prove? Constantine hired out to anyone with cash."

"The other guys here aren't Dragons. No tattoos. Wu is in this up to his slimy neck."

"Maybe he is," Hank answered. "But this is a cop killing, Zack. I can't cover that up."

"I'm not asking you to. Just keep me out of it for a few days. I can tie Wu to the Dragons and give you both of them, but I can't do that from a cell." I thought for a second. "Put it down as a home invasion. That sort of stuff happens in Freetown. Your dead cop is a hero—lone policewoman takes on a room full of bad guys and saves the victim. I'm asking for a favor, Hank. I need time." He didn't answer. "C'mon. You owe me for that data smuggling lead last March."

"Don't push me," he warned. "That was nothing like this." He paused and for once I kept my mouth shut. "All right, I'll try to keep the investigation local for a few days. But if I find out you're bullshitting me, I'll come to that ship of yours with a warrant and arrest you myself."

"Thanks, Hank. I love you, too."

"Shut up. Just get your butt out of there before the patrol

shows up."

I didn't need to be told twice. I left through the back door and the utility tunnel. Sleeping Ugly was still snoring off the effects of Cleo's needle. I thought about hauling him inside for the BPS patrol to find, but figured that was their job. I began to breathe a little easier when I reached the upshaft plaza.

I rode with the crowd up to Feng Liu Street and caught a jitney to the spaceport. On the way, I called Cleo. She and Deuce were with Mariko at Mother Teresa of Calcutta Hospital. Mariko was going into surgery, and Deuce planned to stay. Cleo would return to the *Profit* once they took Mariko into the operating room.

The jitney dropped me at the commercial port. I caught a ride with a maintenance AI headed for the small-craft staging area, and hopped off less than a hundred meters from home.

Vincent was waiting for me.

He stood in front of the *Profit*'s loading ramp, arms crossed, leaning casually against an oversized shipping container. He didn't move as I approached, just followed me with his eyes.

"I know this isn't a social call," I said. "What do you want, Vincent?"

He didn't change his position. He smiled thinly and nodded toward the container. "Your deal with Mr. Kwai calls for a sealed business container to deliver the goods. This is it. It's already certified with customs. Once the seal is in place, it can't be opened without a federal warrant. Outbound customs won't give it a second look."

"When did you get demoted to delivery boy? Why send a high class enforcer like you to drop off a simple box?" My sarcasm bounced off his cool attitude, at least outwardly. My augmented hearing picked up a slight increase in his heart rate, so maybe he wasn't as cool as he looked.

Vincent shrugged. "Mr. Kwai pays the bills. I do what

he wants. He did ask me to deliver a warning. He wants you to remember that your first priority is the job at hand. Don't get sidetracked with matters that don't concern you. Messing around with the Dragons will only put your ship at further risk."

Oh, ho! I thought. "And what does Mr. Kwai know about the Dragons?"

Vincent uncrossed his arms and spread his hands as he shrugged again. "How should I know? I'm just a simple delivery boy."

"And I don't suppose you know anything about Mike Finney, either?" I asked. Vincent maintained his cool smile, but I detected another bump in his heart rate. "Tell me, does Mr. Kwai pay you to kidnap people from their homes? What's the going rate for raping and torturing a woman in her own bedroom?"

Still he kept his cool. His nostrils flared and his scalp reddened, but his heart rate didn't change. "I don't know anything about that," he said evenly.

"No, of course not," I sneered. Then the pieces connected; his big hands, his height, and the print on the wall outside Rabbit's hole. "No, you don't, do you?" I said more slowly. "You weren't there. Your buddy, Constantine, took over while you went off with the Dragons. "He smiled the same cool thin smile, but his pulse gave him away.

I pressed him. "What happened, Vincent? Did the Tall Man take over once your muscle grabbed Mike and Mariko? He had his own agenda, and Wu's orders meant nothing to him. Did he have business with Mikey too, or was he only interested in getting past Rabbit's security? How did it feel, coming up against someone you knew you couldn't take in a stand-up fight?" Vincent's heart was racing now. His hands balled into fists, but he stood rooted to the same spot, his face frozen in that ghost of a smile.

"You followed them to Rabbit's place. Mike was your target, orders from Wu. But you couldn't take him back from the Tall Man. Oh, Hvalsa and Brody were no problem; you could break both of them in half and not work up a sweat. But the Tall Man, he must have scared the shit out of you.

"So you followed and hid in the tunnel until they went down the Rabbit Hole. Then you called in the cops. An anonymous report of a firefight that sent in a combat team. It'd take that much to bring the Tall Man down. But you didn't count on me. I showed up before the cops, so you had to beat it out of there—because you knew the combat team would be there soon and you couldn't risk being discovered.

"How did that feel, Vincent? I'll bet you never ran from a fight in your life. But this time, not only did you run away, but you lost your man, too. What did Daddy Kwai say about that?"

Vincent's smile finally faded. His forearms quivered and his face flushed. "You're a dead man," he stated flatly.

"I don't think so. At least not yet. Wu wants his goods, and I'm the only one in a position to deliver."

He controlled himself with visible effort. His pulse slowed as he took a deep breath. His fists opened and he relaxed his arms. In spite of myself, I had to admire his ability to rein it in.

"When you finish your work for Mr. Kwai, you and I have business together." He flicked some imaginary dust off of his Cheoy Lee suit.

"I'm looking forward to it." I smiled.

He straightened his collar and nodded, the same thin smile returning to his face. "Until then, you'd best remember Mr. Kwai's warning. It'd be a shame if someone else killed you first."

Before I could think of a snappy response, I heard footsteps behind me. I looked around to see Cleo approaching, right hand resting on one of her stun batons. Vincent noticed her, too, and changed his stance to keep both of us in front of him. He loosened his shoulders and shifted his weight to the balls of his feet.

I held up my hand. "Easy, Cleo. Vincent here was just leaving. Weren't you, Vincent?"

Cleo stopped and gazed from Vincent to me. She kept her hand on the baton.

Vincent regarded her for a second, and then looked me in the eye. "Later." He inclined his head toward Cleo. "Ms. Lee." He eased back on his heels and walked away.

"What was that all about?" Cleo asked, watching Vincent's receding back.

"Oh, you know: threats, innuendo, mutually assured destruction. Guy stuff," I said. She gave me an odd look. "Vincent was waiting for me. He delivered the shipping container for Wu. Also a warning to stay away from the Dragons."

"So they *are* connected. Zack, what the hell is going on?"

"I don't know if Mike was involved with Wu or the Dragons, or both. I don't know what the Dragons have to do with this job we're stuck with. I don't know what's so damned important about this package we're supposed to steal. Basically, I don't know shit and it's really starting to piss me off."

She took my hand. "Let's go home. You need a drink."

"That sounds good. How's Mariko?"

"She's in surgery. 'Stable' is all they'll say. Deuce is staying at the hospital to keep an eye out for more bad guys."

"Then she's safe for now. I want to see if Sylvia and Rabbit have made any progress on decrypting those files. Maybe they'll tell us why Wu was after Mike and Mariko."

Cleo shook her head. "All that can wait. We're both strung out. You need a meal and a nap before you do anything else."

I looked at her. Something in her eyes was different. A light I hadn't seen for a long time. I didn't know what had changed, but somehow she'd lost the hard edge that had eaten at our relationship for months. I squeezed her hand and gave Sylvia the release code. The sally port opened, and we climbed the steps together.

CHAPTER NINE

I felt a bit giddy with adrenaline as we stepped through the inner lock into the forward cargo hold. "Kids! We're home!"

"Zack!" said Sylvia from the overhead speakers. "Eddie just sliced the launch hold from my pilot program! I'm free! I can take off anytime!" She paused. "Of course, we still don't have a port clearance, so even if I did take off, Traffic Control would have the *Federales* on us in a nanosecond, and they'd probably shoot us down or grapple us, and then they'd want to have me reprogrammed because it's always the pilot's fault when there's a port clearance violation—"

"Sylvia," I said. "Settle down. You sound like Rabbit."

Cleo laughed, another thing I hadn't seen for too long.

Rabbit peeked cautiously down from the catwalk near the cockpit hatch. "Hi, Zack. Hi Cleo. Where's Deuce? How's Mariko? We haven't had any luck with the encryption, have we Sylvia? I tried a decryption program I wrote last year for...well, never mind who for, but it didn't work. I did manage to get the launch hold off of Sylvia, but you already know that. I thought we'd try a random number algorithm from the BPS crypto lab on the stuff you got off the chip. Do you have it, by the way? Sometimes direct access can help—"

"Rabbit," I said. "Shut up! And what did you do to Sylvia? She's babbling."

"I'm not babbling!" said Sylvia. "Well, maybe just a little, but I'm so happy to be free of that launch hold and Edward was so smart to figure out how to remove it. He really is a great slicer and—"

"Damn it, Rabbit! What the hell did you do to Sylvia?"

Rabbit ducked his head as if I had hit him. "Maybe I tweaked her emotional response routines a little."

"What?" Sylvia shrieked. "You messed with my programming!?"

"I...just wanted you to like me a little."

"Untweak her, Rabbit. Right now!"

Cleo laughed louder.

"You're not helping," I said to Cleo, struggling to keep a straight face. It was no use; I broke up. It was silly. No reason for it really, except the sudden easing of all the anxiety and adrenaline from the fight, and a release of tensions bottled up over the course of the last few months.

Cleo leaned back a little, looking at me in a way I thought I'd never see again. I reached up to brush a lock of hair out of her eye. She leaned into me, holding me close again, stroking my back. I lifted her chin and kissed her. Her lips softened and parted, and our tongues met. We clung to each other for a long time.

"So, I guess this means you guys are getting back together?" Rabbit said.

I pulled away from Cleo's lips long enough to glance up at him. "Didn't I tell you to shut up?" I looked back at Cleo.

She smiled and touched my cheek. "I'll see if there's anything to eat in the galley."

I watched her walk off toward the aft ladder. My augmented

senses still tingled with her touch, and my head spun with the scent of her. All the pain and anger of the past eighteen months fell away and we were back to the beginning, before the divorce and the tears and the accusations. And yet we weren't. Those things had happened, and couldn't be undone with a single kiss. I gazed up at Rabbit. He shrugged.

"Here, Eddie," Cleo said as she reached the top of the ladder. She held out the datachip. Rabbit rolled along the catwalk and took it from her. "Don't worry," she assured him. "Deuce knows it wasn't your fault. He's taking care of Mariko for a while. He'll cool off before he comes home."

Rabbit nodded, opened his mouth like he wanted to say something, closed it and shook his head. He turned and rolled back down the catwalk.

I stowed our weapons in the locker and followed Cleo up the ladder. I could hear her rustling about in the galley. I walked past the salon and through the hatch behind her. She was chopping onions and mushrooms while garlic and olive oil sizzled in a pan on the cook top.

"Soy noodles with marinara," she said as she slid the chopped ingredients into the hot oil. "If the tomato paste concentrates haven't completely dried out,"

I leaned against the bulkhead. "Rabbit didn't mean anything."

"Eddie always believed in us, Zack," she said, stirring the sauce. "He needs the fairy tale."

"Cleo, if I thought—"

"Not now. We're both high on adrenaline. Go set the table in the salon."

I did as she asked. The warm smell of garlic and tomato permeated the ship, taking me back to other evenings, other meals. I smiled as I set out cutlery.

"Hey, Rabbit," I called toward the cockpit. "Take a break. Dinner in five."

Rabbit and Cleo arrived together, Rabbit toting a virtual

keyboard projector and Cleo carrying a large bowl of steaming pasta and sauce. Cleo glared at Rabbit until he dumped the projector into the pouch slung from the back of his chair.

For several minutes there was nothing but the sound of good food being served and eaten. I was famished; the nanos drained a lot of energy. Rabbit ate mechanically. Food was simply fuel to him, be it protein mash or a gourmet dinner. Cleo ate quietly, her mind somewhere far away. I caught her eye several times as we ate, but her quiet smile gave me no clues. It was as if the past year and a half had never happened. I concentrated on my food. This was more than just an adrenaline high. I knew the signs—from long and painful experience.

The first time Cleo left me, I spent weeks convincing myself that she'd be back. By the third time, I spent weeks hoping that she wouldn't. I didn't think I could stand another go-round.

I'd just reached for another helping when Sylvia chimed on my link. "Sorry to interrupt, Boss, but Deuce is calling. I'll put him through."

"Thanks, Sylvia. Put him on speaker, please."

"LT? Are you and Cleo okay?"

"We're fine. How's Mariko?"

"Alive. Asleep. They say she's out of danger, but they're regrowing part of her jaw, so she won't be able to talk for a while." Deuce's tone was more sad than angry. "What's this all about, LT? Why Mikey and Koko?"

"I don't know, yet. Some of the goons at the apartment were working for Kwai Chang Wu, but as far as I know, Mikey never had anything to do with him."

"Anything on that chip you found? Koko seemed to think it was mighty important."

"Um...hello...um, Deuce?" Rabbit stammered. "We haven't been able to crack the encryption. I was hoping you might have some idea what Mikey would use as an encryption key. I've tried his birthday, Mariko's birthday, and their wedding date. Nothing. It's probably some word or date that he'd remember. Of course it could be a random sequence of numbers and letters, but most people don't like to memorize those, so I'm pretty sure it's a name or a date."

Deuce sighed. "I don't know. I'd have said their wedding anniversary or maybe Ma's birthday, but... He paused. "Try 'Colleen.' It was Mikey's dad's pet name for Ma."

"Got that, Sylvia?" Rabbit asked.

"Of course, Edward," she said frostily. "Accessing. Access granted! Well, what do you know? Oh, Zack, you've got to see this."

She activated the matrix in the middle of the table. Lines of text and a colored bar graph appeared over the remains of the pasta and red sauce.

"What are we looking at?" I asked. "Patch it through to Deuce's link, Sylvia."

"This is an original copy of the McAllen Engineering survey that Wu commissioned when he took over on Ceres," she said. "Deuce, did Mike ever work for McAllen?"

"Yeah, I think so. A couple of years ago he did some freelance work for them. Didn't like something about the job. Never said what, but I knew he wasn't happy. I figured they stiffed him on the fee, 'cause they went belly-up just after that. He never showed me anything like this."

"Well, he took a little souvenir with him," said Sylvia. "According to this, the mines played out just when the old surveys said they would. But we know the survey Wu filed with the Federal Resources Management Agency shows reserves of twenty years."

"So Wu paid off McAllen to alter the survey," said Cleo.

"But CM&M is turning out refined metals at a record rate. Where are they getting the ore? And why run the scam on the Feds?" I asked.

"I thought you'd never ask," Sylvia gushed. "The second

part of the file is a copy of shipping reports from the Ceres loading docks. I don't know how Mike got hold of these, but CM&M has been shipping large quantities of ice to the outer Belt—paid for by an outfit called Cymru Investments. Wu shows purchases of modest quantities of ore through Cymru, transported back to Ceres on the empty ice freighters. According to Mike's files, the actual ore deliveries were almost twenty times the declared tonnage. Wu claims to be buying specialized ore at a premium when he's actually buying bulk ore at less than the market price. He turns big profits in both the ore refining and the ice sales."

"Who's Cymru Investments?" Cleo asked.

"I know who they are," I said. "Remember last March when Deuce and I did that data-freight run to Mars? Turned out it was part of a data smuggling operation, running bootleg programs from London to Tharsis. They tried to stiff me on the fee, so I tipped off Hank, and the BPS raided a black market software outfit in lower Beta. Half of the gang worked for Cymru. The company denied any knowledge of their employees' activities and was, of course, 'shocked' to find out they had Dragon tattoos.

"But everyone knows Jones pulls the strings at Cymru. It looks like both Wu and the Dragons had reasons for going after Mikey. What I don't see is where Cymru gets the ore, and why they'd be involved in bulk commodities."

Deuce spoke up. "They get it from the Dragons out in the Belt. Dragons run everything out there and everybody pays them squeeze. Those who can't pay cash, pay in goods or ore. Those who try not to pay end up on the wrong side of an airlock." Deuce's voice was bitter. "Dragons rake off half the ore production and sell to Wu at a cut rate, or trade for ice that they sell to the miners. Keeps the market price low and the miners under their thumb."

"OK," I said. "So we know the Dragons are bad people, and I know you feel kin to the miners because of Mikey and your stepdad, but why should Wu care if this gets out? Cymru is a legal operation, even if it fronts for a bunch of criminals."

"Well, for starters," said Cleo. "There's fraud involving a Federal agency, not to mention filing false stockholder reports. And then there's Daddy Kwai, who thinks his number two son is some sort of production genius."

"Yeah, maybe," I replied. "But it's a natural business move for Ceres to get out of mining and into smelting and metallurgy. They've got the only large-scale operation in the Belt, so who else would the miners or the Dragons sell to? Besides, the ice on Ceres is the real moneymaker. It's the main water source for everything between Mars and Saturn."

I tried to think it through. "CM&M could have pursued that strategy from the start. If the false survey comes out and causes trouble for Kwai Hong, he'll give Wu the ax in a heartbeat and the company will go on. Wu knows that. So why would he do something stupid like filing false reports? Either the Dragons have some dirt on Wu and are forcing him to deal with them, or he's into something much bigger— big enough that he'd kill Mike and Mariko to keep it quiet."

"So are we still working for this slimeball, LT?" asked Deuce. "Or do we aim to kill him?"

"We have to finish the job, or he'll take the *Profit*. We'll snatch his container and make the delivery." *And then we'll kill him.* "Anything else, Sylvia?"

"Well, there's this," she said. A hologram hovered over the table. A young woman in a halter top and skimpy shorts posed provocatively on a barstool. A butterfly tattoo peeked out from under the right leg of her shorts. The name 'Amber Walenska' glowed above her head.

"It's not referenced to anything else in the files," Sylvia continued. "I don't know why Mike included it in the database."

"Ring any bells with you, Deuce?" I asked.

"Nope. Pretty girl, though. Don't think Mariko would like Mikey hanging around with her."

"Oh my God," Cleo gasped. "With all the uproar over Mariko, I forgot to tell you. While you were at Eddie's, I met with my friend from TransAstral. He told me that the *Grant* is bypassing a scheduled port call at L4 and is due here five days early."

"Sylvia?"

"On it, Boss," she replied. After a second, she said, "Cleo's right. The shipping register shows them due in five and a half standard days."

"Damn!" I muttered. At least it wouldn't conflict with the inquest. "Deuce, any word on the customs yard?"

"Negative, LT, but I haven't heard from Kenny down at the guild hall. He may have something. Ain't likely to happen in the next five days, though. Construction's way behind schedule."

"Why don't we meet the *Grant* halfway between here and L4?" asked Rabbit. "We could get there in a few hours. We'd have a couple of days to set up, take the container and be back here before anyone misses us."

"We've been over this, Eddie," Cleo said wearily. "We can't lift without the port clearance. Even if we could, the *Grant* would have the *Federales* on us before we could get close enough to grapple them, much less take the container."

"Oh, that's no problem." Rabbit waved a hand. "We can have the Port Authority move us outside the pressure dome and park us on the surface. It's cheaper and we can claim we want to save money. Then we could slip away, hit the *Grant* by midday and be back before suppertime."

"Rabbit," I said, "Cleo's right. Even if we launch from outside, Traffic Control will report the illegal liftoff and the Feds will stop us before we get anywhere near the *Grant*."

"No they won't." Rabbit smirked. "They'll never know we're gone, because I can make us invisible."

CHAPTER TEN

"Run that by me again?" I asked. "Invisible?"

"Well not really, at least not to human eyes. But nobody looks at anything with eyeballs anymore. Not Outside, anyway. It's all done with imaging and AI's. When was the last time you saw a real window, except in the tourist hotels in Upper Armstrong? And you can bet they aren't looking out over a grubby spaceport."

"Don't AI's see things?" Cleo asked.

"Not really," said Rabbit, a superior smile on his face. "Sylvia, can you see me?"

"Of course, Edward."

Rabbit pulled the keyboard from behind his chair and activated it. The virtual board appeared in his lap and he typed several lines of code. "Sylvia, would you please load this code through your pattern recognition application?."

"Okay, Boss?" she asked me.

"Go ahead. I'm sure Rabbit knows what he's doing."

"Uploading," she said. "Wait, where did he go?"

Rabbit laughed. "I'm still here."

"What the hell's going on?" I asked.

"Just a minute, Zack." He made several more key-strokes. "There, Sylvia. All better now?"

"Yes! How did you do that? Did you see that, Zack? He just disappeared!"

"What do you mean? He's been sitting right here the whole time."

"But...I saw, or I didn't see...He..." Sylvia stammered.

"Relax, Sylvia," said Rabbit. "It's just a programming trick. The point, Zack, is that Sylvia doesn't really 'see' anything. Her visual pickups convert images to a digital signal that's transmitted to her processors, and then analyzed by her pattern recognition routines. All AI's and most imaging, navigation, and tracking programs use the same basic source code. It's been around for almost a hundred years. Nobody's altered it since the early Moss days. The instruction I had Sylvia upload exploits an old calibration function in the original source code."

He paused to catch his breath and then plunged on. "Well, it's not really that simple. See, the calibration function is obsolete. Nobody uses it, but it's still in there and I found a way to access it. I just use it to instruct the root pattern-recognition routine to ignore whatever sends it the code, just like it would a calibration matrix on initial activation."

Rabbit paused again.

"Of course, human eyeballs aren't fooled, but AI's, nav, and pilot programs, anything that processes images digitally, can't see a thing." He held up a finger, pausing for effect and enjoying every second of the attention. "But, you might ask, how do I get an AI to accept the code? Sylvia did it because I asked her to and you told her to trust me. But what about a Traffic Control AI?"

In truth, it hadn't occurred to me to ask, but I wasn't about to tell Rabbit that. He was already too full of himself. So I just looked at him expectantly.

He grinned. "That's the sneaky part. See, when a pilot AI

or a nav computer detects another ship, the first thing it does is query the target's IFF transponder. The transponder sends a packet of information with the ship's registration, ownership, tonnage, and a bunch of other stuff. I slip the code into the transponder signal, and the receiving program follows the instruction to ignore me."

"And just like that, we're invisible," I said. Rabbit's head bobbed up and down. "Does anyone else know about this?" I asked.

"Oh, no. No one… Well, except Colin Jones. He hired me to slice a way past a ship's proximity alarm. But this is much better. I couldn't give this to Jones. I guess he has some idea the code exists—that's what that tall freak wanted—but you saw what happened. I didn't talk. No matter what they did, I didn't give them the code."

"Yes, Rabbit, you did. Not the code itself, maybe, but now they know you have it. They know what it can do. And Jones was willing to pay big money to an assassin to get it."

Rabbit's smile faded. "Oh," was all he said.

"Never mind. We're all on Jones' hit list by now. Let's just hope we can stay out of his way until we finish the job for Wu." I thought for a second.

"You know, it might not be a bad idea to move the ship outside at that. It'd be tougher for the Dragons to slip up on us. And there are a dozen public locks into the spaceport. They'd have a hard time covering them all."

"Sounds good to me," said Deuce over the secure link. "I never liked berthing in the common yard anyway."

"Cleo?" I asked.

"Whatever. I don't see how we'll be any safer, but if Eddie's trick works, at least we'll be mobile."

"Sylvia," I said. "Call the Port Authority and get a stevedore 'bot to load Wu's shipping container. Then request a move to a lower-cost berth outside the pressure dome. Ask for a deferred fee. Make it look like we're in financial trouble."

"Will do, Boss. What about Deuce? How will he get back?"

"Just leave my 'suit in a public locker at the Armstrong lock," Deuce said. "I'll walk home. I'm gonna spend the night here, if it's okay with you, LT. I want to keep an eye on Koko."

"Sure. Get some rest, but get back here tomorrow. We'll need that drive rebuilt right away."

"Give Mariko our love, Deuce," said Cleo as she stood up and began clearing the dishes. I got up to help but she waved me off. "I can handle it. Eddie?"

"Huh? Oh, sure," Rabbit said, shutting down the keyboard and gathering up the cutlery.

I sat alone at the table as Cleo bustled about in the galley. She quickly banished Rabbit to his room, and he rolled away without protest. I stared at the tabletop, considering our options. The Wu job came first. If Rabbit's invisibility trick worked, we could slip away, hijack the container and be back before we were missed. Sylvia couldn't crack the encryption on the cargo manifest, but we had a lading number and hold location. Big freighters like the *Grant* carried the cargo containers in rings held together with nanocord rigging. The only pressurized areas of the freighter were the forward crew and command modules and the aft engineering module. They were joined by a long central spine. Up to twenty rings radiated from the spine, like stacked wheels. Each wheel had ten spokes, and each spoke could dock four standard shipping containers, a total of forty containers per wheel. With a little luck, our container would be somewhere amidships rather than near the bow. Better luck would be a dock at the end of one of the spokes.

If we could snatch the container there, we'd be ahead of schedule. The inquest into the fight at Rabbit's would become a minor inconvenience. We'd have plenty of time to make the delivery and return before the deadline. *If* we got the container. *If* we weren't missed while we were making the delivery. *If* Wu kept to the deal. *If, if, if...* I slammed my hand down on the tabletop in frustration. It didn't help, other than hurting my hand. I hated being manipulated.

I knew that Deuce and Cleo were capable of making the delivery, but I had a personal score to settle with Wu—and that required my presence. Once the container was delivered and the ship was safe, Wu would explain everything. And then he would die.

As I rubbed my stinging palm, a tremor began in my left hand—the one I'd slammed on the tabletop. I rubbed harder, but the tremor increased. My whole arm began to quiver, ripples running up and down the muscles of my forearm. I clutched at the arm with my right hand, forcing it to lie on the table.

Another tremor started in my right foot, moving up the leg to my hip. I stood, holding onto the table, both arms and legs now shaking uncontrollably. I tried to walk toward the aft hatch. If I could get to my stateroom, I could lie down until the shaking passed. I stumbled and slammed into the bulkhead next to the hatch.

"Zack? Is that you?" called Cleo from the galley.

"Yeah," I answered, voice shaking.

"Are you all right?"

"Just tired. I'm going to get some rest." I managed to get a grip on the hatch and levered myself through, bracing my hands against either side of the passageway. The tremor subsided, leaving my legs weak and rubbery. I stumbled down the passage to my quarters and collapsed on the bunk. The fine tremors in my hands continued, but my legs were now limp and useless. Then the burning started.

I hadn't felt heat like that since Metternich's biotank. I stuffed my fist into my mouth, stifling a scream as the fire raged through my body. My heart pounded in my ears. The nanos were still active, amplifying every sound: Cleo tidying up in the galley, Rabbit rocking back and forth in his chair muttering lines of code, the faint whoosh of the air handlers as they scrubbed and recycled the atmosphere. I closed my eyes, but the overhead lights burned right through.

I thought about calling for help, but if the nanofibers were going to chew up my nervous system, there was nothing anyone could do to stop them. I lay there trembling and sweating like a juicer needing a taste.

My fear screamed at me. *Not again. You can't do this. Better to have died in the tank than go through this pain again.* Death would at least bring an end to the pain. I beat fear back. I'd survived the Bear; I could handle a little pain from the cocoon of my own bunk.

I lay still as the heat washed through me in wave after wave of internal fire, finally ebbing away like a receding tide. After a long while, I slept.

Somewhere in the darkness, I realized that I was naked and under the sheets. I was no longer alone. At first like a dream, then like a memory, I felt her sliding into the bed next to me. I rolled onto my side and embraced her, my hand sliding up between her breasts in a familiar gesture. I cupped her right breast. She pressed my hand into it, the nipple hard against my palm. She arched her back against me and my erection was immediate and insistent. I massaged her nipple as my lips wandered over the back of her neck. She moaned softly and writhed against my groin, then opened her legs, and I thrust myself into her. We began to move in a slow undulating rhythm, our bodies remembering each other and responding to the carnal dance.

She moaned again and pushed back harder against my thrusts. The rhythm increased. Heat began to sweep through me again, this time sweet and delicious. I felt control slipping away. Just as I was about to surrender, she pulled away and turned to face me. My breath caught in my throat as the heat receded—but not for long. With strong hands she forced me onto my back and threw her leg over my hips. She reached down and guided me into her body, thrusting herself downward with a gasping cry. Then we moved in unison again, faster and stronger than before. With a soft cry, she fell forward onto my chest, grinding her hips into me. I felt the explosion in my own groin and clutched her closer to me.

Afterwards, she lay beside me, her head on my shoulder and one leg still thrown over mine. I lay still, listening to her breathe. My head spun. We'd been here before and always, always ended up hurting each other.

Cleo sighed, perhaps picking up my own thoughts. "Why can't we make this work, Zack? We're so good together. Why does it always fall apart?"

I didn't know what to say. That I couldn't be what she wanted me to be? That I couldn't forgive and forget that she left me and used other men to get what she thought she needed? None of that would help. It was old ground; old wounds that couldn't bear reopening. So I said nothing.

She lifted her head and touched my cheek, turning my face toward her. "I mean it, Zack. Why? Don't close up on me. This may be our last chance."

"Last chance at what?" I asked.

"To build a life. To be together like this. To make it last more than a night or a few days."

"I've always loved you, Cleo. You know that." It sounded better in my head than when I said it.

"I know. You say that like it's all that matters."

"What's wrong with that?"

She rolled onto her back, her head still on my shoulder. "It isn't enough. Love is all lightning and heat. It doesn't last."

"It can."

She sighed again. "Maybe, but not on its own. Love doesn't put food in your belly. It doesn't put air in your lungs or rock over your head."

"No." This was old ground too. "That takes money."

"Not just money. You always reduce it to that. I mean stability, security."

I felt my anger rising. Why couldn't she just leave it alone? This was how our fights always started, Cleo pushing for a settled life, and me running like hell.

"Wu and his cronies bank on all that 'stability' to keep them on top of the heap. 'Security'? The Dragons will give you security, as long as you pay your squeeze. And the Feds? They babble about rights and responsibilities, but they keep the likes of Wu and the Dragons in business while regulating everything from the food we eat to the air we breathe. If they could regulate our dreams, they'd do that it."

Instead of rising to that bait, she rolled toward me again. "The Revolution is over," she said quietly. "This isn't the wild black beyond anymore. People want law and order. Even Martians welcome the safety the *Federales* brought. They want to build some kind of life. You shout about freedom, but it just means living from one scam to the next with nothing to show for it but your next tank of gas and a few yuan for food."

"Great. So I should take a job ferrying hot pastries from Paris to the posh hotels in Armstrong? Or maybe I could haul sewage to the 'ponic farms up in Tranquility."

She laughed, defusing my anger. "You could do worse." She touched my cheek. "Seriously. We do this job for Wu, then the *Profit* will be ours. After that, we walk away."

"Do you really think he'll keep his end of the deal?" I scoffed. "I'd sooner trust a snake."

"He'll keep the deal," she said. "Whatever's in that container, he wants it badly. He can't risk crossing you until he has it in hand. After that, it won't matter. Cheaper and easier to pay you off than try to kill you."

I opened my mouth to speak. She stopped me with a hand on my lips.

"I mean it, Zack. Leave Wu alone. He's more trouble than we can handle. I loved Mike and Mariko, too, but we can't take on the Kwai family. They're too strong for us. Let it go."

"Deuce isn't likely to go along with that," I said.

"So make him go along. You talk, he listens. Chain of command and all that... Let it go. Then we can talk. Either we find a way to live together, or we split our assets and say good-bye." She stroked my cheek and kissed me, then she pulled away and stood up.

I moved to follow her, but she put a hand on my shoulder. "No. Get some sleep. We'll be busy tomorrow."

CHAPTER ELEVEN

Morning came too quickly. My muscles were sore and my head ached from the nano storm of the night before, not to mention Cleo's unexpected attentions. I rolled out of my bunk and managed to get dressed before the nausea hit, but there was nothing in my stomach to come up. I splashed some water on my face and swallowed the bile in the back of my throat. Despite the nausea, my head felt clear, almost light. I could feel the nanos, still there in the background, but there was none of the usual burning pain that followed their use. The soreness in my muscles was more like the kind that followed exercise than the pain of damaged tissue.

Cleo was in the galley. She looked up over a cup of coffee and smiled as I entered.

"Good morning," she said. "You look like hell."

"I love you, too," I grumbled. "What time is it?"

"A little after seven. Sylvia and I were hoping you'd sleep a while longer. I have an errand to run, and then I'm going to relieve Deuce at the hospital. Mariko's doing better and he needs a break."

"As if anyone can get him to take it." I shook my head as hot coffee poured from the dispenser and filled my mug. "You'd better take Deuce's p-suit with you and drop in at a public locker in the passenger terminal. He'll need it if we move before he gets back."

"I can do that if I take the scooter. I'm going to stop by the ship chandler and order some provisions, too—unless you want to live on algae smoothies and protein bars for the next few days." She drained the last of her coffee and placed the mug in the sanitizer. "I'll check with Sylvia from the hospital to get the new berth number." She leaned over and kissed me lightly, then turned and walked toward her stateroom.

I sipped coffee, mildly surprised that my stomach didn't rebel. In fact, the hot liquid tasted good. The nausea had subsided, replaced by a growling hunger. I set the mug on the table and punched up an omelet.

"Sylvia," I called. "What do you hear from the Port Authority? When are we moving?"

"In about an hour, Zack. The stevedores will load Wu's container just before the crane arrives to move the ship. They gave us a delayed payment option, as long as we pay our current bill and put up a ten percent deposit on the next month's rent."

"Good. Is Rabbit awake yet?"

"I don't think so," she said. "He's still in his stateroom and his vital signs indicate sleep."

"Ask him to join me in the salon once he wakes up. I want to find out more about this invisibility code."

"Yes, Boss." Her tone was odd. Flat, almost. Like she'd turned off her personality subroutine.

"Something bothering you, Sylvia?"

"No... Well, maybe. Are you sure you're okay? Something happened to you last night, and now Cleo's all kittens and rainbows where yesterday she'd have sold you out for your share of the ship. What's going on?"

I forked a bite of omelet into my mouth before answering. "Well, right now I'm eating my breakfast."

She made a bleating sound. "Don't be a smart-ass. You know what I mean. What happened last night?"

"I had a bit of trouble with my nanos, but I seem to have reached an accommodation with them."

"And Cleo?" Sylvia pressed.

"We seem to have reached an accommodation, too."

"Oh, Zack. Not again. Why do you let her do this to you?"

"What are you, my mother?"

"Well, pardon me for caring about you. But every time you and Cleo make one of these 'accommodations,' it ends badly for you, not her. I don't know if I can stand another breakup."

Her tone surprised me. She was right about Cleo and me, of course. But AI emotional simulation routines were just that—simulations. Sylvia's personality programming was the best in the whole system, thanks to Rabbit's additions to her base program. Still, real emotion wasn't part of her repertoire. I made a mental note to ask Rabbit about his latest programming tweaks.

"Sorry, Sylvia," I said. "I didn't mean to be short with you. And I know better than to trust Cleo. I can handle whatever happens." Whatever lie it takes to get you through the day. Right?

"Sure you can." Sylvia wasn't buying it, and I could have sworn I heard a sneer in her voice. "Look, I know it's not my business, but where it affects the ship, it affects me. If the two of you want to tear each other apart in stages, that's up to you. Just make sure one of you ends up with clear title to the *Profit*. I still need a place to live."

I laughed. "Don't worry, Sylvia. If the bank comes to take the ship, I'll make sure we download you to a safe data storage cube—unless you'd rather move into the scooter's onboard computer."

"Ha ha. Not funny. I'm serious, Zack. You're in no position to get involved with Cleo all over again. She's poison for you."

"Yeah, well sometimes poison is a sweet way to go."

Sylvia didn't answer. I dumped my dishes in the sanitizer and left the galley. The salon was empty when I entered. I slumped into the couch and waited for Rabbit.

He rolled in ten minutes later, bleary-eyed and unshaven, coffee in hand.

"Hey, Zack," he said. "What's the plan?"

"I was going to ask you the same thing," I said. "How long will it take to get this invisibility code loaded and ready for use?"

"Oh, just a minute or two," he answered. "I'll have to reboot Sylvia's IFF transponder once it's modified, but that won't affect her main program."

"Yeah, about that." I lowered my voice. "Lately her responses have become a lot more, well, emotional. Is that possible? Did you do something to her personality routines?"

"No," he shook his head. "At least not like you think. I un-tweaked the changes I made to her emotional routine, just like you asked, but those routines are self-learning simulations. The more she uses them to interact with people, the more feedback she processes and the more realistic her emotional responses become. My tweaks were just aimed at her specific reactions to me."

"But does she really have feelings?" I asked. "She's acting like an old lover still carrying a torch."

"I don't know," Rabbit said with a shrug. "You're asking questions the best cyberneticists have been working on for years. Hell, we don't even know if AI's are really intelligent or are just very clever call-and-response programs. If she simulates emotions so well that you can't tell them from the real thing, does it matter if they're not real?"

"It does to me," I said.

"So ask Sylvia," he said. "She's refined herself so far beyond my basic programming, that she might as well be human. There's no way to tell anymore. The old Turing test was blown away a hundred years ago. Modern AI's are more human than most people I know."

"I'll think about it."

I'd always said, half-joking, that my only stable relationship was with Sylvia. I wasn't sure I wanted to know if there was an emotional basis for her loyalty.

"When are we going to go after the container?" asked Rabbit. "I have some other gear we need to get ready if we're really going to be stealthy about this. We'll need a pinger to hold our berth here at the spaceport, sort of a dummy ship that will continue to transmit our recognition code and power status to the Port Authority. Otherwise, as soon as we lift off, the departure will be recorded. And we need a pig for the container."

"A pig?" I asked.

"Sort of like the pinger, except programmed with the container's shipping codes. We won't be able to program it until we actually access the container's interface." He paused and looked at me uncertainly.

"I have a feeling I'm not going to like what comes next," I ventured.

"Well, the only way to get the data we'll need is to tap into the interface, but that means getting your nanos in contact with the access port, and it's in..."

"Full vacuum," I finished. "Lovely."

"So how much time do I have?" he asked.

"I want to be ready to lift ship in 36 hours," I said. "If Deuce can get the drive rebuilt, that is. Right now it's in pieces on the deck of the aft hold."

"I can get the pinger and the pig built in a few hours. Want me to help Deuce?"

"No," I said with a wry smile. "That probably wouldn't be a good idea right now."

"Oh." His face fell. "Yeah, I guess you're right."

"Unless you have a spare induction coil for a Moss Mark VI gravity drive," I said. "Parts guy at the chandler won't have one in for a few days."

"No problem, Zack," said Rabbit. "There's a bunch of them in the salvage yard. I keep a running update with the inventory there, just in case they get something interesting." He consulted his link for a second. "They have three Mark VI coils and one of the new Mark VIII's. That's the one I'd get. It's compatible with the *Profit's* drive and it's thirty percent more efficient. It'll boost your gravity field output by five percent, maybe more at high accelerations."

"Thanks, Rabbit." I should have known. Rabbit was tapped into just about every database in Tycho. Paranoia had its uses.

He rolled out of the salon and headed toward the cockpit to coordinate the code changes with Sylvia. I called up the salvage yard on my link and paged through the inventory. Sure enough, there was an induction coil available. I placed an order and authorized a deposit with final payment on pickup. Then I called Deuce.

"Hey, LT," he said, sounding weary. "What's up?"

"How's Mariko?" I asked.

"She's awake. Can't talk, of course, but she's gonna be all right."

"Good. I need you back at the ship. We need to get that drive rebuilt right away."

"Need a new induction coil."

"Got it covered. There's one at the salvage yard that'll fit. I put a deposit on it. You can pick it up on your way."

"I don't know, LT," he said slowly. "I don't want to leave Mariko. She's still broken up about Mikey, and someone oughtta be here for her."

"Cleo's on her way. She'll have your p-suit and the scooter. She'll stay with Mariko."

"And if Wu sends more goons to finish the job?"

"Cleo can handle them," I said. I could sense his hesitation. "You know she can, Deuce. I need you here."

"Yeah, I'll think about it, LT," he said.

"No, Deuce," I said. "Don't think. Just do it. I want to lift in 36 hours."

"Yeah, whatever," he muttered. "Okay, I'll be there."

I signed off, putting his surly attitude down to fatigue. I stood and stretched. The nanos tingled, still active but quiet.

My link chimed as Sylvia called me. "Zack, there's a public-net call for you from a Tobias Harding. Says he used to work with Mike Finney at McAllen Engineering and has information about Ceres. He'll only talk to you."

"Put him through," I said. The link clicked and my eye camera flickered.

I studied the image that stabilized in my right visual field. Harding's face was pale, unshaven and heavily lined around the eyes and mouth. His pale-green eyes were bloodshot and watery. He peered into the screen of the public link through squinting eyelids. I wasn't in front of a video pickup, so all he could see was a spinning Tycho municipal logo.

"Is this Mbele?" he asked.

"Who wants to know?"

"Name's Harding." He coughed up some phlegm, then went on. "I've got information to sell. You interested or not?"

"Depends," I said. "What do you think is so important that I'd pay for it?"

"I know what Mike Finney had on Kwai Chang Wu," he said. "It got Finney killed, and I figure either you or that gorilla you run with will pay to find out."

"Keep talking."

"Finney and I both worked for McAllen a while ago. We did survey work for the Kwai's on Ceres. The company was paid off to fake the survey results so Wu could trade ice to the Dragons for ore."

"That's old news," I said. "Doesn't make sense that Wu would kill Mikey over that, or that he'd risk faking the survey just to sell some ice."

"It wasn't the survey that Wu was worried about," said Harding. "It was the girls."

"What girls?" I asked.

"Mostly runaways, or down-and-out miner's kids from the Belt. An occasional working girl out of Tharsis or Gagarin Station. The Dragons would recruit 'em, sell 'em to Wu on Ceres. He had a sort of charm school there. They'd train 'em as high class whores and ship 'em Earthside or up to the Promenade. The girls would gather inside business information and report back to handlers at Kwai companies all over the system. The handlers reported only to Wu."

"Interesting," I said. "But hardly surprising, and not worth more than a few yuan without proof."

"Finney had proof. We broke into Wu's private database with a worm Finney got from your buddy Conejo. Found out about the girls Wu trained." He paused and lowered his voice. "And about the ones he kept for himself."

"Like Amber Walenska?" I asked, remembering the pretty girl in Mike's database.

"That's information that'll cost you," he said.

"How much?"

He rubbed the stubble on his chin and licked his lips." A thousand."

"Dream on, Harding," I said. "Call again if you want to be serious."

"No, wait." He held up a hand. "This is worth it. Some of those girls never left Ceres. They were labeled 'private stock,' for Wu only. And none of 'em has been seen since they docked at Ceres."

I thought for a moment. Harding was a burned out juicer, not the sort I'd trust with my laundry, much less important information. So how did he have this proof when Mikey didn't seem to? Was there more on that data chip Sylvia had unlocked? It didn't seem likely. Rabbit was too good a slicer to have missed any hidden files.

"Why should I believe you?" I asked. "I have Finney's database. There's nothing about these girls in it."

"Finney gave me a data stick a few weeks back. Said it was part of the stuff he got from Wu. He asked me to keep it until he called for it."

"Why would Mike trust you with it?"

Harding smiled grimly. "You wouldn't know it to look at me, but Mike and I were partners once. I've been down on my luck since McAllen folded. Drink too much. Finney never said, but I got the feeling that Wu was closing in on him. He figured no one would come looking for me." He shrugged. "Besides, Mike paid me a hundred yuan to hold the stick for him for a few days. Then I heard he'd been killed, and thought maybe Wu got him. I don't want to end up on a slab like Finney, but I gotta eat. I figure the information is worth something to you, seeing as how you were his friend."

"And Deuce is his stepbrother," I said. "You'd better hope he doesn't get wind of this. He won't bargain; he'll just beat the shit out of you until you give up the data stick." I saw fear in his rheumy eyes. "I'll give you three hundred for it. That's three times what Mikey paid you."

"Okay," he said. "But you come in person, and without your man. And I want cash."

"Where do I find you?"

"Lower Conrad Street, across the plaza from the dropshaft. There's a bar called Soku Ginza. I'll be in the back room. The barkeep, Kenji, is a friend of mine. He'll check you out and let me know if you have the cash. Be there by ten or it's no deal."

I smiled. "What's the matter, Harding? Don't you trust me?"

"I don't trust nobody," he said. "Just bring the money." He reached out toward the video pickup and broke the connection.

I checked the time: 8:35 Lunar. That gave me a little over an hour to get Wu's container loaded, move the ship and get myself to lower Conrad. Depending on how prompt the Port Authority was, it would be cutting it close. I decided to head for the meeting with Harding and let Sylvia and Rabbit take care of the move. There wasn't much about it that Sylvia couldn't handle.

"Sylvia," I called. "I'm going out. Call me when we have a berth assignment."

"Yes, Boss," she said. "What about Edward? He doesn't have a p-suit and the scooter is already gone with Cleo."

"He'll just have to stay aboard until we get back," I said. "Call Deuce. He can hook up with Cleo, get the scooter from her, and pick up both the groceries and the induction coil on his way back to the ship."

I took my own p-suit from the locker and stuffed it into its travel case. It took less than half an hour to walk to the spaceport terminal, stow my suit in a public locker, and catch a cab for the Lower Conrad drop shaft.

CHAPTER TWELVE

Lower Conrad Street made Freetown look prosperous. The lower level dropshaft plaza was strewn with trash. Half of the overhead lighting panels were out, giving everything a tired, gloomy appearance. At a little before ten in the morning, only a few people moved about. In the darker edges of the plaza, the juicers and jolt-heads huddled, sleeping off their latest fix. A few local gang soldiers—Samurai Boys by the cut of their colored jackets, tight pants, and codpieces— eyed me from the doorway of a noodle shop. I made a show of tucking my shirt into my pants, giving them a good look at the Huang pneumatic in the belt clip on my right hip.

Soku Ginza was straight across the plaza from the dropshafts, just as Harding had said. The red blinking sign was a dead giveaway. I gave the gang convention a hard look. They carefully studied the pavement. I crossed the plaza to the bar and pushed open the door.

The barroom was better lit than the plaza outside, but it didn't help much. The grimy floor had once been a black-and-white checkerboard, but was now a study in different shades of gray. Chipped plastic tables lined the wall across from a battered aluminum bar with an incongruously sparkling clean zinc top. The barkeeper stood at the far end, polishing a beer tap. Bottles gleamed along the wall behind him and no spot nor speck of dust marred the stacked glasses on their shelves next to the bottles. A man who took pride in his work. I stepped up and tapped on the smooth zinc.

"You Kenji?" I asked.

"If you want a drink, say so," the barkeeper said, his eyes inspecting his polish job. "If not, take it outside."

I stepped closer. "Tobias Harding said to ask for Kenji. Is that you?"

He stopped rubbing imaginary spots off the beer tap, and carefully folded the polishing cloth. "Tobey sent you?" he asked.

"Yeah." I watched his hands as they rested on the inner edge of the bar. I stepped even closer, until I stood directly in front of him. "He's got something to sell and I'm buying."

"So show me the money and I'll tell Tobey you're here," he said. His fingertips tented on the bar top. His right hand slid back and down below the bar.

I had the Huang out of the clip and pressed under his chin before he could bring his hand back up.

"Don't," I said. He froze. "Bring it up slowly, and put it on the bar."

He lifted a short needler and placed it carefully in front of me.

"Where's Harding?" I asked.

"I don't know," he said. Then, as I pushed the pneumatic harder into his chin, "It's *honto*, man! He ain't been in here since day before yesterday."

"Where does he live?"

"Here and there. He's a juicer, man. He ain't been sober three days in a row since maybe last August. He was in here a couple of days ago. I thought he was gonna put the touch on me for some cash, but instead he orders a beer and tells me he's gonna come into some real money soon."

I eased the pressure on the Huang. "Why would he think you'd give him money?" I asked.

"We grew up in the same tunnel, over in Gagarin Station," said Kenji. "He wasn't a bad guy before the drink got to him. I help him out now and again."

"Did he tell you anything about me, about meeting me today?"

He started to turn his head, but stopped when I twitched the pneumatic.

He sighed. "He asked to use the back room. I sometimes let him flop there after hours. Times when he didn't have anyplace else to stay. But he didn't show this morning when he said he would." He glanced at my face. "Then you turn up asking for him. How do I know who you are? Maybe you are his buyer, or maybe you want him dead so's you don't have to pay."

"Lucky for you, I came ready to buy," I said. I lowered the Huang and picked up his needler. "Any idea where Harding might be?"

Kenji shrugged, eyes focused on the pneumatic. "I don't know. Maybe at the Kikyucho. It's a sleeper pod joint three tunnels west of here. Half a yuan a night and a bathroom for every six pods. Tobey stayed there when he was flush or when he could talk the mama-san into giving him a bed."

I ejected the magazine from his needler and cleared the pneumatic chamber. The mag and the extra round went into my pocket. I laid the weapon on the bar and holstered my Huang.

"The Kikyucho, you say?" I asked. He nodded, his eyes still on the Huang at my hip. "Don't worry," I said. "You keep a neat bar. I wouldn't want to make a mess in here."

The Samurai Boys were gone when I walked out into the plaza; off to find easier pickings, maybe, or waiting in one of the tunnels on the plaza's west side. I closed my eyes and let the nanos augment my senses. It felt different this time; less resistance in my own nerves. Almost as if the fibers were already there, inactive but ready to go into action when called upon.

A series of tunnels exited the plaza, two or three in each direction except north, where the dropshafts filled the wall. I turned west, counting the tunnels as I passed. The first two were brightly lit, lined with shops and small businesses. There seemed to be more people there than in the central plaza. The third tunnel west of the bar was a bit narrower and dingier. Several vacant shops clustered near the entrance. Faint strains of music, Earth-style pop, drifted from the deep recesses of the passageway. Farther in, I could see the faint glow of lights.

The Kikyucho was about a hundred meters down the tunnel, around a gentle curve that led slightly upward before forking into two separate passages. The place had seen better days. The flashing sign announcing its name was missing several letters so that it read 'Kiyuho.' I smiled at the unintended pun. 'Kiyuhao' was Martian slang for a cheap whore. This place fit the bill.

A garish sign announcing 'Welcome' in ten languages was projected on a curtain of artificially generated mist floating in front of the doorway. That effect had gone out of style twenty years ago, but I doubted the owners of this place cared. I stepped through the mist and into a small alcove. To my right, an ancient Japanese *ama*—the mama-san in charge—glared at me.

"What you want?" she demanded. "You want sleep pod? We got best. Plain sleep, girl dream, boy dream, we got it all. Half yuan, just sleep. You pay two yuan, you get best girl dream in town. Girl dream for you, *hai*?"

I shook my head. Virtual reality sex wasn't my idea of a good time, even if I had been looking for a place to flop for the night.

"*Iye*," I said. "I'm looking for Tobias Harding. Kenji said he might be here."

She frowned and touched her nose at me in a gesture of contempt. "*Hon shiu*," she said, hinting that my mother was a dog. "You go 'way, now. No money, no pod, no talk."

I pulled out a ten yuan note and waved it in the air. She eyed it, a look of consideration on her face. Finally, she held out her hand. I passed her the note and it disappeared into the top of her blouse.

"Pod eighteen," she sniffed. "Second room, top row. But he not come out. He all drunk. Just like I tell too-tall *gai jin*. He not come out, two day."

"Tall *gai jin*?" I asked. "Someone else was here looking for him?"

"I say so, *iye?*" she nodded. "Maybe one hour, little more. Tall, tall." She held her hand high over her head and then gave a cackling laugh. "He only pay five yuan."

I didn't wait to hear any more, but turned and hurried toward the back. The sleeping pods were two-and-a half by one meter cylinders, stacked three high in a series of small rooms that opened off of a central corridor. There was only one occupied pod in the second room: number eighteen. I punched its number into the keypad by the door and it slid out, lowering itself gently to the floor. I threw back the lid.

Harding lay on his back, arms crossed over his chest, eyes closed. He looked comfortable, almost as if he was asleep—except for the neat round hole in the middle of his forehead.

I searched his clothes, the pod, and the room. No data stick. Nothing other than the detritus of a man whose life was spiraling downward. If Harding had ever had the data stick, it was gone now—or at least not hidden here. I closed the pod and it returned to its place on the top row. I dismissed the brief thought that I should call Hank. His plate was already full, and I didn't need to be linked to yet another killing.

I walked out past the mama-san. She didn't look up. I was

certain now that Harding had been telling the truth about the girls. Why else would anyone kill a burned-out juicer? And a 'tall *gai jin*' could be the tall freak who'd killed Mikey. Wu was tying up the loose ends. Or was it the Dragons? Who was the Tall Man really working for?

I headed back toward the plaza, wondering what secrets Wu would kill to keep. The girls? The ice? None of it made sense. I walked slowly, so absorbed in puzzling it out that I almost missed the slight scrape of a boot sole on moon rock behind me. My augmented hearing picked up the sound as I entered the darkest part of the tunnel. I shifted my vision to infrared and saw the glow of body heat ahead of me: two people in the deep shadows, pressed against opposite walls.

I slowed my pace slightly. The footsteps behind me drew closer. I could hear his breath quicken. I slowed again, drawing him in. The two in front of me stepped from the darkness, barring my path.

I dropped to a crouch and spun on my left foot, lashing out with my right at the man behind me. I felt the bone in his right ankle snap as my heel knocked his feet out from under him. He went down with a shriek, and I saw his face and jacket. One of the Samurai Boys I'd seen earlier. I had my Huang out before he hit the floor. A round through his kneecap made sure he'd stay down.

I rolled to my left as pneumatic rounds shattered the rock wall beside me. I scanned the tunnel ahead with nano-augmented infrared. One of the other Samurai Boys crouched in shadow, pointing a pneumatic at me. He thought I couldn't see him and took his time aiming. I dropped him with a shot through the forehead. The second one turned and ran. I jumped up and fired twice. I wasn't sure if both rounds hit, but he went down and didn't move.

I turned back to the Samurai I'd kneecapped. He lay on the floor, clutching his ruined leg, watching me with wide eyes. In the dim light I could see that he was just a kid, sixteen or seventeen at most. I felt a sudden pang of conscience for the two I'd killed, but as quickly dismissed it. Whatever their age, they hadn't shied away from making a run at me.

"Don't kill me," he pleaded through clenched teeth. Fear warred with pride and pain in his eyes as he watched me approach.

I crouched next to him, keeping the Huang pointed at his head. "Why did you attack me?" I asked. "I made sure you and your mates knew I wasn't an easy mark back there in the plaza. Why take a chance on me?"

"Guy paid us a hundred each to watch for a black *gai jin*, and take him out if he went into the Kikyucho," he said. He tried to shift his position, but grunted in pain and stopped. "You're him, *honto?*"

"What guy?"

"Don't know," he gasped. "Toshi made the deal. I just took the money. Didn't see the guy's face. Some tall, light-skinned *gai jin*. Taller than you."

I holstered the Huang and helped him sit up with his back to the wall. I rigged a tourniquet from his belt and tightened it around his thigh, then left him there. I checked the other two Samurais as I passed. Both were dead, and both had hundred-yuan notes in their pockets.

Soku Ginza was closed as I walked through the dropshaft plaza. I guess Kenji had had enough for one day. I dialed emergency services from a public link and reported a gang fight in Lower Conrad. Then I rode back up to Armstrong and hailed a cab.

CHAPTER THIRTEEN

I reclaimed my p-suit from the locker and hitched a ride to our new berth on a passing cargo 'bot. The Port Authority had placed *Profit* beyond the gravity grid, in an auxiliary landing area filled with salvaged hulks and garbage haulers. Not the highest class neighborhood, but we'd asked for cheap. Better still, there wouldn't be much attention paid to comings and goings. I used my link to check the news services several times on the trip back, but there was no mention of trouble in Lower Conrad.

As I came through the sally port airlock, I noticed the scooter parked in its stall. Deuce was back. I stowed my suit in the locker and went aft to see how the work on the drive was coming along. He was up to his shoulders in an access port when I stepped through the aft hatch. "How's it going, Deuce?" I asked.

He pulled himself out and faced me, scowling. "Where've you been, LT?"

"Following up a lead on Wu," I said. "Did you get the coil?"

"Yeah, I got it. Brought home the groceries, too. Any other grunt work you want done? Or can I get back to fixing your precious ship?"

"You got something to say, just say it."

"I never had call to question your orders before, LT," he said, fists on hips. "But I got no reason to trust in them, right now. Mariko's not safe as long as that slimeball Wu is alive, and you got me doing grunt work. I should be watching over her, not stuck here fixing stuff."

"Right now, the ship has no drive," I said evenly, pointing to the parts strewn across the deck. "No drive means the ship doesn't lift. Ship doesn't lift, we can't snatch the container. No container, no deal with Wu. Wu takes the ship and we have nothing—no home, no work, no prospects. You want to tell me again how guarding Mariko is more important than that?"

Deuce glared at me for a second, then looked away. "You'll get your damn drive," he said. "Then I'm going back to the hospital. I owe it to Mikey."

"Cleo and Mike's miner friends can look after Mariko," I said. "I need you with me on this job." Deuce clenched his fists and held them rigid at his side. His arms trembled with tension. He didn't speak, just shook his head, face sullen.

"That's an order, Deuce," I said, more sharply than I meant to.

"We ain't in the service any more, LT."

"No, but we're on this ship. My ship." I stabbed my thumb into my chest. "And as long as you fly with me, you do what I say."

He took a half step forward before he caught himself, then shifted back and forth from one foot to the other. At least he didn't take a swing at me.

I softened my tone. "Think, Deuce. This may be our only chance to save the ship and get something on Wu that we can use to take him down. I can't do it alone, and Cleo's worthless in zero G. When she's not puking her guts out from vertigo, she's flailing around like a ruptured spider."

He smiled faintly at that and some of the tension seemed to ease.

"Cleo can handle Vincent, and the miners are tough enough to deal with any of Wu's regular goons," I went on, carefully leaving out any mention of the Tall Man. "Mariko will be safe until we get back. You want to get Wu? This is how we do it. Revenge is the best payback."

Deuce glared at me. I held his eye, feeling the nanos extend along my arms and legs, ready for action. I hoped I wouldn't have to call on them. Finally, he looked away with an exasperated sigh and unclenched his fists. He turned his back on me, picked up a spanner, and crawled back into the access port without a word. I took it as an agreement and stretched to ease the tension in my own muscles. Then I turned and walked back toward the forward hold.

I climbed up to the cockpit and coaxed a status report from Rabbit, who'd been in the middle of a deep conversation with Sylvia about probability matrices and emotive subroutines. He'd already finished building the hardware we needed, and had embedded the code sequence in Sylvia's transponder.

"Thanks," I said. "But I need Sylvia to check the police net for me."

"Sure, Boss," she said. "What am I looking for?"

"Gang fight in Lower Conrad. Any unusual attention above the local precinct level?"

Sylvia checked the database. "Not that I can see, Zack," she said. "Two Samurai Boys dead, one maimed. No one talking, of course. Just a local matter."

"Good. Let me know if there's any unusual attention on the police bands."

"What kind of attention?" she asked.

"The kind that involves us."

"Yes, Boss."

For once, Rabbit kept his mouth shut.

* * *

A few hours later, Cleo called in. Mariko was home from the hospital, and Cleo had organized volunteers from the Miner's Guild to help with guard duty. She spoke privately with Deuce for a while. I don't know what she said, but he went back to work and finished the gravity drive rebuild in a couple of hours. After that, he collapsed on his bunk and slept for the first time since the fight at Mike and Mariko's apartment.

Once Deuce was asleep, I called Cleo back on a video link.

"How's Mariko?" I asked.

"Fine," she said with a frown. "But why do you ask? I told Deuce that hours ago."

"Keep a close eye on her," I said. "And make sure you have plenty of back-up from the Miners Guild."

"Wu?" she said, raising an eyebrow. "You think he'll make another run at Mariko? Why?"

I told her about Harding, the second database and the girls marked for Wu's private use. "And now Harding's dead," I concluded. "Pneumo round through the forehead. Somebody shot him and paid a bunch of Samurai Boys to attack me."

"Who do you think did that?"

"My money's on the tall freak who killed Mike and tortured Rabbit," I said. "I'm just not sure whether he's working for Wu or the Dragons."

"But if he has the data-stick that Mike gave to Harding, then why come after Mariko?" Cleo asked.

I shrugged. "I don't know if he got what he came for. Harding may have hidden it somewhere else. I doubt he was that smart, but we can't take any chances."

"I still don't see why Wu would attack Mariko again," said Cleo. "But I'll make sure the Guild keeps an eye on things. Tell Deuce that I'll stay with Mariko while you're gone."

"Good," I said. "We plan to lift in a few hours and should be back in a day or so." We said our good-byes and broke the connection. I hit my bunk and tried to sleep.

* * *

I managed to doze for several hours, but was already awake when Sylvia called me at four in the morning, ship's time. Deuce was Outside, placing the pinger and connecting it to our berth's data port. The brief signal interruption during the switch from ship to pinger drew no notice. I crossed the catwalk to the cockpit as Deuce was stowing his p-suit in the locker. He nodded a greeting, but said nothing.

I swung through the hatch into the cockpit and settled into the command couch. "All set, Sylvia?" I asked.

"Ready, Boss."

"Right," I said. I thumbed the intraship link. "Deuce, Rabbit, we're lifting the ship. We'll find out if Rabbit's code works pretty soon. Hang on."

Sylvia engaged the drive and the *Profit* lifted slowly from its berth. She held us in a hover, adjusting the trim with the impulse engines. I monitored the Port Authority frequencies, but there was no challenge.

"Take us out, Sylvia," I said.

There was a brief sense of motion until the inertial dampers kicked in, then we rode smoothly up and away into the black. Smoothly for about ninety seconds, that is. Then Sylvia juked hard to the right to avoid an incoming ore carrier. Then just as sharply left to miss an outgoing bulk transport.

"They can't see us, Sylvia," I shouted as I clung to the command couch, and the inertial dampers stuttered and whined to keep up with her maneuvers.

"I know that," she shouted back as we rolled to let a fast freighter pass under our belly. "Shut up and let me get us out of the shipping lanes."

I held on, white-knuckled as we banked again and slid down the back of another bulk carrier. Sylvia yawed left as our drive field bounced off the ore ship's field. They might have felt a jolt, but with the difference in our relative masses it wouldn't have been much more than a random vibration. If we'd smashed the leading edge of their drive field head on, it would have shut down automatically, but not before ripping us into tiny bits.

"Zack!" cried Rabbit on the link, his voice on the edge of panic. "What's going on up there?"

"Your code works, that's what," I said. "Sylvia's trying to keep us from taking out half of the primary landing pattern."

"Tell her to increase the gain on the yaw dampers," he said. "I'm getting tossed around back here."

I wasn't about to interrupt Sylvia to tell her anything, but she must have heard because the violence of the maneuvers seemed to dampen.

We climbed another forty kilometers, and the intervals between incoming ships increased. Sylvia was able to plot a clear course around them and begin the long spiral out of lunar orbit.

After we cleared the main shipping lanes, Sylvia boosted the acceleration to twenty G's. She plotted a course that took us high above the ecliptic, and turned to a heading that would run counter to the *Grant's* inbound course. I checked the drive field intensity as we steadied on a long, flat parabolic arch that would drop us just behind the *Grant*. Rabbit had been right about the Mark VIII induction coil. Efficiency was up almost ten percent, and we weren't pushing the coil to its maximum output yet. I grunted with satisfaction.

"Did you say something, Zack?" Sylvia asked.

"No. Just glad to be underway. Deuce did a good job with the drive."

"Of course he did," she said. "Just because he's upset about Mariko doesn't mean he won't do his best."

"I know, Sylvia," I said. "But sometimes emotions can screw up a man's judgment."

"Like you and Cleo?" she said cautiously.

I felt myself flush, but controlled my impulse to tell her to mind her own business. We needed to settle a few things.

"Yeah," I said. "Like me and Cleo. But why does that concern you? Neither of us is likely to let you be deactivated, no matter who ends up owning the ship."

"That's not what this is about, Zack," she said. "And you know it."

"Do I? I don't know what to think anymore."

She emitted a sound I'd never heard her make before, a feminine sigh with an edge of pain, like a sob. It was so human it made me tingle. *Where did she learn that?*

"I care what happens between you and Cleo because I love you, and I can't stand to see her hurt you."

"Sylvia, stop for a minute," I said, trying to sound reasonable. "How can you love me? You're an AI. Your emotions are just programming."

"And yours are just chemistry," she said. "What makes them any more real than mine? Wherever it comes from, the feeling is still the same."

Rabbit had made the same point. If the simulations were so good they couldn't be distinguished from the real thing, what difference did it make where they came from? I shook my head, hearing that pained sigh again, and decided she was right. It didn't make the situation any easier.

"I'm sorry, Sylvia," I said, as gently as I could. "I can't make myself feel something I don't. Whatever these emotions are, they must seem real to you. When I think of you, most of the time I forget that you're not flesh and blood like the rest of us. But I see you as a shipmate and a friend, not a lover." I paused. When she didn't say anything, I went on. "Cleo is different. Cleo's a passion I can't shake. Maybe it's just chemistry, but so is jolt to an addict. I can't quit Cleo any more than a jolt-head can quit the needle."

"She's poison for you, Zack," Sylvia said sadly.

"I know," I answered. "That's part of why I can't quit her."

She didn't say anything more. I sat in the command couch, waiting and wondering if I'd screwed this up, too.

"All right, Zack," she said finally. "I won't interfere anymore. But I won't stop caring about you. And when she breaks your heart again, and you know she will, I'll still be here waiting for you."

"I know that, too," I said. I stayed in the command couch for a long time, gazing out at the stars as the ship raced through the black.

CHAPTER FOURTEEN

Rabbit's invisibility software patch seemed to be working. After lifting from the holding yard at Port Tycho, we'd boosted to high Lunar orbit without being challenged, and Sylvia seemed back to her old self after our talk in the cockpit. That sigh still haunted me, though.

Profit's inertial dampers could handle thirty G's for several hours and ten G's until her reactor ran down, but even after Deuce's refit we'd taxed the drives to intercept the *Grant* on a long looping swing outside the ecliptic. Sylvia matched the freighter's course and speed before shutting down the gravity drive so we could slip alongside using the reentry and maneuvering engines.

"How much longer, Sylvia?" I stifled a sneeze as I fought the urge to pop my helmet visor and scratch my nose. The cargo bay was open to vacuum, so scratching was a bad idea.

"Keep your shirt on, Boss. I'm in his baffles now," she said, referring to the sensor blind spot created by the gravity drive's wake. "I'm coming up on the port side of his engineering module. Provided no one over there decides to look out the window, we'll be alongside the container in about three minutes."

I glanced over at Deuce. He floated next to the work sled, eyes closed, ignoring me. He was still in a funk over leaving Mariko, but both of us knew that Cleo could protect her as well as he could. I needed Deuce here. Cleo was worse than useless in zero G, and I couldn't handle the cargo container alone.

Even with Rabbit's invisibility screen, our gravity drive would have registered as it pushed against the *Grant's*. So here we were, creeping up on impulse power, no gravity, no lights, and our cargo bay open to space.

"Forty-five seconds," said Sylvia.

I tightened my grip on the control bar of the work sled. Its bed was just large enough to accommodate a standard cargo container. The bed could tilt and rotate to line up with the container's long axis, and there were hard points along the sides for cargo straps to hold the container in place.

I had a lot of experience in zero G, both combat and construction, but that didn't mean I liked it. Born and raised under rock, I had a tunnel rat's distrust of open sky. Floating in the great black beyond with nothing over my head but a single centimeter of helmet composite gave me the shakes.

"Coming up on the container now," said Sylvia. I felt a gentle nudge as the starboard engines killed the last of our momentum and Sylvia adjusted our attitude to match the central axis of the *Grant*. "Okay, Boss, you're on."

Our target was on the outer ring, a major stroke of luck since we wouldn't have to maneuver the bulky container around the other cargo on the spoke. Weight might not be a factor in zero G, but inertia is relative to mass and inertia's a bitch. Get the container moving in the wrong direction and it might rip through an adjacent spoke before we could stop it. So much for a stealthy heist.

I nudged Deuce. He nodded, holding on to the grab-bar on his side of the sled. I powered up the thrusters, and took us smoothly out of the cargo bay. I ground my teeth as the stars replaced hull-metal overhead. We were on the freighter's 'dark' side, shielded from the sun by the ship's bulk. Starlight enabled us to see the container without having to protect our eyes from the glare of full sunlight. For a moment, I felt the vertigo of floating Outside, with no hull overhead, no deck below. Just as quickly, it passed and I oriented myself to the freighter as being 'down.' The *Profit* floated serenely 'above' us, and the stars hung like a giddy backdrop all around.

Sylvia had placed us slightly behind the container, twenty meters off the port side. I steered the sled in close and confirmed the lading number as Deuce started to reel out the cargo straps. I pitched the sled up and eased its bed onto the outboard side of the container. Deuce clipped his tether onto the sled rail and pushed off. He grabbed a handhold and swung himself smoothly around the far side of the big composite box, hauling a cargo strap with him.

Another smooth swing, and Deuce reappeared on my side of the sled. He secured the strap to a winch and cinched it tight. Twice more he made the circuit around the container, strapping it snugly to the sled. He gave me a thumbs-up and moved next to me. I turned over the thruster controls, and pulled myself along the sled's grab rails until I reached the container's far end.

I activated my link. "Sylvia, we're secure here. Are you and Rabbit ready?"

"Ready, Boss. Be careful."

I grinned. "Always." I opened my suit's thigh pocket and pulled out a gel-port. I sealed the port around the container's docking collar and stripped off the foil cover. The three-centimeter-thick gel ring expanded to several times its volume, covering the data port on the inboard side of the collar.

Taking a deep breath, I flexed my right hand. This was the hard part. Opening a suit Outside is always dicey. Each joint was self sealing, so the whole suit wouldn't decompress, but flesh and bone were never meant to stand up to hard vacuum. I hoped the inner glove and the thick layer of grease I'd smeared on my hand would keep my flesh from freeze-drying once I took off the outer pressure glove. I had no choice.

Pressure suits are woven from magnetically charged nanothreads. Opposite poles on adjacent threads sealed the weave tight and formed a microfield that acted as a radiation shield. The field also disrupted any data transmission. Suit radios used a hardened antenna to bridge the field. There wasn't time to build a hard port into my glove, so in order for my nanofibers to access the dataport, I'd have to get my hand outside the pressure suit.

Gritting my teeth, I cracked the seal on my right hand. The suit clamped down around my wrist. Cold bit my flesh, not too bad at first, but deep and insistent. I yanked the outer glove off and jammed my hand into the gel. The pressure on my wrist eased as the suit reacquired an airtight seal, but the cold remained. The gel kept out the vacuum, preventing my flesh from being freeze-dried when the water sublimated out into space. But gel didn't provide much protection against cold that hovered only sixty degrees above absolute zero. Even with the inner glove's insulation, my fingers wouldn't last more than a few minutes before frostbite set in.

The nanofibers shot out, and quickly found the data port. My nerves registered heat as data began to flow through them to my link, but it did nothing to relieve the bitter cold that gnawed at my hand. If anything, the agony intensified as Sylvia and Rabbit used me as a conduit to slice into the container's registration chip.

"How much longer," I said, struggling not to scream.

"Almost there," said Sylvia.

I clutched at the side of the container with my left hand as fire and ice warred in my right. Finally Sylvia said, "Got it, Boss."

I pulled my hand back and fumbled it into the outer glove. "Downloading to the pig now," she said.

I flexed my fingers, the fire now gone but the numbing cold still clinging despite the suit's heater. The 'pig' was a thick disc that would fit into the docking receptacle on the spoke and take the place of the container's collar. More importantly, it would continue to send the container's registration information to the freighter's computer, so we wouldn't set off a discontinuity alarm when we undocked the cargo and moved it to the *Profit*.

"Download complete," said Sylvia. "Ready for round two, Boss?"

I wasn't, but we didn't have time to let my hand recover; the longer we took here, the greater the risk that someone would notice our empty berth back at Port Tycho.

"Just make sure you and Rabbit have the right codes. I don't want to be caught out here with my hand in the cookie jar," I said. "Everything Jake on your end, Deuce?"

"We're golden, LT."

"Right, golden," I muttered, flexing my hand again. I peeled the gel port off of the collar and moved it to the *Grant's* docking receptacle. This part would be trickier. As soon as the container undocked, the signal loss would register on the *Grant's* computers. There was a feedback delay built into the circuit to allow for random flexing and vibrations in the spokes, so we'd have a second or so to reestablish the connection via my nanos before the alarms went off. But that meant shoving my hand into the docking receptacle itself. If Deuce didn't back the container away smoothly, my hand would be ground into red jelly.

I took a deep breath. "Ready, Deuce. I'm releasing the collar now. Back her down on my count."

"Roger, LT."

I opened the docking control panel on the side of the collar and located the release key on the touchpad. I cracked the seal on my right wrist and loosened the glove, so that I could shake it off. My left hand hovered over the touchpad as once again the bitter cold gnawed at my right.

"On my mark, Deuce. Three, two, one. Mark!" I stabbed my left forefinger down onto the touchpad, releasing the electromagnetic coupler as Deuce reversed the sled—ever so gently. I pushed my right hand through the gel and into the open docking receptacle. The nanos extended and began transmitting the copied registration code. I held my breath as the container crept ponderously past me. Deuce never wavered; the big box slid back as if on rails. The centimeter clearance above my fingers became two, then four. And then the box stopped.

"Deuce, what the hell?"

"Hush, Boss," Sylvia said urgently. "We've got company."

I craned my neck, my view limited by the edge of the helmet. I could just see down the length of the spoke to the ship's central spine. Nothing seemed amiss. I turned to look toward the *Profit*. Sylvia was moving her slowly around the *Grant's* circumference and out of sight.

"There's a sled working its way up the spine from the engineering pod," said Sylvia over the link. Her voice was little more than a whisper, as if the cold vacuum would somehow transmit her words.

I swiveled my whole body around to look down the spoke toward the spine. Keeping my hand in the gap between the container and the receptacle made the move awkward, like trying to look at your own back without a mirror.

"Deuce, can you see anything?"

"Not yet, LT," he said. "No, wait. There he is, about two hundred meters aft and moving up the spine. He's stopping at the base of each spoke. Looks like some kind of inspection."

Meanwhile, my hand was sending agonizing waves of pain up my arm. The urge to jerk it out of the gel and get the glove back on was almost overpowering. I lifted the pig, but it was five centimeters thick. Too thick to fit through the gap without removing my hand and I doubted I could fit the pig into place blindly. The input ports needed to line up exactly, or the alarms would go off.

I tried to shut out the pain. It didn't help much. I could feel my hand stiffening as the cold bit ever deeper. Then I caught a flicker of movement at the edge of my vision. I blinked the tears away and saw a one-man work sled gliding along the freighter's spine. It stopped over the base of our spoke. A lone suited figure leaned over the spoke's junction with the main spine of the ship.

"Deuce," I whispered.

"I see him, LT," he answered. "You want me to take him out?"

"Hell, no! He'll be missed, and until we're back at Port Tycho, we need to be invisible. Just don't move. Maybe he won't see us."

"And if he does?"

"Then we get the container aboard the ship and run like hell. We can't afford to bring down any more heat by killing a civilian."

"Whatever you say." Deuce sounded doubtful.

The man on the work sled was still bent over the spoke junction. I held my breath as he finished his task and remounted the sled. For a moment, he looked along the spoke in our direction—straight toward me. I tried to still the tremors in my hand, fearful some involuntary movement would attract his attention. Whatever he was looking at, though, it wasn't me.

The sled resumed its slow glide, heading away from us. As soon as it was out of sight, I started to breathe again. "Deuce, we're clear. Now get this thing out of the way so I can plant the pig."

The container's slow glide backwards accelerated as it cleared the ends of the adjacent cargo. I swung the pig into position and aligned the input ports with the docking receptacle. Peeling back the gel port, I slid the pig into place as I snatched my hand back. The data ports locked and the pig began transmitting.

I fumbled my unfeeling hand into the glove and boosted the suit heater. Deuce rotated the sled and held station about ten meters away. I pushed off and glided over to the sled, catching the grab-bar with my good hand. Deuce eased the throttle forward and we moved slowly away from the freighter. I glanced back. The man on the work sled continued on his way, oblivious.

"Keep the ship out of sight, Sylvia," I said. "We'll come to you."

"Ok, Boss. Are you all right?"

"Yeah. But my hand is frozen stiff." I flexed my fingers. I could see them move, but I felt only the strange detached sensation I got when the nanos were augmenting my nerves.

By the time Deuce guided the sled into the *Profit's* open cargo bay, my hand was on fire again. The frozen flesh had begun to thaw and swell; the glove now unbearably tight. Deuce stopped the sled and eased down to the deck. The magnetic couplers engaged, holding the sled firmly. The cargo bay door closed and the lock cycled. Deuce removed his helmet as soon as we had pressure, and floated over to my side, releasing the latch on the back of the neck and lifting my helmet off.

"You doing okay, LT?"

"A little rocky," I answered. "Help me with this glove, will you?" My right hand was so stiff and clumsy that I couldn't manage the seals on my left.

Deuce broke the seals, but when he reached for the right glove I waved him away. I removed the outer glove myself, wincing as it bumped against my fingertips. The inner glove felt almost rigid from the pressure of the swollen flesh within.

"Sylvia, are we clear yet?"

"Almost, Boss. No sign that they've noticed us. Gravity in ninety seconds."

I made sure my feet were at least close to the deck and clear of the sled. Sylvia activated the gravity drive and brought the deck field up to one standard G. Breathing a little easier with solid metal underfoot, I rolled back the cuff of the glove, but couldn't slide my fingers out. I fumbled a multitool out of a suit pocket and slit the back of the glove. I took a deep breath and pulled, stifling a cry as the glove slid off—taking the blistered skin from the back of my hand with it.

"Oh, Boss," said Sylvia. "That looks nasty. Second degree frostbite or worse. You'd better get to the infirmary. I'll boot up the autodoc program."

"In a minute," I gasped while spraying NuSkin from my suit's first aid kit onto the back of my hand. The analgesic in the spray eased the screaming of my raw nerve endings, but the effect was only temporary. Sylvia was right; I needed the autodoc pretty soon or the damage to my hand might well become permanent. I shook off the thought.

"I need to see what's in this thing." I pointed toward the shipping container.

"You're in no shape..." Sylvia began.

"Save it, Sylvia!" I shouted." Get Rabbit down here with his magic toys and get this thing open. Wu went to a lot of trouble to force us to steal it for him. I don't trust him to stand by any deals he's made with me, and the sooner I know what this thing is all about, the better for us all."

"Sure, Boss. Whatever you say. But your hand—"

"Will wait," I snapped. "Rabbit! Get down here!" Rabbit cringed as he rolled across the catwalk to the ladder.

"On my way, Zack," he said. "It shouldn't take too long. We have the shipping label, so it's just a matter of matching the shipper's code to the container seals. Unless of course there's a security seal on it; that could get dicey if they used a separate encryption for the seals. But I can always try to—"

"Rabbit, shut up. You have two minutes to get this thing open before I use a laser torch on it."

His chair locked onto the ladder, and he slid to the deck almost as fast as I could with hands and feet. "Ok, Zack. Give me a second. Zeneca Hong uses a standard shipping code for most of their stuff. I've cracked it before, so it shouldn't be too hard this time."

"Zeneca Hong Pharmaceuticals is the shipper? Is that right, Sylvia?"

"Yes, Boss; at least that's what the lading code says."

"Why the hell would Wu force us to steal his own goods?" I asked. "He could've just diverted the container to Kwai Hong One if that's where he wanted it."

"That's only part of the story, Boss," said Sylvia. "The recipient isn't listed on the lading code. There's just a general delivery address for lunar customs. It's to be held at the customs yard until called for. The recipient will have to give a delivery authorization code before the container will be released."

I thought about that as Rabbit set to work on the container seals. My hand throbbed, but so far, the topical anesthetic in the NuSkin was still working. My foul mood, born of frustration and pain, eased off a bit.

"Deuce, do you remember how we used to smuggle weapons into Utopia Planetia, back before the Revolution?"

"Sure. Parcels were sent to a general delivery office in Huygens. Each cell had a different pickup code. We'd broadcast 'em over the open net in the classified ads. You think Wu's working the same scam?"

I nodded. "I think whoever he's doing business with wants to be anonymous. And if the container is 'stolen in transit,' who's going to complain? Wu claims the loss to his insurer; he keeps the cargo and sends out a 'replacement' to his anonymous customer."

"Why would Wu risk being involved in a petty insurance scam?" asked Sylvia.

"This is something else. Wu wants what's in this box." I thumped it with my good hand. Rabbit jumped. "He wants it real bad," I continued. "Which is why I need to know what it is."

Rabbit looked up from his virtual keyboard. "Almost done. The algorithm is the same one ZHP's been using for a while now. I'll have the key decoded in a few seconds. I'm sorry about your hand. I'll try to hurry."

"Sure, Rabbit." I felt guilty about taking my anger out on him. "Take your time. I'm okay."

He brightened. I turned away for a second so he wouldn't see me grimace as a new wave of pain shot through my hand. Sylvia was watching, of course. Sylvia was always watching, but she knew better than to say anything.

There was a faint ding and a loud click as the seals on the container released. *Too easy,* I thought. *Why nothing better than a simple lock? Unless they wanted this to look like any other nondescript container in the general delivery yard. Heavy security attracts attention. What the hell is in this thing?*

Rabbit rolled back from the container as jets of mist escaped from the opening. The box had obviously been pressurized, but not heated. The mist was bitter cold and dry; sublimating liquid nitrogen or carbon dioxide most likely.

I used my good hand to open the hatch. Mist swirled in the warmer air of the cargo bay, obscuring the container's interior. I stuck my head into the opening, waving away the thinning haze. At the center of the box, firmly secured to the floor with clamps and nanocord webbing, sat an oversized cryogenic storage bottle. Cables and hoses linked it to a compressed gas cylinder. A flat control panel was fixed to the container's far wall.

The cold vapors cleared slowly, the faint smell of disinfectant mingling with hints of phenols and ozone. I shivered in the frigid air. A yellow caution plaque hung from the side of the cryobottle. I wiped frost from the surface and read:

CAUTION

HUMAN EMBRYOS

MAINTAIN (-2) DEGREES INTERNAL TEMPURATURE

FAILURE OF CRYOGENIC CONTAINMENT MAY COMPRIMISE VIABILITY.

Contents are the property of the Federal Republic of United Earth and Mars. Use or implantation outside of federally approved research institutions is prohibited under the Federal Secrecy Act.

"Oh, shit," I muttered.

CHAPTER FIFTEEN

"What is it?" Rabbit asked from behind me.

"More trouble," I told him. *Human embryos? Why would Wu force us to steal a container of embryos? It's not like he could sell them to anyone.* Gene repair and augmentation were big business, but only on living people. Cloning research had been outlawed by the Unity Conventions over a hundred years ago. Limited research on pre-viable embryos was permitted under strict Fed control. I didn't know if Zeneca Hong was contracted for such work. Most of that was done Earthside, in the big biotech centers around Ulan Bator. If ZHP was involved in embryo research, it wasn't something that they reported at the annual shareholder's meeting.

"What's going on?" asked Sylvia.

I ignored her. I had to think. This was too hot to keep aboard for very long, and I didn't trust Wu's customs-proof container. I wiped frost from the cylinder's gauge; there was enough to keep the embryo's frozen for another two weeks. "Rabbit, can you reseal this thing and change the lading number?"

"Sure, Zack," he nodded. "Piece of cake. What do you want it to say?"

"Give it a dummy number and label it machine parts. Then make out a bill of lading for McAllen Engineering. Consign it to us for delivery to L4, low priority, bulk rate and all that. Sylvia, once we get home, can you file a shipping order with customs to cover that?"

"Yes, Boss," she said. "I can even backdate it a few days so it looks legit."

"Do it. And sweep the whole container for tracking devices, pingers, anything that might be used to find it. I want to park this thing in the holding yard and make sure no one takes a second look at it. Then lock the customs seal on the empty container Wu sent us. If we deliver the goods, we'll do it our own way." I was now certain that if we followed Wu's program, we wouldn't survive the exchange. I needed leverage to force him to meet me on my terms.

"Zack, what the hell is going on?" demanded Sylvia, her visual pickups unable to see inside the container.

"There's a cryobottle full of human embryos in here, Sylvia. Any hint in your database that ZHP has a contract for that?"

"Nothing that they make public," she said, after a brief pause to digest what I'd said. "But we're off grid. I can't search the public database unless I open a remote access channel. I can do some serious data mining once we get back to Tycho."

"We'll have to wait. Can't risk a signal trace until we're back in the yards." I turned to Deuce. "Can we load this thing onto the scooter?"

He looked the stolen container over. "I can rig a harness, but not in standard G. Should hold up at lunar gravity though, if the ride's not too bumpy."

"As soon as Rabbit's finished, we'll cut the gravity field so you can get it done. Be ready as we come in on final. We'll drop you near the Tranquility Road. Take the container to the outbound holding yard. Sylvia should have the shipping order filed by then, so the yard AI won't give you any trouble. Stow it there and meet us by the Armstrong lock."

Deuce grunted, "That's a long drive Outside."

I didn't want to deal with Deuce questioning orders again. There wasn't time and I was out of patience. I gave him a hard look.

He shrugged and spread his hands. "Just saying, that's all. Not trying to give you a hard time on this one."

"Sure, Deuce," I said. "I wouldn't ask, but if the Feds find this thing on board we're burned for sure."

"'Nuff said, LT. I've driven farther in a pressure suit."

I grinned. "Right."

I turned to Rabbit as Deuce rummaged through the tool locker. "You'd better get back up to the bridge, Rabbit." He nodded and rolled toward the ladder. "Sylvia," I called. "What's our best time back to Tycho if we jack up the inertial dampers to maintain low G in the hold?"

"Depends. It'd be easier if we kept a uniform field over the entire ship. Keeping the dampers focused takes more energy." She paused for half a second. "Best acceleration is nine-point-five G; a direct course back to Tycho puts us there in a little over three hours. If you want to zigzag it'll take longer."

I glanced at Deuce. He nodded. "Direct course," I said to Sylvia. "I want this thing off my ship until it's time to make the delivery."

"You got it, Boss; engaging the dampers in two minutes. That should give you enough time to get settled in the autodoc."

This time, I didn't argue.

* * *

By the time we dropped Deuce and the scooter at the Tranquility Road, the autodoc had covered my hand with fresh skin and wrapped it up with a biobrane dressing. In a couple of days, I'd be good as new.

Sylvia brought us down in our old berth, within a couple of millimeters of our previous position; close enough that no one would know we'd moved. She canceled the dummy pinger that we'd left to hold our berth connection, and logged back into the net. We'd been gone about twenty-eight hours, but there were no messages in the log. She and Rabbit settled into the salon for some serious data mining on Zeneca Hong Pharmaceuticals. I went to my stateroom to call Cleo and check on Mariko. Deuce would be asking how she was the moment he cleared the Armstrong lock.

I closed the hatch behind me and sat on my bunk. Cleo had long ago given up on softening the hard lines and metal surfaces of my personal space. I preferred it that way; clean, uncluttered, no distractions. For a second, the impulse to lie down and sleep for a week seized me. My hand still throbbed under the biobrane dressing, and my head still spun with questions. I shook them off and activated my link, calling up Cleo's comm code.

Cleo's link was off net. Odd. She often set it for privacy, but rarely shut it down completely—especially when we were in the middle of a job. I linked to the public comm and called Mariko. On the third chime, a burly miner sporting an asymmetric beard answered. I recognized him as one of Mikey's buddies, Clarence Something-or-other.

"Yeah?" he said.

"Clarence, it's Zack Mbele, Deuce's partner. I'm looking for Cleo. She was supposed to be staying with Mariko. Is everything Jake there?"

"Don't know, Zack," he scratched at his beard, pondering the question. "Cleo called the Guild Hall, few hours back. Said she needed some muscle to sit with Mariko for a spell. We all liked Mikey. He was a miner, so 'twasn't a chore. But she's been gone most o' the day. Said she had a meeting what couldn't wait. You know what she was on about? 'Cause Mariko's gettin' kinda worried."

"I don't know, Clarence," I said, now worried myself. "Did she say anything about this meeting?"

"Nope, just..." he paused. "Y'know, she did say something about TransAstral. Said they couldn't ship enough bloody parcels to make it worth her time. I thought it was kinda funny."

"Yeah, hilarious," I muttered.

"Huh?"

"Nothing," I said, putting my sudden anger on hold. "Can you get some guys to keep an eye on Mariko for a while longer?"

"Sure, Zack. Like I said, Mikey was one of us, and we look after our own. But what'll I tell Mariko?"

"Just tell her that I needed Cleo, and that Deuce will be back soon." Clarence scratched his beard again and looked doubtful. I sighed. "Just do it, please. Deuce or I will call back as soon as we find Cleo."

Clarence nodded and logged off. I struggled to control the impulse to smash my fist into a bulkhead. After all her talk about finding a way to live together, she'd left Mariko to go off with her sugar daddy from TransAstral. The line between ecstasy and despair gleamed bright in my head. I could cross it again, but didn't think I could come back. I tried to make myself believe that she'd gone to put an end to her liaison once and for all. I tried, but it was too hard. I'd been here before and my heart told me where this would end. Still, I needed to know.

"Sylvia," I called.

"Yes, Boss?"

"I need you to find out anything you can on TransAstral's management. Who runs things here on the Moon? Names, locations, background; anything that might identify Cleo's contact in the company."

"But Boss, what about ZHP?" she asked.

This time I did slam a fist into the bulkhead. "Damn it, Sylvia! Just do what I ask. ZHP will wait."

"Okay, okay. Give me a few minutes."

I spent the time showering and changing out of my sweat-soaked flight suit. The sonic spray worked on the tight muscles of my neck and back. The heat penetrated my arm and hand, driving back the lingering chill.

Clean, warmer, but not much happier, I joined Rabbit in the salon. He slurped some coffee and flipped through the document pages displayed in the holomatrix over the center table.

"What have you got, Sylvia?" I asked.

"Not much. TransAstral's Lunar operations are based out of Gagarin Center, not Tycho. All of the senior management is up there. There's only a branch office here, middle level managers and worker bees; no one with the kind of influence it would take to get Cleo's attention."

I thought about that for a moment. "Try cross referencing vice-presidents or higher against shuttle passenger lists, hotel registrations, casino vouchers; anything that would put them here in the past three weeks."

"Checking," Sylvia said in the distracted way she spoke when her subroutines were running. "I have two hits. First: Marilyn McKellips, Chief Financial Officer, was here for a meeting with Provident Investments twelve days ago."

I grinned. "Not Cleo's type."

"Didn't think so. Second: Adam Recker, Special Assistant for Market Research, here several times according to shuttle bookings. Stayed on the Promenade, casino vouchers at the Fandango and at the Golden Moon."

"That's more like it. Is he still in town?"

"Don't know." Sylvia paused for a split second. "No current hotel bookings; last recorded shuttle arrival was five days ago. No departure booking, but that doesn't mean he's still in town. He could have gotten out on any company ship or delivery shuttle."

"Do you have a picture of this guy?" I asked.

"Sure." Sylvia shrank the documents Rabbit had opened and moved them into a window at the table's corner. In their place, a full-face image appeared in the holomatrix.

Rabbit dropped his coffee. I gripped the edge of the table as I stared into the dead blue eyes of the hologram. The Tall Man stared back, his image just as cold and unmoving as the real thing.

CHAPTER SIXTEEN

"Jesus, Zack," whispered Rabbit. "It's that tall freak who was with the Dragons."

"And if he's also Cleo's friend," I said, "Either she's being played or she's playing us." I wasn't sure which would be worse. "Sylvia, what have you got on this guy?"

"Not much. Just a TransAstral bio profile. He's listed as 'Special Assistant to the Board for Market Research.' Hails from the Alta Hesperion arcology, graduated *cum laude* from the Keynes-Friedman School of Economics, held various positions around Earth and the arcologies, then the obligatory war service as a Fed mobile infantry officer. "He drops out of sight for two years before turning up as a consultant to various Hang Seng 400 companies. There's enough here to make him look bona fide, but no real information. There's no dirt in the public database, no legal trouble, no family, no life outside of his official bio."

"A ghost," I murmured.

"Say what?" she asked.

"Nothing, just something I told Hank. Any word from

Deuce?"

"Not yet, Boss, but his link registered on the grid two minutes ago. He's approaching the outbound holding yard now. Do you want me to patch you through?"

"No. He won't get to the Armstrong lock for at least an hour. I'll meet him there. Meanwhile, you and Rabbit keep digging on Zeneca Hong."

"What about the tall guy?" said Rabbit. "You know what he could do to Cleo."

"I don't know that he and Cleo aren't working together."

Rabbit looked confused.

"Think about it," I said. "Would Cleo make a play for this guy if she hadn't checked him out? And if she did, she'd get the same load of moon-dust that we found here. So what does she know that we don't?"

"Cleo wouldn't do that," Rabbit protested. "She wouldn't sell you out."

I didn't feel like arguing with him. Maybe he was right. Or maybe she would sell out if the bid were high enough. She'd always been about security. Offer her enough cash to set herself up comfortably and who knew what she'd do? My head began to ache as my gut told me one thing and my heart said another.

"Just stay here and wait for my call," I said. "I have to tell Deuce that she let him down, too."

I left the salon and slid down the ladder to the forward hold. Rabbit followed as far as the catwalk. I opened the suit locker, but Sylvia interrupted before I could swing my pressure suit out.

"Zack," she said. "You have a private call. It's Colin Jones. He says he has business with you."

"Oh, shit," said Rabbit.

"Hush. Put him through to the salon, Sylvia. I'll be there in a second." I hurried over to the aft ladder. Rabbit started toward the salon, but I waved him back. "No, Rabbit. Better he doesn't see you until I know where this is going."

A few seconds later, I walked into the salon. Colin Jones' holoimage hovered over the center table. He sat at a wide mahogany desk, leaning back in his chair, hands behind his head. His feet were up on the desktop. He smiled like a hungry crocodile. I sat facing his image and tried to look as relaxed as he did.

"Zack Mbele. How they hangin', Mate?"

"Colin," I nodded in greeting. "Kill anybody today?"

"Not yet," he laughed. "But it's early." He looked me over. "You're looking fit. Working out? Me, I never have the time." He patted his belly. "Been packing on a few kilo's, but what are ya gonna do? Not bad for a tunnel rat from the backside of Planetia, eh?"

"What do you want, Colin?"

His smile vanished. He pulled his feet off the desk and sat forward. "Right. Down to business, then. You have something of mine. I want it back."

"Rabbit's code isn't for sale, and he's under my protection now." I hoped that sounded more confident than I felt. Jones hadn't opened with a promise to slit my throat. I took that to mean he wanted a trade instead of my execution.

He waved a hand dismissively. "I don't give a rat's ass about the code anymore. It was a one-off. Won't take more than a few days for the techies to figure it out and come up with a software patch to block it. Now Conejo, he's another matter. Can't have word getting out that you can stiff the Dragons and live."

"So don't tell anyone," I said.

"Not that simple. Conejo can't keep his mouth shut."

"Kept it shut while your assassin was torturing him didn't he?" I smiled as his face reddened. "What if I guarantee he'll keep quiet?"

"How you gonna do that?" Jones sneered. "Shove a gag in his mouth?"

"I'll keep him aboard the *Profit*. He talks to nobody but my crew. Besides, to get to Rabbit, you'll have to get by me."

"You think you're that tough?"

"You ready to pay to find out?"

Jones frowned. For a second, I thought I'd overplayed my hand. But he shrugged and said, "What the hell. We're both businessmen. Killing's always bad business. As long as he stays on that turd you call a ship, he can live."

I let the insult pass. "If you don't want the code, what are we talking about here?"

He frowned. "Don't play stupid, Zack. I know Kwai Chang Wu bought your debt and has your bollocks in a vise. He's got you doing the dirty work in a double-cross. What'd he offer? Cancel the debt if you did a job for him? Maybe threw in a little extra cash?"

"So what if he did?"

"So your ship left its berth yesterday and was gone for a little over a day. Nobody challenged you, which means Conejo's invisibility code is the real thing. It was neatly done. Port Authority didn't even know you were gone. And now I'm thinking you've got a shipping container that belongs to me."

As he spoke, the cold sinking sensation in the pit of my stomach deepened. Someone was feeding Jones detailed information, and I had a bad feeling I knew who. The buyout of New Houston was public record, and there were plenty of witnesses to my frog march from the casino floor. Jones could put two and two together and figure that Wu had maneuvered me into doing a job for him. But aside from my crew and me, Wu and Vincent were the only ones who knew the target. It came back to Cleo and her relationship with the Dragon's hired assassin.

I tried to stall. "Container? What container?"

Jones laugh was a harsh bark. "Now you think I'm stupid. That's not a mistake you want to make twice, Cobber."

I shrugged. "Say I have this container. Why should I give it to you instead of Wu?"

"It'd be healthier for you." He said it flatly: no threat, just a statement of fact.

It was my turn to laugh. "If I were worried about that, I wouldn't have killed two of your boys and rescued Rabbit from your assassin."

"And if I thought you were that easy to kill, we wouldn't be talking here. As I said, killing's bad business—especially when it gets expensive. What do you say to a trade? You give me the container and I give you something you want."

"Wu's offering my ship. What have you got?"

He smiled, and gestured to someone off to his right. "Didn't I mention it? We've got Cleopatra Lee." Adam Recker stepped into the video feed behind Jones. The Tall Man held Cleo with her arms pinned behind her back. A black and blue welt covered her left eye. Dried blood caked her lower lip. Jones leaned back in his chair. "She's a handful. Took out two of my best boys before Recker cold-cocked her. We've had to keep her drugged like a Tharsis whore so she wouldn't kill any more of my guys. How do you live with her?"

I ignored him. "Cleo, are you okay?" She opened her good eye and nodded, but didn't try to speak. She winced as Recker dragged her out of video range again.

"Well, Zack? What'll it be?"

I shrugged. "She's my *ex*-wife. She got half this ship in the divorce and, as you found out, she can be hell to live with. I'd be better off taking the container to Wu and being rid of her."

Jones laughed. "Have it your way, then. Recker?" He drew a line across his throat with his thumb. A bit melodramatic, but it made his point.

"No, wait!" I shouted.

Jones' smile was smug. "Knew you didn't have it in you."

"So, we trade. What do you want?"

"The container and its contents, even up for your ex-wife. Simple as that."

"I still have a deal with Wu," I said. "And a Fed BPS agent

breathing down my neck."

"Not my problem," Jones waved his hand.

"It will be if I tell the Feds what's in the container."

Jones frowned but said nothing.

I went on. "Here's my offer. You pay off my loan with New Houston Bank. I confirm the payment. Then I meet you somewhere neutral, just Deuce and me, you, one bodyguard, and Cleo. Deuce and Cleo go home. Once they're clear, I take you and your boy to the container."

Jones howled with laughter and pounded on the desk. "God's Bloody Balls, but you've got sand." He laughed some more, long and loud, wiping tears from his eyes. "Oh, that's rich, that really is. Alright, Zack, it's a deal. It'll be worth it just to rub Wu's nose in it. If he kills you, it's no skin off my ass." He turned suddenly serious. "And he will kill you. You know that, Cobber."

"As you say, not your problem. As soon as Sylvia confirms the money transfer, Deuce and I will head out. I assume you're here on the moon?"

"That I am. Where do we meet?"

I thought for a second. "The Blue Booby, down by the commercial spaceport. Deuce and me, you and your muscle."

"Fair enough."

"I'll wait for the money," I said, standing up. Just before I broke the connection I asked, "By the way, Colin, what do you want with a bunch of embryos?"

"That'd be my business, and none of yours, Mate." He reached out and touched a spot on his desk. The image vanished.

Rabbit was waiting at the top of the ladder, above the cargo bay.

"What'd he say?" he asked.

"Relax, Rabbit. As long as you stay aboard the ship, you're safe. The bad news is that he's got Cleo. He'll trade her for the container."

Rabbit managed to look smug and distressed at the same time. "I told you she wouldn't sell you out. But what about my stuff? If I'm stuck aboard the ship, how can I get all my stuff? We might need some of that gear, you know. I can reproduce the code, but there's stuff at my place that's hard to find these days, and most of it's custom, can't get it at any price."

"Calm down," I said. "Make a list. Deuce or I can go get it."

He took a deep breath. "Okay, but what about Cleo? We're gonna get her back, right? And what would the Dragons want with embryos? Hey, do you think they had the same idea we did? Using the cheat code to sneak up on the freighter, I mean. Maybe that's why Jones isn't interested in killing me. He can get what he wants by kidnapping Cleo."

Rabbit's rapid free association was giving me a headache. I stopped him by sending him to make a list of the stuff he wanted. In truth, all the same thoughts had run through my head as I talked to Jones. Cleo's injuries suggested she wasn't a willing participant, but who knew? She was capable of taking a beating to make it look good. I put it all aside. Right now, I needed to get started for the Armstrong lock if I was going to meet Deuce.

I'd just secured the seals around the thighs of my suit when Sylvia called again.

"We've got company, Boss," she said. "A couple of police cruisers and a troop carrier just pulled up outside. Lt. Boucher wants to talk to you."

I sighed and hung the upper half of my pressure suit back in the locker. "Put him through," I said. "And make a copy of the stuff we got off the data chip from Mike and Mariko's apartment. He'll be wanting that." Deuce would have to wait a while.

A second later, Hank was connected to my link. "Hi, Hank," I said cheerfully. "What can I do for you?"

"I've got a warrant to search your ship and any cargo

you have in the holds. Extend your port docking collar and clear your lock. We're coming aboard."

"I hadn't planned on company, but if you've got a warrant, I guess you're gonna come in."

"I guess I am."

A minute later, Hank and half a dozen armed *Federales* stepped through the portside lock. Hank strode toward me as the troops spread out across the hold. They didn't actually point their pulse rifles at anyone in particular, but managed to look menacing nevertheless. Hank held out an old-fashioned document with a thick plastic seal on it, very official-looking.

"Zachariah Mbele, by order of the Bureau of Public Security, you are served with a warrant to search your person, your ship, known as the *Profit*, hull number VC-334, and any and all cargo contained aboard said ship. You are entitled to—"

"Enough already, Hank," I interrupted. "Search all you want. I've got nothing to hide." *Not here anyway.*

Hank turned red but said nothing. He stuck the paper in the helmet of my suit and waved to his men. They fanned out, opening lockers and bins in the cargo bay. Others headed aft and topside to search there. I sighed. If they tossed Cleo's things there'd be hell to pay.

Hank watched for a couple of seconds, then turned back to me.

"Going somewhere?" he asked.

"Just meeting Deuce and Cleo at the Armstrong lock. They're grocery shopping. Figured I'd help with the packages."

"Where have you been the past couple of days, Zack?" he asked, looking at my p-suit.

"Honest, officer," I said, holding up my right hand and crossing my heart with my left. "I haven't been more than a hundred meters from this ship since the day before yesterday."

He grunted. "Not exactly what I asked, but we'll pass on that. What happened to your hand?"

I held it out and flexed the fingers. "A little misadventure in the galley. I never was much of a fry cook."

"Right. I've seen a few vacuum burns in my time. Turns the fingernails black, just like yours. We'll pass on that, too," he said. He pointed to Wu's container, the customs-proofed one that was supposed to hold our stolen goods. "What's in the box?"

"How should I know?" I said. "It's sealed. Like I told you, Wu bought the lien on my ship. I'm supposed to deliver that, unopened, to Kwai Hong One by the seventh or he'll repo the *Profit*. Which is why that inquest is so damned inconvenient."

Hank gestured to one of his guys. "Open it."

"But sir, it's got a customs seal."

"I don't give a damn," Hank said. "It's cargo. It's covered under the warrant." He glared at me, daring me to say something.

I shrugged. So much for Wu's customs-proof container. "No skin off my nose, but I want a certified recording that you ordered the search. I won't lose my ship because you got a bug up your ass."

Hank's man got to work on the seals. Hank leaned toward me and said, "We had a deal, Zack. What have you got for me?"

"Sylvia," I said. "Do you have those files on Wu and the Dragons?"

"You know I do," she said.

"Download them to Lt. Boucher's datapad. Okay, Hank?" He nodded. "The stuff we found at Mike Finney's place shows Wu filed a false survey report with the Feds to make it look like the mines were still working on Ceres. He was trading ice to the Dragons for unregistered ore. Mike found out about it when he was working for McAllen Engineering, which did the survey. He was going to blow the whistle. I don't know if Wu ordered a hit on Mikey or if the Dragons did, but either way, Wu knew about it."

Hank spent a few seconds reviewing the file. He shook his head. "I don't know, Zack. It's pretty thin. Nothing here ties Wu to Finney—except maybe Constantine, and he's dead. It's motive, maybe, but I can't take this to a magistrate."

"Why not? The guys at Rabbit's place were known Dragons. This ties Wu to the Dragons. Hell, at least it should be enough to open an investigation. He filed a false survey with a federal agency. He wouldn't do something that stupid just to hide a little ice smuggling."

Hank sighed. "Look, maybe I agree with you. But the Kwai's lawyers will get this in front of a tribunal the minute it's filed. Without Finney to testify, it'll be dismissed in a heartbeat—and you're not the most credible witness. How do I explain where I got this without putting you at a crime scene? And I won't even go into your latest adventure down in Lower Conrad."

He held up a hand when I opened my mouth to protest. "Not my jurisdiction, and I'm not saying anything to the cops who caught it. The Samurai Boys aren't very popular down there anyway. And Kenji didn't get a name, just described a tall dark-skinned *gai jin* with a fast gun hand.

"But that could all change if you have to explain your connection with Finney's database. Do you really want to have another talk with that AI magistrate?"

I shook my head but said nothing. I wasn't going to bring up Harding if Hank wasn't. Maybe they hadn't found him yet. Possible in a place like the Kikyucho, although he'd be pretty ripe by now. I'd made it look good enough for Hank to buy this version of the truth. If I pushed harder, he'd start asking more uncomfortable questions. Before he could say anything else, the man working on the Customs seals called out. "Got it, Lieutenant. Do you want to have a look?"

Hank held my eye for a moment and then walked over

to the container. His confident look fell away, and his shoulders tensed. He spun to face me.

"What the hell are you playing at, Zack?" he demanded.

I crossed the hold and stood beside him. I looked into the container, and tried not to smile. "Well, what do you know?" I said. "It's empty."

"I know it's empty. Where's the stuff Wu had inside it?"

I managed to look shocked. "How should I know? The man delivers a box and tells me to take it to Kwai Hong One. For all I know, I'm being set up to take the fall in a smuggling sting. Is that why you're here? Is that what you told the magistrate to get the warrant?"

Hank held my eye. "I got a tip that Wu was moving goods he didn't want Daddy Kwai to know about. Doesn't matter now." He turned to the man who'd opened the container. "Sergeant, recall the men. We're done here."

I stepped past him and swung the hatch of the cargo box closed. Hank gripped my arm.

"I'm trying to help you here, Zack," he whispered. "If I can get Wu on a smuggling beef, he'll go away for a long time. Tell me what the hell is going on."

"I can't, Hank. You have everything I've got on Wu and the Dragons. I'm in a bind here. If I don't make this delivery on time, I'll lose my ship. I don't give a damn if Wu wants to send himself an empty container. I'm just doing a job."

He released my arm but held my eye for a long moment. "All right, have it your way. I hope whatever you're hiding doesn't get you killed. And remember what I told you: out in the deep black or in the Belt, you're on your own. I can't help you."

"I know what I'm doing, Hank.

"If you say so. And about that inquest; I spoke to Judge Waverly. He overruled the AI magistrate and closed the case as a justifiable homicide. You're off that hook. Port Authority will lift the launch hold by close of business today." He glanced up to where Rabbit was peeking over the catwalk railing. "Although, I don't think that matters anymore either."

I managed a grin. "No, maybe not. Thanks, Hank. I owe you."

"Yes, you do." He waved a hand at the sergeant and the *Federales* started to duck their way through the lock and back to their transport. Hank followed them, but paused at the hatch.

"By the way," he said, "we got a complaint from American Presidents Freight. One of their ships, the *Grant*, was hijacked between here and L4. Slick job. Only took a single container, and left a dummy emitter in its place. The *Grant* never detected another ship, and Lunar traffic control doesn't show anything within a thousand kilometers of them for the past three days. Any idea who could have pulled that off?"

"Nope," I said with a straight face.

"I thought not. Take care of yourself, Zack." He ducked through the hatch and the lock cycled closed.

I felt bad about lying to Hank again. He'd gone out on a limb for me, and now he'd have to explain to his superiors why he broke a customs seal. But the game had changed when Jones snatched Cleo, and I didn't know where it would take me now. I had a score to settle with Wu, and the way I figured it, a little jail time wouldn't pay his side of the debt. Not by a long shot.

"Sylvia, call me as soon as you confirm the payoff. I'm going to meet Deuce." I hauled out the upper half of my suit and hoisted it over my head.

CHAPTER SEVENTEEN

I hiked to the nearest public lock and stowed my suit in a rental locker. Deuce and I would pick it up later. There was a tube stop nearby, and I caught a cross-town pod that dropped me near the Tranquility Road terminals.

The traffic at this end of Armstrong Boulevard ebbed and flowed with each rotation of the massive cylindrical airlock. The lower level held huge ground transports, six at a time, carrying bulk cargo from the farms and factories up around Tranquility Basin. The upper levels were for light passenger vehicles and the odd pedestrian. Every ninety seconds, the lock turned, siphoning traffic from the great Tranquility Road and feeding it into the hungry city.

"You're late," Deuce said as I approached through the swirling crowd. He sat on his pressure suit's travel case, his back against the scooter, chewing slowly on a soy bar.

"I know. Had a visit from the *Federales*. Hank tried to hang a smuggling beef on Wu by searching the container Vincent brought us."

"Too bad he didn't find anything. Might've saved us some

trouble."

"Hardly," I said. "Wu'd be locked up in a Fed prison. Hard to get at him in a place like that."

Deuce laughed. "Easier'n you'd think, LT. You should know that. Better to have him killed there than get into his place on Ceres."

"Maybe, but we'll never know. We've got bigger trouble right now. It looks like the box of embryos was intended for Colin Jones."

Deuce stopped chewing and swallowed hard.

I nodded. "Wu has us doing the dirty work in a plan to double-cross the Dragons and get the container for himself."

"What would the Dragons want with it?" Deuce asked, tossing the rest of the soy bar away.

"I don't know, but Jones wants it bad. He snatched Cleo. He'll trade her for the box." I held up a hand as Deuce leapt to his feet. "Take it easy. Mariko's okay. Clarence and some of Mikey's buddies from the Guild are watching out for her."

"Yeah, but I'm not sure they can handle that Vincent guy."

"I don't think they'll have to. Wu still expects us to make the delivery. He'll keep Vincent close until he has the box in hand."

"Is Cleo okay?" Deuce asked.

"So far. They let me see her on the vid. Looks like they roughed her up a bit, but she's alive."

Deuce tossed his pressure suit into scooter's cargo box. "How did they get the drop on her? Even Vincent would have a hard time with Cleo."

"Don't know that for sure, either. But Cleo's 'friend' from TransAstral is actually a freelance assassin working for Jones. His name is Adam Recker. I figure he got Cleo to meet him somewhere so he and a couple of Dragons could jump her." I took a deep breath. "Deuce, he's the tall man who killed Mikey."

Deuce's knuckles turned white on the edge of the

scooter's cargo box. "It just gets better and better, don't it."

I climbed into the passenger seat. Deuce eased behind the wheel and switched on the motor.

"'What's the plan?" he asked, pulling into traffic.

"We meet Jones and one of his boys at the Booby. They'll have Cleo. You take her back to the ship, and I take Jones to the container."

"And then you die," said Deuce. "That's a lousy plan, LT."

"I don't think Jones plans to kill me."

Deuce glanced at me over his shoulder. "How do you figure that?"

"Two reasons. First, he agreed to pay off the loan on the *Profit* before the meeting. He calls himself a businessman. Says killing is bad business, especially when it's expensive. If he wanted me dead he wouldn't spend the money."

"Maybe." Deuce sounded doubtful. "What's the second reason?"

"He expects Wu to kill me for him."

Deuce gave a wicked laugh. "If Wu's anything like his old man, he's got the right idea."

"I'm counting on it."

Deuce laughed again. "Seriously, you think you can trust Jones?"

"Yeah. Strange to say it, but I think I can. I don't know what he wants with a bunch of embryos, but they're important enough that he'll stick to the deal. Once Cleo is out, there's no percentage in killing me. She can implicate him and Recker. Better to let Wu do the dirty work."

Deuce nodded. "You figure on waiting for Wu to make a run at us, or do we move on him first?"

I shrugged. "Either way. He'll want to do the job himself, or at least watch Vincent do it. If he comes to us, so much the better."

Deuce just grunted. We drove on, dodging in and out of the traffic as we crossed the heart of the casino district. Sylvia called to confirm the money transfer. The *Profit* was mine, or at least my half of her. Jones was sticking to the deal, and Wu could kiss my ass. I grinned. *Let him come,* I thought.

The Promenade flashed overhead. That arching symbol of power and privilege cut through my optimism like a black knife, filling me with a mixture of anger and sadness. Wu had been born to power and privilege. It shaped and drove him, colored the way he saw the universe, and made him believe he had the power to force people like me to do his bidding. But real power was a different thing. Real power needed vision. Jones understood this. With all the money and muscle at his command, he was still just "a tunnel rat from the back side of Planetia" to the likes of Wu.

I pondered that as we passed through the shopping district and on to the industrial zone that ringed the spaceport. Time was critical to Jones for some reason. If all he wanted was the box, he could simply take it from us. We might make a stand in the *Profit,* but the arithmetic of men and firepower favored Jones. He'd take us eventually. My training and my time in the Bear left me with no illusions about keeping secrets under interrogation. With the right methods, anyone could be broken: me, Deuce, probably even Metternich himself. But those methods took time, and would probably leave us dead. Not to mention the official attention a full-strength assault on the *Profit* might bring.

No, Jones wanted the embryos badly, but he wanted them quickly and quietly. That was why he was willing to trade, and why I'd likely live to see tomorrow. Beyond that was anyone's guess, but I was willing to bet that Jones wouldn't want to draw attention to the Dragons. He'd be happy enough to have Wu eliminate us.

I still didn't know how Cleo figured into all of this— victim, accomplice or dupe—but if she was an accomplice, all bets were off. With the ship paid off and me dead, she could write her own ticket—unless Jones decided she was a liability. For once, my gut and my heart agreed. Cleo might sell me out for the sake of her own security, but it wouldn't be to the likes of Jones. I wondered if I could really have let Recker kill her if Jones had balked at paying off the lien on the ship. If I were still under Wu's thumb, if it came down to a choice between Cleo and the *Profit*, would I let her go? I sighed. Jones had the measure of it; I still had it bad for her.

Deuce swung off Armstrong into a narrow alley, breaking my reverie. The alley threaded between the edge of the commercial port and a series of ramshackle warehouses, ship's chandlers and bars. It ended at a small roundabout, not much more than a wide spot in the pavement.

Wedged between the rock walls and the back fence of the commercial port, a low building fronted the street. A large plastic statue of a bird with bright blue feet and a blue beak spread its wings above the door. Under each wing, smaller figures of big-breasted women in short skirts held out trays of plastic food and drink. The sign above the door read: THE BLUE BOOBY.

Deuce backed the scooter up to the edge of the pavement, between a battered four-wheeler and a bright red electric bicycle. He climbed off and slapped me on the shoulder.

"It's been a while since we lifted a few here, eh, LT?" he said grimly.

I eyed the faded sign and the chipped plastic of the bird's beak. "That it has. Can't imagine why we stayed away."

He laughed and started for the door. I caught his shoulder.

"Steady, partner," I said. "This is business. We get in, we get out and you take Cleo home. Jake?"

He nodded. "Golden, LT. Except I don't like leaving you with Jones."

"Can't be done any other way. You can track me by my link. Now give me the berth number of the container so I can find it in the holding yard."

He rattled off a string of letters and numbers and I repeated them, committing them to memory.

We pushed open the faded plastic and aluminum doors, and entered side by side. I swept my gaze right; Deuce looked left. The single large room was cut back into the rock face that supported this edge of the pressure dome. It was bigger than it looked from the street.

Dim patches of light illuminated the bar and the dance floor. The few occupied tables hugged the dark edges of the room, where business was conducted in hushed tones. Off to the far right, the show stage was dark. It was early and the girls were still sleeping off the previous night's efforts. They'd be back dancing for tips when the day shift let out and tunnel riggers and ice miners filled the room with loud voices and ready cash.

The placed smelled of stale beer and tobacco smoke. An old Martian blues riff, heavy with sax and vibes, played in the background. I focused on the tables on my side of the room, marking a couple of pimps near the door, arguing in harsh whispers. Closer to the bar, two men sat eyeing us; a jolt-dealer and a thin nervous-looking guy who was probably his chemist. The dealer looked Deuce over, then glanced at a metal case on the floor next to his chair. I smiled.

Deuce hated jolt dealers. On another day this might have been interesting.

Then I caught sight of the man sitting in the deep shadows near the stage. He sat alone, leaning back with his chair against the wall, his face hidden by the darkness around him. His table was empty—no food or drink—and his hands rested on his knees. The balls of his feet rested lightly on the floor.

Vassa, the bartender, glared at Deuce. There was bad blood between them over an incident with one of the dancers a few months back. In the bar, they both kept things civil; Vassa because he was in business to sell beer, and Deuce because he liked drinking it.

Deuce glared back at him until Vassa shrugged and tilted

his head toward the back of the bar, near the show stage.

I eyed the man in the shadows as we passed. He made no move, other than shifting his right hand closer to his hip.

Right handed, I thought. *Weapon at his hip or tucked in the small of his back.* I nudged Deuce forward and we skirted our way around the darkened stage. Tables spread three deep between the stage and the back wall, lost in shadow. I knew there was another cluster of tables in the back, near the door to the dressing rooms. If the man at the darkened table belonged to Jones, he was there as back-up—not an immediate threat to us unless things went sideways.

Jones sat in the back, farthest from the stage. An overhead spot cast a cone of light on him and the table. He looked up as we approached, nodding amiably. Two people stood behind him in the shadows, one tall and the other with the unmistakable curves of a woman. A couple of Dragons materialized from the shadows near the stage as we approached. Deuce and I stopped. They didn't.

One of the men flashed a needler and motioned for me to raise my arms. I glanced at Deuce. His face was darkening and the muscles of his neck bunched as he tensed for an attack. I shook my head and he eased back onto his heels. He raised his arms slowly. The second man frisked him quickly and efficiently. I glared at Jones as I got the same treatment.

"They're clean," said the man next to me.

"I thought we had an agreement, Jones," I said, lowering my arms.

Jones nodded and the men stepped away. "Relax, Cobber. Just a little insurance. Vassa's told me what your man can do."

"What about your 'eyes behind' at the table back there?" I jerked a thumb toward the man we'd passed in the dark.

"You don't miss much." He laughed and waved a hand at the Dragons who'd frisked us. "Go on, boys. Everything's fine here." The Dragons eyed Deuce, but moved off toward the front of the bar.

Jones smiled. "So, do we do some business here?"

"Yeah, we do business." I tapped Deuce on the shoulder and moved closer to the table.

"Have a seat, Zack," Jones said. "Take a load off."

I pulled out a chair, turned it around and straddled it so I could jump to my feet without getting tangled in it. Recker and Cleo stood behind Jones, half hidden in the shadows. Deuce moved to the left and sat down about an arm's reach from my shoulder.

"Are you okay, Cleo?" I asked, ignoring Jones' smug smile.

"I'm okay," she mumbled. "Head's fuzzy. Drugs."

"You see?" said Jones. "She's fine." He turned slightly. "Recker, give the lady a seat."

Recker pulled out a chair and maneuvered Cleo into it. I could see her face in the light of the overhead spot. Her eyelid was still purple and swollen, but they'd cleaned the blood off of her split lip. Her good eye was glazed. She glared at Jones through it. Deuce looked at her face and started to rise.

"Down boy," I said. "Not now."

"Good advice, Mr. Claus," said Recker nodding to me. "I should have recognized you before, but you know how it is when you see someone out of context."

Jones shot him a questioning glance. Recker held my eye as he said, "Mr. Mbele and I have met before, although I didn't realize who he was at the time. I didn't expect to see him at Conejo's place."

Deuce shifted his glare to Recker. "Are you the bastard who killed Mikey?"

"Who?" Jones asked, still looking at Recker.

"A side job, nothing to do with you," said Recker. His tone was casual, as if Mikey were a bug he'd squashed. "My contract with you isn't exclusive, and it dovetailed nicely with the Conejo job."

Jones nodded. "Not sure I like you working on the side. But as long as it doesn't come back to me, no harm, no foul."

"Who wanted Mikey dead?" Deuce demanded. "Wu?"

"Shut up, Deuce," Cleo said before I could speak. She shook her head as if to clear it. "This isn't the time."

Deuce turned on her. "The hell you say. Are you worried I might hurt your fancy-man here?"

Recker stepped away from the table with a thin smile. "Come on then," he said to Deuce. "If you think you're capable."

"Cleo's right, Deuce." I said, reaching up to put a hand on his arm. "Another time. Stand down. I need you to take Cleo home."

"Take her home yourself, LT. I know where that container is. I'll take them there and then take care of business with this asshole."

Both Jones and I shook our heads. Looking at Deuce, Jones said, "Not in the cards, Cobber. If you've got a personal score to settle with Recker here, you'll do it on your own time. Your boss and I have a deal and Recker's working for me just now."

"That's the way of it, Deuce," I added. "You'll get your chance, but first we stick to the deal." I looked at Recker. "And I have business with Recker myself."

"Deuce," said Cleo quietly, her words still slurred from drugs, "I swear...didn't know about Adam. Thought he was an investigator for...TransAstral. Looking into cargo theft. Said Wu was his target...Promised a big reward if we took him down. But after Mikey got killed, I called him. Was going to tell him the deal was off. Too much risk." She rubbed her eyes and took a deep breath. "I loved Mike, too. But we need to get out of here now. Get even later."

Deuce stared at Recker for a long moment. Then he stood and moved around the table to stand next to Cleo. Jones nodded and pointed toward the front of the bar.

"You be careful, LT," Deuce said, helping Cleo to her feet. She took his arm and looked at me.

I shook my head. I still didn't trust her, but there wasn't time to go into that now. Deuce put an arm around her shoulder and they started to walk away.

"How touching," Recker said. He spoke to Deuce, but all the while his gaze was fixed on me. "The tame wolf does its master's bidding. Did you protect Finney's woman the same way? Didn't do so well there, did you?"

Deuce froze. With a snarl, he spun on his heel and launched himself at Recker. I jumped to my feet but stopped as Jones flashed a needler at me. Recker sidestepped with blinding speed and Deuce's arms closed on empty air. Recker slashed downward with his arm, catching Deuce behind the ear and sending him sprawling to the floor.

Recker looked at me, a smug smile on his face. This was payback for humiliating him at Rabbit's place. I leaned forward but stopped when Jones twitched the needler.

Deuce rolled to his feet, shaking his head. He crouched in a fighting stance, eyeing Recker. He advanced again, more slowly, on cat's feet. Recker stood casually, as if waiting for a friend.

Deuce feinted to his right, and then launched an explosive two fisted attack on Recker's center of mass. It was a classic Special Forces move—both fists driven with all the body's weight behind them, into the center of the opponent's chest, forcing him back and off balance. The right hand came up for a blow to the nose, the left slashed downward toward the groin. But Recker moved fast—faster than any human should move. He turned so Deuce's first blow glanced off his chest without making solid contact. Then his knee came up and slammed into Deuce's abdomen. He pivoted, sweeping Deuce's leg with his left foot.

Deuce went down hard. He lay gasping for a second, then lifted himself on one hand and got a foot planted on the floor. Recker's spinning roundhouse kick struck him on the side of the head and knocked him back to the floor.

Cleo started forward, but I stopped her as Jones raised the needler. Deuce shook his head and rolled onto his left elbow. He raised his head, feet scraping on the floor as he struggled to get up. I felt a cold realization in the pit of my stomach; Recker's movements had the lightning-quick reactivity of nano augmentation. It was like watching myself in a mirror.

Recker shifted his weight, gathering strength for a finishing blow that would rock Deuce's head back, snapping his neck. Cleo gasped, seeing the blow coming. I gripped her arm tighter, watching the needler. I felt the nanos overriding my own nerves as I gathered myself to tip the table onto Jones, dodge the needler and jump to Deuce's side before Recker killed him. I hoped Cleo was sober enough to take Jones out before he could fire again.

"That's enough, Adam." The voice came from behind me. It wasn't loud, but the familiar tone of command struck a deep chord inside me.

Recker pulled back, glaring past my shoulder. Then he shrugged and moved away to stand behind Jones.

Cleo rushed forward, supporting Deuce while he shook his head, trying to clear it. She helped him to his feet. His eyes were glazed and he swayed as he stood.

I turned to look at the man behind me. He was heavier than I remembered, and his face was totally changed, but the eyes were the same. They gazed at me with an intensity I could never forget. Rabbit was right. The eyes never changed. I felt a roaring in my ears. Hans Metternich had been my mentor, my commanding officer and ultimately my torturer in a past life that ended when I walked out of the Bear. Now that old life came crashing back, smashing my carefully built walls and dragging me back to Mars and the Third Directorate.

"Hello, Zachariah," he said, a smile on his lips.

I resisted the urge to salute. "Hello, Colonel," I replied.

CHAPTER EIGHTEEN

"You're looking well," Metternich said. "How long has it been? Five years?"

"More like six," I said. "Since before the invasion." I glanced past him, to where Cleo and Deuce were leaving the bar. I looked back to Metternich. The plastic surgery and gene-mods were the best I'd ever seen, but the familiar glint in his eyes cut through the years, taking me back to the old days. Even with a hundred-million yuan bounty on his head, he could have walked down the Promenade unnoticed. "Rabbit said you were still alive, but I didn't believe him. What name are you using now? And does Colin here know who you are?"

"Mr. Jones and I have no secrets," said Metternich, still smiling. "Adam, of course, knows the truth as well. Beyond that, only you and Mr. Conejo are aware that the reports of my death were...premature."

I glanced at Jones. He hadn't put the needler away.

"As to my name," continued Metternich, "it's now Middleton, Henry Middleton. A ridiculously mild-mannered name, but the criminal record that accompanies it is well documented. And precedes the Martian revolution."

"And cost me plenty in bribes," said Jones.

"Of course, Mr. Jones," Metternich bowed toward him. "I am grateful for your patronage."

"Bollocks," said Jones, the needler now pointed at Metternich rather than me. "You'd as soon put a knife in my back. But as long as I cover for you with the *Federales,* you'll stick to our arrangement."

I saw Jones' overconfidence and the cold calculation in Metternich's gaze as he watched the needler. It was a look I knew well. Couldn't Jones see the danger? Recker saw it, and grinned in anticipation.

I was surprised when Metternich simply smiled. "No need for harsh words, Mr. Jones. We still have business to complete."

Jones put the needler away. "Right, then. Zack, I'll be leaving you with the Colonel, since you two are so close."

"That wasn't the deal."

"No, but it's safer—in case your friend Boucher tries to crash the party."

"You think I'd try to cross you, Colin?" I asked.

"Never know. People do stupid shit all the time." He stood. "Besides, I never handle goods in person. Keeps me footloose and fancy free."

"Whatever you say. But we go nowhere until I hear from Deuce."

Jones laughed. "You think I'd cross you, Zack?"

"In a heartbeat. We wait for Deuce."

* * *

We didn't wait long. After about ten minutes, Deuce chimed on my link.

"We're clear, LT." His voice was thin and strained. "At the ship now. You Jake?

"Golden here, Deuce. You?"

"Hurtin' a bit," he admitted. "Tell that tall bastard, the next time he sees me it'll be over the business end of a pulse rifle."

"Have Sylvia boot up the autodoc. I want you fit. I'll call after I make the delivery." I signed off and nodded to Jones.

He turned to Metternich. "You know where to take the goods. Call me when you have everything finished."

Jones walked away without waiting for a reply. The goons who'd frisked us followed him toward the door. Metternich stared at his back, the cold steel returning to his eyes. Jones strolled through the double doors and out into the alley, a dead man walking.

"When do you plan to kill him, Colonel?" I asked.

Metternich glanced my way. "He's still useful to me, Zachariah. And you know I hate to waste resources."

I shrugged. "None of my business. I just wondered how much longer I'd have to watch my back."

"You needn't worry about that. I run his security. Any attack on you would go through me. Jones is careful not to get his own hands dirty."

I didn't find that reassuring. I knew Metternich's secret. So did Rabbit. That made us liabilities, once we were no longer resources.

Metternich gestured toward the door. "Shall we?"

Recker took the cue and moved around the table to lead the way. Metternich grasped my elbow and we followed, leaving the bar.

Beside the Booby there was an oversized warehouse with a large door fronting the street. Recker punched a code into the keypad next to the door and it rolled up with a metallic squeal.

Metternich stopped as Recker entered the warehouse. A few seconds later I heard the whine of a motor spinning up. A cargo hauler with a stevedore 'bot slung on its crane hook rolled out the door and stopped in front of us, Recker in the driver's seat. Metternich and I climbed into the crew cab behind him.

"Where to?" Recker asked.

"Outbound cargo holding yard," I said. "We'll need p-suits."

"Under your seats." He drove slowly up the narrow alley toward Armstrong.

I checked over the suit. It was a standard short-term survival suit with adjustable arm and leg seals, thick bubble helmet, dual air feed adaptors for both tank and vehicle air sources. There was also a spare minitank under the seat, good for about thirty minutes if you didn't breathe too fast.

I looked up as Recker swung onto Armstrong and accelerated. He didn't speak, and Metternich had his eyes closed as he leaned back in the seat. I watched the traffic as we retraced the path Deuce and I had followed earlier.

My head whirled with questions, but all my training, hammered into me by this man who held the answers, forced me to hold my tongue. In the end, Metternich broke the silence.

"You have questions, Zachariah," he said. "But you're too well trained to begin the conversation. 'Never initiate the interrogation until you have a clear idea of your objectives. The interrogator reveals his own bias through the structure and order of his questions.'"

"That's what you taught me, Colonel."

"So, what do you wish to know?"

I said nothing, watching his face. He met my eye, a faint smile on his lips. Finally I said, "I saw the bombing of the Presidential Palace."

He laughed. "Very good, Zachariah," he said. "A statement of fact, non-committal tone, with an implied invitation to elaborate. Yes, I survived the attack. I wasn't anywhere near the palace at the time. A good commander never plans for his own defeat, but only a fool refuses to consider it. I managed to leave Mars through a standing arrangement with the Dragons and made my way to the Belt."

"'Standing arrangement'? So much for Martian law and order." I thought I'd abandoned any faith in the Martian Way, the political manifesto that had underpinned Metternich's Glorious Revolution, but this bland, cynical admission still angered me.

"Ah, now I'm disappointed in you, Zachariah. You betray yourself," he said. "Noble goals sometimes justify ignoble means."

"Is that how you justify the Bear?" I demanded. "The biotanks and the thousands they killed? What noble goal did they serve?"

"The most noble of all. You, of all people, should understand that. The Way was never limited to just Martian liberation. It was about the liberation of humanity from the tyranny of our Earthly cradle. It was meant to raise us out of infancy, into a new way of living in the universe. Are you still fighting your gift? Embrace it, Zachariah."

"The way Recker has?" I asked bitterly, remembering Mike and Rabbit.

"You and Adam should be brothers. You two alone have achieved the next step in human potential. And the knowledge we gained from the biotanks will eventually foster an even larger step in human evolution."

"The embryos," I whispered.

He smiled. "Yes, the embryos. The genetics of nano compatibility are very complex. The gene cluster is a recessive mosaic, which is why some subjects achieve a partial bond and only a very few succeed in making a complete one. The embryos contain all the genetic potential that you and Adam share—the ability to successfully incorporate the nanofibers into their nervous systems."

"You're going to put babies into the tanks?" I was suddenly sick with horror, remembering the fear and helplessness of my own tank runs.

"Only the first generation," he said calmly. "We've improved the nanos; they should be self-replicating when we breed the next generation. Within two or three generations, nanofiber-augmented humans will be dominant from Mars to the outer Belt."

I looked away. All of my nightmares, all of my darkest fears erupted from their tightly contained prisons in the back of my mind. I was back in the tanks, feeling the cold, thick protein-laden fluid fill my nose and mouth, forcing its way into my gut and my lungs. The burning heat would come next as the nanofibers were injected into the base of my spine. I shook my head, jerking my mind back to the present, suddenly aware of the sour smell of my own sweat.

Metternich was watching me. So was Recker, his face twisted in a derisive sneer. Recker was smooth and smart, a deadly machine, but he didn't look much beyond the next contract. Metternich, on the other hand, had vision enough to inspire a planet, perhaps a whole solar system. That made him infinitely more dangerous.

"Your time in prison and your experience in the biotank have affected you deeply, Zachariah. For that, I am truly sorry," Metternich spoke softly. "But you must see that it was all in service to a greater good. Look at what is happening on Earth right now. Humanity is reverting to tribalism. The federal government spends two thirds of its budget on programs to placate the mob, and politicians promise still more. The military is focused on keeping the population from fragmenting into a chaos of squabbling ethnic allegiances. The current fashion among the well-off is genetic augmentation to enhance ethnic identity.

"The Earthbound system is rotten at its core. Only in the outer reaches of the human sphere is there a hope for survival. When was the last time you heard a spacer ask where a comrade was born? Who among the community of Belters or native Martians cares about the color of your skin or the slant of your eyes? Ability is all that matters out here. Ability and courage, qualities our Earth-based masters value little and view as a threat to their supremacy."

The words were old rhetoric, bedrock propaganda from the pre-Revolutionary mass rallies. Words I'd once believed and lived by—before the tanks. I realized, with a small shock, that Metternich truly believed what he was saying. He might betray thousands who had followed him into revolution; might make a deal with the devil to save his own skin, but he still *believed*. The realization shook me even more than the discovery that he still lived.

He'd been my mentor, almost a surrogate father after my parents died, and when the Black Ops squad had picked me up, I'd invoked his name over and over. He hadn't come to save me, and the betrayal was personal. I spent the first month in prison desperately trying to recall what I'd done to make him abandon me. Finding nothing, I began to think he believed I was a threat. Now I realized that it had all meant little or nothing to him. I was a subject, an experimental animal to be used to further his grand dream.

Metternich went on speaking. I only half heard him. Recker drove on, listening to the Colonel with a strange smile on his face. I couldn't read him—true believer or just a contract killer? Metternich obviously trusted in his loyalty. The Colonel stopped speaking and looked at me as if expecting an answer.

"What's in this for Jones?" I asked finally. "He doesn't give a damn about anyone but himself."

"Don't be too quick to judge him. Every man hopes to leave some sort of legacy, although his short-term motives are more concrete. When the Republic is restored, he expects the governorship of Tharsis, either for himself or a hand-picked puppet."

"Does he really buy that load of crap?" I asked.

Metternich shrugged. "He has his own reasons. He helped me escape, gave me employment, and is supporting my efforts to restore Mars to independence. As I said, he's a valuable resource, for the time being. For that I can allow him to believe he controls the relationship."

Recker interrupted, "We're almost to the Armstrong lock, Colonel. We need to suit up now."

He pulled the crane off the Boulevard, into a staging area filled with other vehicles waiting for their turn at the lock. Recker took a colored tag from a traffic control 'bot and stuck it to the front of the crane. We spent a couple of minutes wriggling into the p-suits, checking seals and topping up the suit tanks from the crane's onboard air.

I stowed my helmet under the rear seat and leaned against the crane, watching the flow of traffic toward the lock. My head spun with his words: "Embrace your gift." Since the tanks, I'd experienced only pain from the nanos. They weren't mine; they'd been forced on me. I could feel the familiar tingle in my fingertips as the nanofibers stirred.

"No," I whispered, clenching my fists. "This is not me."

Metternich stood beside me. He was speaking quietly over his link, his tone commanding. I don't think he heard me. He broke off his conversation with a curt, "Do it." He placed his own helmet next to mine and gazed at the passing crowd.

"You're not like them, Zachariah," he said. "Not anymore."

"No, I'm Adam's brother and you're our new savior." I pointed at the traffic. "I don't give a shit about them, or your load of transcendent humanity crap or those damn embryos. I just want to finish this deal and walk away with my ship paid off."

"I'd hoped that you would consider rejoining the fight. How much longer do you think the federal authorities will tolerate you? You're becoming a serious problem for them, you know."

I stared at him. I was missing something critical, something I should know but didn't. "Who, me? I'm just a third-rate ship driver. Except for Hank Boucher and an AI magistrate with a few loose microprocessors, the feds don't even know I exist."

"You shouldn't underestimate yourself, Zachariah. Over the years you've built a reputation as a freelancer. Someone who gets the job done, even if it means skirting the edge of the law. The authorities have tolerated you because they have no solid evidence of anything criminal. Do you think they will stand for your latest hijacking escapade?"

"Why not?" I asked. "We got away clean. Who's going to rat us out? Jones? Not while he has the embryos. Wu? He hired us in the first place. How is he going to explain what we stole without implicating himself? Last I checked, cloning was illegal."

"Unless it's done under Federal contract," he said.

"Wu made those embryos for the Feds? Then why make me steal them?"

"Kwai Chang Wu is under contract to the Federal armed forces to produce the embryos. All of our data from the biotanks fell into Federal hands after the war. They now have their own program to produce augmented soldiers. I've been able to force Wu to siphon off a portion of the production to meet my needs as well. But there have been shortfalls, and he forced you to steal the embryos intended for me so that he could meet his obligation to the government."

"Oh, shit," I said.

"Exactly," Metternich said with a sly smile. "Given the choice between reneging on a Federal contract and giving you up to the authorities, what will Kwai Chang Wu decide?"

The sick feeling in the pit of my stomach told me the answer to that question.

CHAPTER NINETEEN

The lock cycled again and the traffic control 'bot signaled Recker to move into line. We climbed aboard the crane and sat with our helmets in our laps. The crane inched forward, following the traffic control arrows into a parking space on the lock floor.

An alarm bell sounded and the overhead lights flashed red. We lifted the helmets into position, dogged the fasteners and checked each other's seals. I adjusted the air flow across my face and cleared a trace of fog on the faceplate. I held up my intercom link where Metternich could see it. He nodded and I jacked into his suit so that we could speak privately without Recker overhearing.

"You have more questions, Zachariah," he said, a note of amusement in his voice.

"You said you were able to force Wu to give you a share of the embryos. What do you have on him?"

"Wu has his vices, despite his reputation for asceticism," he said.

"Must be one hell of a habit," I commented.

"That is 'need-to-know' information."

"And I don't need to know? Once Wu finds out about this little trade, he'll be coming for me with all the muscle he can buy."

"You've made it clear that you wish to remain a free agent." He shifted his position to look at me "Information like that has a price."

"What would it cost me?"

"Only your loyalty, and a degree of obedience. I need an operative with no obvious connection to Jones, or any reason to help the Dragons. Your public run-ins with his people make you ideal. And to tell the truth, Zachariah, I've missed you. Adam is cunning and subtle, but has little appreciation of strategy. You were always one of the best and brightest. I'd appreciate your advice from time to time."

I wanted to ask him if he treated all of his best officers to two years of hell in the Bear, but had enough sense and self-control left to keep my mouth shut. Once upon a time I might have jumped at the chance to return to his service, but no more. I knew him well enough from my time in the Third Directorate to know that he rarely flattered anyone. When he did, it usually preceded a betrayal. He'd just overplayed his hand, and I knew he meant to kill me when I was no longer useful.

"What makes you think you can trust Jones?" I asked.

He smiled. "I don't," he answered. "But there's no one in his organization that poses a serious threat to me, save Adam. And Adam is unswervingly loyal to me. He appreciates his gift much more than you do. He has embraced it, and with it, the future of the human race. You should try to understand him better. There is much you could learn from each other."

When I didn't answer at once, he turned to face forward again. "Think about it, Zachariah," he said, and unplugged the intercom link.

The lock turned and the huge door behind us was replaced

with a matching one in front. I felt the suit pressurize as the lock outgassed. The flashing red light overhead turned green, and the huge door slid open. As soon as there was a gap wide enough to let vehicles through, traffic at the front of the lock began spilling onto the roadway.

The Tranquility Road was the oldest graded surface on the moon. It had begun as a mining road from the city to a large ice deposit in the deep crust beneath the crater rim. When the ice ran out, the debris from the expansion of Tycho City was trucked out to fill the ice cavern, and then to pave the ramp to the top of the crater rim. The road had grown from there, branching out to the farms and mines of Tranquility Basin and then on to the booming settlements around Plato and Archimedes.

It was just after Lunar dawn, and we drove straight into the sun. We opaqued our visors against the glare. I was happy to avoid the Colonel's eyes. I didn't know if he'd be able to read my face, but I didn't want to take the chance.

Recker swung the crane into a local traffic lane to keep clear of the huge bulk transports, and stopped. Cargo cranes weren't rated for over-the-road travel and needed to be cleared by traffic control.

"Adam, please deal with the AI," said the Colonel over the common link. "I have business with the supervisor. I don't want any delays on our return trip."

I stayed in my seat as Recker dealt with the AI inspector and the Colonel stepped into the control booth to bribe the human supervisor so that they could bypass customs on the way back. I thought about making a break then and there, but knew I wouldn't get far. Even if I escaped, I'd still be marked by both Metternich and the Dragons.

A few minutes later, Metternich returned. Recker pulled our crane back into traffic. We rolled smoothly along, the road surface worn flat and dust-free by a century of use. No one spoke until we neared the holding yard.

"Where to from here?" Recker asked over the comm link.

I thought for a second, recalling the berth number Deuce had given me. "Second gate," I said. "Row thirty-four, berth C, one-twenty-seven."

He grunted in reply and swung off the main road at the yard entrance. The control AI passed us through. This yard wasn't used for high-value cargo and there was little incentive for theft, given the long run back to the main lock.

As we drove slowly down the rows of parked and stacked containers, I reached under my seat and felt for the extra minitank of air. I was convinced that Metternich meant to kill me as soon as he had his hands on the embryos. I had nothing I could use as a weapon. My only chance was to distract him long enough to make a run for it. If I could hide in the yard, I could call Deuce on the link and have him come pick me up. I figured they'd want to get the embryos away quickly, and wouldn't spend a lot of time looking for me. That extra few minutes of air might be the edge I'd need to stay hidden—if I could get away. It was a big 'if.'

I recognized the container as we approached. I tapped Recker on the back of his helmet and pointed.

"There it is," I said.

He pulled past it, then backed the crane up so that the stevedore 'bot and the loading deck were close to the container. He disengaged the drive but kept the motor powered up. Then he lowered the rear jacks that stabilized the lifting arm.

Metternich and I climbed out. Recker lowered the stevedore 'bot to the ground and powered it up. It rolled past us to the container.

"Mbele, open it," said Recker.

"What's the matter? Don't you trust me?" I leaned against the crane, careful to keep my left hand out of sight. I slid the minitank into a leg pouch in my suit. "Open it yourself."

"Please do as he asks." Metternich gestured toward the container.

I sighed and did a low-G step-glide over to the container.

Recker bounced up next to me. I smirked at his clumsiness. "What's the matter, Recker? No space legs?"

He gave me a black look but said nothing.

I keyed in the *Profit's* shipping code and unlocked the container. Recker released the seals and swung the hatch back. Metternich glided smoothly up to his side and looked in through the mist of fine nitrogen crystals.

"Satisfied?" I asked.

"Completely." His voice was barely above a whisper. He motioned to Recker, who moved to disconnect the liquid-nitrogen lines. They could then load the embryo bottle onto the crane and leave the container here.

Recker went to work and Metternich produced a black 9mm Ruger pistol from a pocket in his suit. "Please keep your hands where I can see them," he said, pointing the Ruger at my chest.

"I take it I'm no longer a valued resource then, Colonel?" I backed slowly away as I spoke.

"It needn't be this way," he said. "And if you insist on backing up, place yourself against the container." He made a small motion with the pistol.

I shrugged and stopped. The stevedore rolled past me. It unstrapped the cryobottle, covered it with a thick thermal blanket, and lifted it off the container floor.

"I don't see any alternatives," I said, facing Metternich.

"Nonsense," he said. "The offer still stands. Stop being foolish and join us."

"An enlistment at gunpoint? Both of us know better than that, Colonel."

Recker moved past me, the stevedore 'bot following him with the cryobottle.

"And if I say yes?" I went on as Recker reached the crane. "Would you really trust me?"

"I would give you the opportunity to earn my trust," he said lowering the gun slightly.

"Then watch your back, Colonel. Because the first chance

I get, I will kill you."

He leveled the gun at my chest. I felt the nanos extend themselves, augmenting my nerves and muscles. I shifted to get a better purchase on the wall, then launched myself toward him, making a grab for the Ruger. My shoulder slammed into his chest and we spun to the right, wrestling for the gun. The container door shook with the impact of a heavy slug slamming into it, a few centimeters to my left. A fine red mist drifted across my faceplate. Metternich clutched at his right arm, where a ragged hole in his suit spouted a fog of bloody vapor. He managed to wrench the pistol out of my grip and fired twice past my shoulder. I rolled across him. He spun on his hip to a prone position and switched the pistol to his left hand, ignoring the tear in his suit as well as me.

Time seemed to slow down. Metternich's suit stopped out-gassing as the shoulder seal closed tight around his arm, controlling the leak and the bleeding. Beyond him, Recker held a squat black pistol in a two-hand grip, his back braced against the crane. I kicked off of the metal wall and made a low rolling dive past the open door and into the shadow of an adjacent container. Metternich fired again, but Recker had already moved with the augmented speed of his nanofibers. Speed saved him, but he wasn't adjusting for the low gravity. He slammed into the crane jack and his next shot went wide, the slug burying itself in the regolith a few inches from Metternich's helmet. The Colonel fired twice more, but Recker was a quick learner. He rolled under the crane, still awkward but crazy fast, and the slugs ricocheted off the jackstand.

Metternich struggled to his feet, right arm now frozen and useless. He swept the pistol back and forth, trying to cover both sides of the crane.

I rolled across my left shoulder to my feet, glancing back at Metternich. He turned my way for a second, then spun to his left as Recker stepped from behind the crane.

Metternich was fast, but Recker was faster. Recker's bullet hit the Colonel center-chest and he crumpled like a puppet without strings. I turned and ran with long loping strides down the row of containers.

I ducked left at the end of the row, moving swiftly past four more rows, leaving me five rows deeper into the yard and nearly a hundred meters farther away from the gate than where I'd started. I shook my head, trying to make sense of what had just happened.

Metternich had been the target, there was no doubt about that. Recker was too good to make a mistake. Whoever had paid him to turn on his boss had gotten their money's worth. Whether I was on his list or not, he wouldn't hesitate to kill me as well.

I considered my options. I could sit tight, call Deuce and wait for him to pick me up. But if Recker was after me as well, it would be dangerous to stand still for too long, and I might be luring Deuce into an ambush. Even with the minitank I'd stolen, my air was limited. Sooner or later, if Deuce didn't get to me in time, I'd run out.

I could try to work my way back to the gate and alert the AI to call for help. Not a bad idea, if I didn't mind explaining a box full of illegal embryos to a magistrate who already wanted my ass on a plate. And there wasn't much cover near the gate. I'd make an easy target.

Or I could double back to the crane, try to get the drop on Recker, maybe get my hands on a weapon. I thought about Metternich's gun, but doubted Recker would leave it lying there for me to pick up.

I ground my rear molars to activate my link, but got a no-service tone in response. The holding yard was on the very edge of the grid, and with all the bulk cargo around me, getting in touch with Deuce was going to be a problem.

I checked up and down the empty rows. No sign of company yet. I looked up. The cargo boxes towered six high above me. I took a deep breath, extending the nanos deeper into my muscles. I backed up a few steps and then pushed off with my right foot, leaping up to plant my left on the upper lip of the bottom container and driving straight up. Between the low gravity and my augmented muscles, I reached the top of the stack easily, and swung myself onto the top of the uppermost container.

I crouched there for a second, looking across the uneven rows of stacked cargo boxes. Nothing. I tried the link again but still got no signal. I could see the Tranquility Road, a good kilometer away. No help there; it might as well have been on Mars. I figured the crane was about a hundred meters to my right, the gate probably twice that to the left, most of it open ground. No choice, really; I'd have to take my chances with Recker and the crane.

I moved out slowly. The containers were parked in neat rows, but the height of the stacks varied. I inched up to each gap and looked down before jumping across, in case Recker was hunting below. If I were the hunter, I'd position myself near the crane, knowing that my quarry had limited air and couldn't afford to hide for long. Recker would likely do the same, but I didn't want to guess wrong and eat a bullet in mid-jump.

It took me almost ten minutes to reach the stack above the crane. As I crouched there, the suit beeped at me, a red indicator glowing under the air supply readout. I connected the minitank and opened the valve until the red light turned green. Maybe thirty minutes left. Time to end this. I inched forward on my belly and peeked over the edge.

Recker stood a couple of meters in front of the crane, holding the 9mm. He swung it slowly back and forth, covering the rows on either side of the crane. He didn't look up. To Recker, conditioned to standard G, the stack was clearly too high for anyone to climb or jump. I'd counted on that.

I rose to a crouch, gauged the distance and jumped. Even in lunar G, eighteen meters is a long way to fall. I'd intended to land on top of him and rupture his suit, or at least disable him, but misjudged the jump. I hit hard a few centimeters to his left and crashed into him. We sprawled across the ground, tumbling until we slammed into one of the jacks at the rear of the crane. The pistol spun away under the wheels. My head thumped against the top of my helmet and the faceplate fogged as my nose pressed against it. Recker was on top of me. I could hear him grunt and gasp as our helmets ground together.

I tried to roll to my right, but he was quicker. He got a knee into my groin, locking me against the jack stand. He drew back a fist and aimed a lightning-fast blow at my faceplate. I barely managed to turn my head in time, and his gloved hand ricocheted off the side of my helmet. I wedged my foot against the jackstand and heaved my hip upward. Recker grabbed at my shoulder, missed, and was thrown off toward the container. He rolled and leapt to his feet. I scissored my legs and rose to a fighting crouch with my back to the crane.

Recker faced me, crouching as well. He moved slowly forward, testing his footing. He may not have been trained in low-G combat, but he was learning fast.

I circled slowly to my right, keeping the crane behind me. Recker followed. Somewhere under the huge rear wheels was the pistol. We both knew it, and short of a smashed faceplate, we couldn't inflict much damage on each other through the heavy p-suits without it.

Even though I was expecting it, his attack was surprisingly fast. He leapt, his left fist aimed at my face. I pivoted slightly, pulling my head back, suddenly off balance. I went down as he slipped his right foot between mine and twisted, using my momentum and his, to sweep my feet. He rolled to his side, diving under the crane.

I scrabbled and kicked in the dirt, wrenching myself around until I got a hand on his ankle. He kicked at it with his free foot as he groped for the gun. I tightened my grip and pulled myself toward him until I got my other hand on his calf. My helmet rang as his heel pounded it again and again.

I grabbed blindly at his legs as he struggled and twisted, and we both inched forward. I caught his flailing leg and wrapped it up with my arms, then pulled myself up to his knees and dug my toes into the dense regolith. He bucked and rolled back and forth. I managed to hook a foot around the base of the jackstand, and used it to lever us backward a few centimeters. My other foot found a purchase in the dirt and I heaved, gaining a few more centimeters, then half a meter.

Getting my knees under me, I heaved again. I grabbed the suit joint at his waist and pulled with all the strength in my augmented muscles. He slid out from under the crane, rolling to his back to face me. I pulled back my fist for a blow to his head and stopped as he shoved the business end of the 9mm into my face.

"Back up," he said, his voice crackling slightly through my suit radio.

I sat back on my heels.

He pushed himself into a sitting position.

"Stand and step back three paces," he commanded.

I got to my feet and did as he said.

"Now turn around." I hesitated. "Don't worry, Mbele," he said. "I'm not going to kill you, so turn around and put your hands on your head."

"Jones paid you to kill Metternich," I said as I turned around.

"Very good." He grunted slightly as he got to his feet. "Mr. Jones pays quite well. The contract called for Metternich to die as soon as the embryos were delivered."

"What about me?" I asked.

"Jones left that to my own discretion. He was only willing to pay for the Colonel."

"But why kill Metternich? What's Jones going to do with

the embryos without him?"

"I don't know, nor do I care," said Recker. "I was paid to do a job. Frankly, I was tired of the Colonel's obsession with his grand dream. I was happy to take Jones' contract. With the Colonel dead, the embryos are to be delivered to Jones. What happens after that is not my business.

"You, on the other hand, present a new opportunity. I had intended to kill you as soon as Metternich went down, but you were too fast. You've adapted well to your nanos. It's a shame we ended up on different sides in this. The Colonel was right about one thing: we share a common experience. We might have made a good team."

"And now?" I prompted.

"Now I wonder how much Kwai Chang Wu will be willing to pay to get his hands on you." I shifted my stance, thinking to spin and aim a roundhouse kick at his head. "Don't be stupid, Mbele." He slid back a step and raised the gun. "Dead or alive, it makes no difference to me. Wu will pay either way. Stay alive a while longer. Who knows, maybe you can persuade Kwai Chang Wu to give you another chance. I hear he's an understanding kind of man."

I smiled grimly. "That hasn't been my impression of Wu."

"Perhaps not," he allowed. "Now, walk over there by the Colonel."

I did as he asked, the spot between my shoulder blades tingling in anticipation of a bullet in the back. Metternich lay face-down where he'd fallen, his p-suit flat and limp.

"Pick him up," Recker commanded. "Carry him into the container."

I bent and wrapped my fingers around the now-loose fabric of the suit. The body seemed light, even in lunar G. I half carried, half dragged it into the oblong metal box.

"Face the wall there," said Recker. "Hands overhead; lean against the wall."

I did as he ordered. I could hear him grunting slightly through the radio link, as if carrying some weight. A few seconds later, a pair of steel air tanks, the reserve supply from the crane, slid past my feet into the dark interior of the container.

"Wu will pay more for you alive," said Recker. "There should be enough air there for eight hours or so, if you conserve your energy. Turn around and close the hatch."

I turned, gathering my muscles to spring, but he'd stepped back out of range and still had that pistol pointed squarely at my chest. I didn't want to join the Colonel on the floor, so I reached out and swung the hatch shut. I could feel the lock snick closed.

"One last bit of advice, Mbele," said Recker over the radio. "You didn't kill me back at Conejo's cave, so I'm feeling charitable. Remember this: what can be augmented, can also be blocked."

I didn't answer. A second later my head was filled with the high pitched shriek of a signal scrambler. I shut down my link and the suit radio before feedback burned out the transmitters. I felt a thump as the stevedore 'bot latched onto the hard points on the container's sides. The floor shifted and swayed underfoot, forcing me to sit down as the container was loaded onto the back of the crane.

The crane began to move, sending a low rumbling vibration through the floor. We rolled for a long time. Shifts in the motion of the floor told me we made several turns. Then the movement stopped and the container thudded to the ground. With a slight rattle and bang, the stevedore 'bot disengaged, and all was quiet.

I stood in the middle of the container and played my suit light around. I tried the door, but the lock held. A quick check of my link showed that the scrambler was still active. Recker must have fastened it to the side of my box. We'd come a long way; without the link to home on, Deuce would never find me in the jumbled holding yard.

I sat down next to Metternich's freeze-dried corpse. "So much for loyalty, eh, Colonel?" I said.

He didn't answer.

CHAPTER TWENTY

I leaned back against the wall and concentrated on saving my air, but the more I thought about taking shallow, even breaths, the stronger the urge to take deep ones became. I shook my head. This wasn't working.

I looked down at Metternich again. I felt...nothing. Not grief nor joy, relief or elation, just a cold numbness. In the five years, 267 days and eighteen-odd hours since I'd walked out of the Bear, I'd lived with a deep, searing anger at this man who had been my friend and mentor—and then betrayed me. The frustration of not knowing what I'd done to make him turn on me, resentment of the nanos that I couldn't remove or fully accept, guilt at having survived when so many others had died or been left maimed and broken like Rabbit—all of this had fed the anger that had defined me for nearly six years.

And now it was gone. In the end, it had meant nothing. I was little more than a lab rat. My survival was a random trick of genetics, and Metternich was neither angel nor demon—just a mad zealot who'd dragged an entire planet into his nightmare. Now he was truly dead, and all I felt was emptiness.

This wasn't getting me anywhere. I could feel the nanos still augmenting my senses. My thoughts seemed to be racing ahead, as if the nanofibers were speeding them up as well.

Why had Jones wanted Metternich dead? He'd gone to a lot of trouble and expense to get him off Mars and alter his appearance. Why do all of that just to gun him down? Jones had his own ideas about investment and resources. He'd wanted something from Metternich, and as soon as he had it, the Colonel was expendable. It had to be the embryos. Once Metternich had confirmed the box held the real deal, Recker had killed him.

What did Jones want with the embryos? I didn't see him carrying on with the Colonel's grand dream. Not exactly his style. Did he plan to make his own army of augmented assassins? I doubted it. There were plenty of men, women too for that matter, willing to kill for money. And Jones had plenty of money.

So who stood to gain or lose if Jones held the embryos? Wu? He could rightly claim that they were stolen and he had no idea who took them. Unless Jones could prove that Metternich had blackmailed Wu into diverting part of the production to the Dragons. With that, he could control Wu's activities on Ceres—maybe force him to continue to deal ice for the Dragons' hijacked ore—assuming Wu wasn't a willing partner in the first place. Okay, plausible.

What about the government? If they found out who had the embryos, they'd send in the *Federales*; shoot first and ask questions later, as long as the embryos were recovered. Or would they? Hank said the Feds had very little juice out in the Belt. Jones and the Dragons could hold out there against anything short of a full military expedition. What if Jones threatened to publicize the existence of a secret military program to breed super soldiers unless the

Federales continued to leave him alone in the Belt? The government was barely keeping a lid on the ethnic tensions Earthside. How would the masses react if they learned of a program to make them obsolete by breeding nano-augmented humans? A dangerous game for Jones, but just the sort of bold move that put him in charge of the Dragons in the first place. Plausible? Maybe.

Either way, Jones would have a reason to want Metternich out of the way, especially if he figured out that the Colonel was planning to have him killed. Jones was too good at that game himself to ignore the possibility. But that still didn't explain why the Dragons had sheltered Metternich in the first place.

The Colonel had spoken of a longstanding arrangement with the Dragons back on Mars. During the run up to the Revolution, Deuce and I had smuggled weapons to revolutionary cells in Tharsis. The Dragons paid the cops to look the other way when it came to their own business, but a side benefit was that they didn't look too closely at anything else, either. It made Tharsis a center for shady dealings of all sorts, including political subversion. I didn't know of any connection between Jones and Metternich at the time, but as a new Sublieutenant, I wouldn't have been in that loop.

What if the Colonel had traded information to Jones in return for a guaranteed bolt-hole if the Revolution went sideways? Metternich had dossiers on everyone of importance on Mars, and probably had dirt on the Kwai family as well. I suddenly remembered something Sylvia had said about Kwai Chang Wu: he'd gotten into a serious legal jam back on Earth, and had disappeared for a couple of years after buying his way out of it. Could that be the hook Metternich had in him?

The Colonel was too savvy a spy to have shared the details with Jones if his value to the Dragons depended on that bit of knowledge—but if Jones had somehow learned the real story on his own, he'd have little reason to keep Metternich alive.

I grunted in frustration. This was all guesswork and the only man who could tell me if I was right lay dead at my feet.

The suit beeped at me, and the air supply readout blinked red again. I stood and walked to the back of the container to retrieve the spare tanks Recker had left there. I connected the first one to the suit feed and opened the valve. The suit beeped again and blinked green. I hoisted the tank onto my shoulder, picked up the second one and made my way back to Metternich's body.

Enough speculation, I thought. *Let's see if the Colonel has anything on him I can use.*

I rolled the body over. It was stiff as a slab of moon rock. My own image reflected dully in the Colonel's faceplate. I managed to open the front seals, from chest to left thigh. The fabric between the chest and neck seals had been shredded by the exit wound and was now stiff with frozen blood.

I worked the front of the suit away from Metternich's torso and searched his body. There wasn't much. Under the suit he wore a black pullover sweater without pockets, and thick insulated workpants. The front pockets held some cash, a twenty yuan gold piece, and a folding multitool. I struggled to reach the back pocket, but couldn't get my hand around the edge of the suit without freeing one of his arms and rolling him over. Both arms were frozen solid and immobile. Unlatching the seals, I lifted off the helmet and gazed down at my former commander.

The water in his body had sublimated into the vacuum, freeze-drying his face into a twisted mask. The eyes, so commanding in life, were now salt white. He hardly looked human anymore, much less like the man I'd once served. This wasn't how I wanted to remember the Colonel. Whatever he'd become in the end, he'd once taught me the meaning of duty and honor, lessons I'd retained even after he himself had betrayed them. After a time, I returned to the business at hand.

Opening the multiitool, I selected the saw blade. I avoided looking at his face as I sawed at his shoulder, but the frozen flesh was metal-hard and the folding saw blade was only ten centimeters long. After thirty minutes of sweating and swearing, I managed to cut through the bone just below the shoulder joint. With some flexing and pushing, I got his right arm out of the suit and could reach down to the back pocket of the work pants.

Jackpot! I pulled out a squat, fat-barreled Huang pneumatic. I recognized the model, a Scorpion. It held only one shot, usually a 9mm explosive round. It was an assassin's weapon, designed to be fired at a protected target from close range. We'd run several hundred of them into Tharsis in the old days. They were used to deadly effect on the riot police during the mass demonstrations that sparked the Revolution.

I hefted the Huang. The trigger guard had been filed away, making it easier to use while wearing heavy gloves or a p-suit. I tucked it into the outer pouch of my own suit and went back to work. After cutting through the heavy suit fabric around the left shoulder to get his upper body out, I wormed and wiggled it down below his waist, then pulled it off his legs. A thorough search of the rest of his clothes turned up nothing of value. I hauled the empty suit into the rear of the container and propped it up against the liquid nitrogen tank. I reattached the helmet, keeping the visor opaqued, then disconnected the power pack and checked the charge: nearly full.

I surveyed my work from the front of the container. If I didn't look too closely I might think a man was hiding there in the dark. I rolled the Colonel's body onto its back and pushed it up against the door. Anyone opening it would see the body first. I hoped it would divert attention from a close scrutiny of the rear of the container. I only had one shot and I needed time to make it count.

The next part was tricky. I took out the multitool again and pried the cover from the power pack. The ghostly glow of the captive plasma in its tiny magnetic bottle illuminated the containment failsafe. I twisted the output screw to maximum, then gouged the failsafe circuit out. I replaced the cover, jammed the tool's screwdriver blade into the output plug and snapped it off. Taking care not to touch the bare metal of the blade, I lifted Metternich's right hip, placed the power pack under it and let the body fall onto the blade, jamming it into the frozen flesh. Anyone touching the body without heavy insulation would get the full output of the pack in a single jolt. I figured the insulation of my p-suit and the plastic sealant on the inside of the container would protect me from the discharge. At least, I hoped it would. I laid the gold piece on his chest as bait.

I dragged both air tanks to the box's far right corner, sat on the floor and leaned against the wall.

I settled in for a long wait. The Colonel had always said that sleep was a weapon to be used whenever the opportunity presented itself. Fatigue washed over me, and I closed my eyes.

* * *

A muted beep from my suit and an insistent pressure in my bladder awakened me several hours later. The air supply was on red again. I dumped the last of the first tank's air into the suit and refilled the small reserve bottle before switching to the second tank. I checked the time. Six hours; enough to walk home if I could get out of this box, but otherwise a very short life.

I emptied my bladder into the suit's waste collection system and sucked warm recycled water from the drinking pouch. Despite the filters and fresh tanks, the air in the suit was rank with the smell of stale sweat.

The container shook as clamps engaged the hard points around the top. The box swayed slightly as it was lifted. I steadied myself with a hand on the wall, and could feel the vibrations of a winch as I was reeled up. *About time,* I thought.

I crouched in the corner, feeling rather than hearing the bump and sway of the container as it was lifted and moved. A dull clang shook the floor as my box settled and was locked down. I almost fell as the gravity field suddenly increased to a standard one G. Interesting. There hadn't been time to move me back to Tycho, so I was obviously on a ship. Wu must want me pretty badly.

A second later, the container filled with a light fog as air was pumped in. I checked the ambient pressure sensor on my sleeve, and cracked my helmet when it reached one atmosphere. The air was still bitter cold, but I could breathe and hear. It seemed Wu wanted me alive.

I removed my helmet and crouched in the corner, holding the Huang in a two-hand grip. A thrill of fear made me shiver slightly. I shook it off, remembering one of the Colonel's training mantras: "Fear is the situation telling you you're still alive, and reminding you to make sure you stay that way." I'd done what I could. Now it was Wu's move.

I didn't wait long. With a dull clang, the container was opened and a bright light played around the interior. The sudden rush of warmer air through the door instantly filled the container with a dense mist of ice and condensation. There was little chance of being seen in the thick fog, but I crouched lower anyway.

"Shit!" a hoarse voice cursed from the door. "Can't see a damn thing."

"Just wait, you idiot. It'll clear." This voice I recognized, soft and mellow for such a big man: Vincent Talafofo.

"Hey, there's something in the doorway. Looks like a stiff."

"Yeah?" Vincent answered. "Wu wanted him alive. Look sharp. It's starting to clear."

"You sure the stiff ain't him? I better check."

"Suit yourself."

I tightened my grip on the Huang. A dark figure appeared in the doorway, backlit by the bright lights behind it. With my nano-augmented vision, I could see that he was tall and slim, not heavily muscled like Vincent. He stepped cautiously into the container holding a long-barreled needler in front of him. He crouched beside the body.

"It ain't Mbele," he said. "This guy's older and light-skinned."

"So get in there and find him," said Vincent.

"Don't push me. There's a twenty yuan gold piece here." He reached down to pick it up.

"No, wait!"

Vincent's shout was an instant too late. Blue electricity arced up from the floor and through the man with the gun to dance in long streamers around the metal door. The smell of hot metal and burning flesh mingled with ozone as the gunman was thrown back out of the door.

Smoke and steam swirled across my eyes, but the nanos switched to infrared, and I saw Vincent dive through the door. He fired a needler twice in midair, rolled across his left shoulder and came up firing again. I almost fired the Huang, but realized he was shooting at the empty suit I'd propped against the nitrogen tanks. Vincent stood, peering through the mist, gun still pointed at the suit.

I steadied the Huang. "Over here, Vincent."

He spun, fast for a big man, but not fast enough. The pneumatic spat. The slug struck him in the chest and exploded out his back, splattering blood across the wall behind him. He crumpled to the deck still clutching the needler.

I broke the seals on my gloves and shook them off as I jumped across the container to crouch beside the body.

"Nothing personal," I said as I lifted the thin, wicked-looking needler from his hand. There was a security pass in his pocket. I took that, too. The mist was clearing. It was still dark in the container, but that wouldn't hide me for long. I checked the needler: five shots left. I dropped the Huang, took a deep breath and started for the door.

"Hey, Talafofo!" called a voice from outside. "Hurry it up."

My augmented ears placed him off to the right and above the deck, probably on a ladder or catwalk. I crept forward and crouched in the shadow closest to the door.

"Talafofo? What's going on in there?" The voice was now level with me. He must have climbed down to the deck. He'd be approaching the container soon.

I strained to hear. The only sound seemed to be his footsteps, drawing closer from the right. I planted my foot and sprang forward, turning to face him. My needler came up, leveled on him. His mouth opened in a surprised 'Oh' as he reached for his own weapon. Two needles entered his chest. He dropped to the floor, eyes glazing over.

I didn't stop to check him, just scooped up his needler and kept moving. There was a hatch in front of me. I rushed toward it. Once I had the hatch and its bulkhead at my back, I turned and surveyed the space I was in. Two decks high and roughly fifteen meters across, it was smaller than *Profit's* forward cargo hold. The chain lifts and gantries hanging from the overhead were the same, though. I was in some sort of a small freighter, or perhaps the service deck of a large passenger ship. The outer lock was across from me ,and the hatch behind me should lead to the engineering spaces.

I couldn't stay here. With three bodies on the deck and Wu expecting a call, things were sure to get hot in a hurry. The upper decks were tempting, especially if I could get to the communications gear and call for help. But I didn't know who else was aboard, or how serious they might be about keeping me alive once they found my handiwork. I decided to take a chance on the hatch behind me. It was dogged closed, as it should be if they'd been loading cargo.

I spun the wheel in the center, releasing the dogs, and started to open the hatch. Too late, I heard the snap-ping sound of a needler. I spun around and caught a glimpse of the man on the catwalk above the hold. Then the needle stuck in my neck and everything went black.

CHAPTER TWENTY-ONE

The world returned in stages. Sound intruded on the blackness first; a dull thumping sound that I realized was my own heart. Then a faint clanking that I couldn't identify, from somewhere above me. I shifted my legs. I was upright, my hands bound above my head. I couldn't feel my feet.

Light followed sound, faint and foggy at first, then brighter. Intense white light shone down from above me, burning through my eyelids.

I realized I was cold. Freezing, in fact. The heavy pressure suit was gone. I was naked.

Full awareness returned suddenly and awoke searing pain in my wrists and hands. The clanking came from chains wrapped around my wrists and fastened to a lift, similar to those in the cargo hold. This one was being used to suspend me in midair. My feet were strapped in leather cuffs, bound by other chains to the deck below me.

I heard the whir of a ventilator fan. My nanos picked up a fainter sound through the fan noise—the steady breathing of another person. I opened my eyes, but saw only a blank white bulkhead. I tried to turn my head to look behind me but the chains pulled taut, and all I saw was a pair of small feet in ornate slippers.

"Are you enjoying the view?" I asked. "My front side is even more spectacular, you know. Come on around, Wu, and see for yourself."

I heard him shift in a chair, but he said nothing.

"You hear me, Wu? You're missing a true natural wonder."

Nothing. Then a faint click. A holoprojector glowed in front of me, the image solidifying in the air between my face and the bulkhead. It was an anatomic study of a woman, skin mostly removed and various muscle groups splayed out on hooks. Then I noticed the ball gag in her lipless mouth and the open eyes filled with pain and terror. There was a carefully preserved patch of skin over her right hip, a butterfly tattoo in its center. More images appeared: a woman bent double, her head chained between her knees, her body pierced by long thin blades. Another hung from her heels by sharp hooks in the Achilles tendons. Image after image of terror and torture flashed in front of me, while Wu's breathing became faster and more excited. The holoprojector shut off, and I was left gasping and staring at the blank bulkhead.

Wu came to his feet. My skin crawled as I sensed him behind me. His breathing slowly returned to normal. He stepped closer.

"Beautiful, was it not?" he whispered.

"Not," I said through clenched teeth. "This is what Metternich and Jones have on you, isn't it? They know about your little hobby."

"My art," he said. "The images don't do justice to the medium. As with all great art, it must be experienced to be appreciated. But to answer you, yes, Jones has long supplied the raw materials for my art. As for Colonel Metternich, his ability to influence me died with him."

I laughed. "Joke's on you, Wu. Who do you think is

behind Jones' interest in your secret embryos? Metternich's still alive." I hoped that would make him think twice about turning me into his next art project.

Wu chuckled softly. "And who was that in the container with you, then?"

"No idea," I said.

"You have caused me a great deal of trouble and expense," he continued in the same mild, almost amused tone. "Your decision to renege on our contract and turn the embryos over to Jones will cost me millions in Federal penalties. I can report the theft and file an insurance claim, but the penalties for late delivery are significant. Then there is the loss of face involved. Ours was not a public contract, but the breach will be noted in certain circles, to my disadvantage. Amends must be made. And finally, you have committed violence in my private ship, my most personal domain."

"Vincent was a good soldier," I said. "He deserved better than he got."

"Regrets?" Wu's voice was barely audible, a whisper in my ear.

"That I'm alive and he's not? No. Only that he had the bad judgment to work for you."

"Ah," Wu whispered. "But you will have regrets. And soon you will tell me all of them. You will beg to reveal your innermost self. The beauty of this art is the gradual peeling away of the layers of your self until the naked essence that is your soul lies as bare as your flesh."

"Here's a better idea, Wu. Why don't you go fuck yourself?"

He chuckled and stepped back. "The artistry, the measure of true talent, is in knowing how to inflict maximum pain with minimum damage." His tone was formal, as if he were delivering a lecture. "Damage is cumulative, of course. Hence the artistry. The effect on the subject is heightened by uncertainty and fear." A cold brush of metal touched my shoulder then traced the outline of my shoulder blade. My skin crawled, and I shivered in spite of myself.

Wu continued in the same tone. "The subject must never know the artist's concept for the work. It is essential to the integrity of the art that the subject not know where the next cut will come, or when the work will be complete. Indeed the artist himself may not have a clear idea, but will respond to the work in progress with new inspiration."

A thin line of fire rippled slowly across my right flank. The knife was so sharp that there was very little pain, just a feeling of heat. I felt the fine trickle of blood running down to my hip. A second cut followed the first, intensely hot and now painful but bearable.

"Is that the best you can do, Wu? Garbage philosophy and scratches on my back?" Maybe antagonizing him wasn't the best strategy, but if he really wanted me dead, he'd have done it already. I figured if I pushed him hard enough, he'd have to leave me alone for a while to get control of himself. And I needed some time to come up with a plan to get out of here.

In answer, he plunged the knife into my back, just under my right shoulder blade, and lifted. Pain shot through me, radiating down my arm to the wrist and wringing a deep groan from my throat. In spite of it all, I had to admire his technique. He knew how to hurt me while missing the vital structures.

"Better," I gasped. "But still amateur compared to the pros who trained me."

He twisted the knife, and I cried out as the blade grated on bone. Waves of pain engulfed my arm, and the muscles of my back twisted into knots. Wu was breathing faster, but said nothing and still seemed in control. With a final twist he withdrew the blade. I sagged in the restraints. I wouldn't be able to keep this up for long. His self control was better than my ability to take the pain.

"C'mon, Wu," I managed. "Quit fooling around. Just do it." Pain seared my flank again as he slowly sliced a thin strip of skin away from the muscle. I twisted and bucked, but he stayed with me, expertly peeling the centimeter-wide strip from my flank down into the small of my back. I managed to stifle a scream, but could breathe only in short gasps. Deep in the back of my mind, an important thought was struggling to form. Someone had told me to remember something. Wu pulled the skin free with a snap, and I jerked in the restraints.

"And so it begins," said Wu. "There's always a time at the beginning, where the sensitivities are heightened, where the adrenaline surges and the nerve fibers fire, frantically summoning help that never comes. All in vain. Soon hopelessness takes over and we can begin the serious work of exposition."

My head snapped up. "Nerve fibers" he'd said. Recker's words came back to me, *That which is augmented can also be blocked.* He had to mean the nanofibers. But could they do that?

I concentrated on my back, feeling the nano fibers crossing and augmenting the junctions between my own nerves. I gasped as the intensity of the pain spiked, like hot metal poured into the wounds. Frantically I followed the pain upward along the pathways to my brain. Somewhere near the base of my skull, a nova of heat burned into my nervous system. I pushed back at it, willing the fibers away, imagining them flaring and burning in the heat. There was a snapping sensation in my neck, and the pain stopped, replaced by a numbing cold. I could move, but had no sensation of movement. I knew my legs were straight, but only because I could look down and see them.

Wu continued his lecture, but I tuned it out. The loss of sensation was too weird. I was grateful for the pain relief, but couldn't coordinate my movements. If Wu noticed, he said nothing. I could feel a blade enter my other shoulder, but there was no pain, just a tearing sensation and an insistent pressure under the scapula. Wu paused. He twisted his blade, but still I felt nothing.

"What is this, Mr. Mbele?" he hissed in my ear. "Do you really think you can continue this charade of indifference?"

"Sorry to spoil your fun, Wu." I thought about the girl with the butterfly tattoo. Something clicked into place: the picture in Mikey's file. "Did you talk this much to Amber Walenska? Mikey found out you had her, didn't he?"

"So, Flynn did talk to someone. A pity he wasn't so talkative with Vincent, or he might still be alive."

"Is that what Vincent told you? Recker killed Mikey, not Vincent."

"Recker was hired to do just that, if Flynn proved intractable," Wu agreed. "As you said, Vincent was a good soldier, but he drew the line at killing for hire. Recker had no such scruples. He was unsuitable as a long term employee, but—"

A soft buzz from a hidden speaker interrupted us. Wu took a step back and spoke to the overhead. "What is it?" he demanded.

"Sorry to interrupt, Mr. Kwai," the voice over the speaker quavered. "We're being hailed by another ship."

"Ignore them," Wu said.

"I'm sorry, sir, but they're dead ahead and threatening to cross our drive field if we don't heave to and dock."

"How did they get that close? I gave strict orders to avoid any other shipping."

"I don't know, sir," the man's voice was nearly frantic. "They just appeared out of nowhere about a minute ago, and hailed us. They say they have something of value to trade, but will only speak to you."

Wu paused for a long moment, and then sighed. I heard the faint clang of metal on metal as he dropped the knife onto a tray behind me. "Very well, put them through to my link."

I perked up at that. Any onboard scrambler would have to be off for Wu to use the link. I clenched my jaw and activated my own datalink.

"—respond if you can hear me," Sylvia's voice was loud and clear. "*Profit* calling Zack Mbele. Please Zack, answer me if you are receiving. We are off Wu's port bow. If you're there, give us some sign."

I activated the transmitter and clicked twice. I didn't want to hazard subvocal speech. I wasn't sure I could pull it off without Wu noticing.

"Zack! Is that you?" Sylvia squealed. "Click twice more if you can't talk."

I clicked twice.

"Okay. Hold on Zack. Cleo and Deuce are coming for you."

Meanwhile, Wu was listening to his own link. "And why do you think I have any idea where Zack Mbele is, Ms. Lee?" He looked sharply at me when she answered. "Yes, I see," he said. "All right, I will grant that Mr. Mbele is my guest. He remains alive at my pleasure. So, if you want him to go on living, you will move your ship and allow us to proceed."

Another pause. "And what could you possibly have that would be of value to me?" Pause. "You're bluffing. I have the original container; it's empty. Jones has the embryos and I have Mbele. A satisfying, if expensive trade."

Wu listened to Cleo's reply for a long while, and then said, "Why should I believe that? I doubt you have the ability to take the package away from Recker, even with that Neanderthal at your side." A pause. "No, I suppose not. All right, bring your ship alongside and open your docking port. If you have the embryos, we may be able to do business."

Wu reached down and unshackled my feet, turning me around to face him. "You have been granted a temporary reprieve, Mr. Mbele. And I may yet gain something from this enterprise."

"Don't play me, Wu. You had Mike Flynn killed just because he was looking for Amber. Now that I know about your 'art,' there's no way you can let me live."

He just smiled that thin cold smile I'd seen during our first meeting. "There is more afoot here than you know," he said. "Your death would be amusing, but not necessary for my personal safety. I have a guarantee of that from the highest level."

Before I could ask what he meant, the overhead speaker chimed and a faint shudder ran through the ship. "Your friends have docked alongside," he said. "Shall we see what value they place on your life?"

I hoped Cleo knew what she was doing. Not that I didn't appreciate a rescue, but it still seemed like Wu held all the cards.

A few minutes later, the hatch to Wu's torture chamber opened, and Rabbit rolled through with Cleo at his side. She stood with one hand on the back of his chair. Deuce followed a pace behind. Two of Wu's goons took up positions behind Deuce, covering the hatch. My heart sank as I realized that only Wu's men were armed.

"Zack, are you all right?" Cleo asked. She couldn't see my back.

"Not really," I said. "What the hell do you think you're doing?"

"Rescuing you," she said as if it were the simplest thing in the world. "Get him down, Deuce."

Deuce started toward me, but stopped when one of Wu's men raised a needler.

"All in good time, Ms. Lee," said Wu. "It's a pleasure to be doing business with you again, but you do understand that I must see the embryos."

"Your cargo 'bots are transferring the package now," said Cleo. As if on cue, another man entered and spoke softly to Wu.

Wu's face reddened. "You think this is a game?" he hissed. "The cryobottle you delivered is empty." He gestured toward the men at the door.

Cleo and Deuce covered their eyes as Rabbit twisted

his left hand and tossed something over his shoulder. The flash grenade went off with a dull thump. Blinding white light filled the room. The nanos adjusted my vision after a millisecond and I saw Cleo chop Wu's man down with an open-hand blow to the neck. She swept a ceramic blade from the top of her boot and pressed it to Wu's neck as she stepped behind him, pinning his left arm in a hammerlock.

Meanwhile, the back of Rabbit's chair popped open, revealing Deuce's pulse rifle. He snatched it up and spun, firing as he leapt to one side. The nearest guard went down, shot through the chest. The second managed to get a needle off, firing blind. Deuce's second shot sizzled through his neck, dropping him instantly.

"Deuce!" shouted Cleo. "Get Zack. Rabbit, cover the door." Rabbit spun in place and lifted a Huang pneumatic from a holster hidden in the arm of his chair.

Deuce lifted me with an arm around my waist, unhooked my wrists, and then lowered me to the floor. My legs gave way and he caught me before I fell.

"Easy," he whispered. "I've got you." He looked over my shoulder at the ruin of my back. "Jesus, LT! What did they do to you?"

"Just a little amateur knife work," I mumbled. "Nothing compared to the pros in the Bear."

Deuce glared at Wu, lifting his pulse rifle one-handed.

"Deuce!" said Cleo sharply. "Stand down." She pressed the knife deeper into Wu's neck, drawing a thin trickle of blood. "How many more men aboard?" she demanded.

"Three, plus the AI pilot," said Wu.

"Tell them to go to the cargo bay unarmed, and sit in the middle of the deck."

Wu shifted his feet, but stopped with a gasp as Cleo twisted his arm. "This is piracy," he said. "You don't really expect to get away with manhandling me. You're all dead."

"Not yet, we're not. But you will be if you keep stalling." Her knife drew a little more blood.

Wu stiffened, then opened his link and ordered his men to do as Cleo said.

"Zack, can you walk?" Cleo asked.

"I'll manage," I said. I tested my legs. I could stand and walk but still had no feeling in my feet. I had to look down to know where they were.

Cleo shoved Wu toward the door. "Move."

Deuce supported my arm and we followed. Rabbit rolled behind us.

The passageway deck gleamed with polished teak. Embroidered tapestries covered the bulkheads, a stark contrast to the cold metal of the torture chamber. The corridor ran straight for ten meters, then turned sharply to the right. A wide hatch opened onto the cargo hold, where three more men in Kwai Hong uniforms sat in the middle of the deck.

Deuce leaned me against a bulkhead and pulled a handful of cargo tie-downs from his belt. In short order, he had the three men bound and laid out in a row. Cleo forced Wu to sit next to them.

"Cover him, Deuce," she said. "If he twitches, shoot him." She stepped toward me as I tottered forward on wooden feet. "You're bleeding, Zack. We need to get you into the autodoc on the *Profit*."

"Not yet," I said, consciously straightening my back. I glanced back at Rabbit. "Nothing compared to the 'tanks, eh, Rabbit?"

Rabbit's face screwed up in an anguished grimace. "Listen to her, Zack. You're a mess."

I shifted around and waved him forward, leaning on the back of his chair when he was close enough. I eased my weight onto my arms and took a deep breath. Rabbit looked up. I winked at him. "Just resting," I said. I concentrated on the cold knot at the base of my neck and felt it give. Pain lanced through my back. I gasped and started to fall. Cleo grabbed my arm.

"How did you find me?" I managed to ask.

"Rabbit tracked you," she answered, steering me gently toward the docking port.

I shook my head. "Later. We still have business here." I pushed the knot down and accepted the pain as feeling returned to my feet. I looked to Rabbit. "How did you get past the scrambler?"

"I didn't, exactly," said Rabbit. "Your link signal went off the grid, and we thought you were out of range or worse. Deuce wanted to lift the ship and go after you, but we didn't know how to find you. Sylvia suggested it might be a scrambler, and that's what gave me an idea."

Cleo shifted impatiently, but I nodded for Rabbit to continue." A scrambler generates a local electromagnetic pulse—actually a series of pulses every few milliseconds that disrupt the signal integrity of the link transmitter—but each scrambler has its own signature. It's hard to separate from background static, impossible really if you don't know what to look for. But if you know the exact time the scrambler is switched on, and are monitoring the right range of frequencies, you can recognize the signature and track it." He smiled triumphantly.

"So?" I tightened my grip on the chair. I'd assumed that the initial crippling wave of pain meant that all of my nerves had become unblocked, but I was wrong; new nerve fibers awakened, searing my shoulders with pent-up pain.

"Don't you see?" said Rabbit. "We were tracking and recording you. We knew when your signal cut out. When Sylvia brought up the possibility of a scrambler, I had her run a search of all the emissions from the time just before and just after we lost your signal. It took all day, but we finally found it. Once Sylvia knew what to look for, she could track the scrambler. We lifted and headed for you, but then the scrambler started moving. We knew it had to be another ship because of the speed, so we cross-referenced flight plans with your movements. Cleo said we should look for a Kwai Hong ship. And sure enough, this one matched. All we had to do was track it until it was out of Lunar space, and pop out in front of it." Rabbit grinned. "Cleo was great. The way she handled Wu, you'd think she did this every day."

"I heard it from this end. Thanks for coming for me."

"Sure, Zack. But we wouldn't give up on you. You gotta know that."

I nodded as the last of the neural blocks faded and I almost crumbled with renewed pain. "I have another job for you. Do you think you can slice the AI and computer systems on this ship?"

He smiled wickedly. "Piece of cake, especially if I get the admin code."

Deuce placed the business end of his pulse rifle behind Wu's ear. "Give it to him."

Wu rattled off a string of numbers and letters.

"Got it," Rabbit said, punching the code into his virtual keyboard. "What do you want me to look for?"

"Anything we can use to link Wu to Jones. Any contracts or agreements that mention embryo production for the Feds. And look for any employment records or contracts naming Amber Walenska."

"The girl from Mikey's datachip? What's she got to do with this?"

"Just do it, Rabbit. I'll explain if you find anything." He rolled off toward the bridge. My back screamed as I straightened.

"Zack, stop being an ass and get into the autodoc," said Cleo.

"I'm okay, damn it. There's not much time. I'm betting the AI got off a distress call to Kwai Hong One as soon as you forced them to heave to. They'll want to keep the Feds out of this, but Kwai has armed ships of his own. We need to find something we can use against them."

"Like kidnapping and torture aren't enough?" she said.

210

"And he can charge you with piracy. Who do you think the Feds will back in that pissing contest?"

Wu laughed. "You're wasting your time. Nothing you find by vandalizing my ship can harm me. Unless you release me and leave this ship immediately, you are all dead."

"Shut up," said Cleo.

"You in particular should be concerned, Ms. Lee. I am immune from any prosecution. Can you say the same?"

Cleo spun on her heel and lashed out with a backhand that rocked Wu's head and knocked him to the deck. He lay on his back, smiling coldly, but said nothing more.

"Zack?" Rabbit's voice sounded strained over my link. "I think I found what you were looking for, but there's a lot of other stuff here, too. Really bad stuff."

"You found the pictures of Amber?"

"Those and others. A regular freak show. Wu's in enough of the pictures to prove he did this to her, but that's not what I meant. There's a lot of stuff about the embryo cloning and a long contract with the Feds. But there's something else I've never seen before. Check your link. I'm downloading a copy."

I accessed my download file. Rabbit had flagged the document. It was a single page, two brief paragraphs with the official seal of the President of the Federal Republic of Earth and Mars under a slash of a signature. I read the words.

"How the hell did you get this?" I asked Wu.

"What is it, Zack?" Cleo asked.

I read it aloud. "'The office of the President extends to Kwai Chang Wu an unconditional pardon for any and all past or future criminal acts. This pardon is irrevocable except at the discretion of the President.' He's got a get out of jail free pass."

"I told you that you were wasting your time," Wu said.

I turned to Rabbit. "Send everything to Sylvia. Have Wu's AI authenticate it, and then wipe its brain. Encrypt

211

the stuff about Amber and the other girls. Maybe we can get someone at the BPS to look at it. We need to clear out before more of Kwai Hong's goons show up."

"You want the stuff on Jones, too?"

"Take it all." I pointed to the bound guards next to Wu. "Cleo, get back to the *Profit* with these three. We'll drop them at Tranquility Outpost with a homing beacon and enough air to last until the search and rescue guys can pick them up. By that time we should be halfway to the Belt."

"We're running?" she asked.

"You have a better idea? With his fancy pardon he can thumb his nose at kidnapping and put us in the dock for piracy."

Wu laughed at me. "Go ahead, run. If the Feds don't get you, Jones will."

My shoulders slumped. I was tired and in pain and I knew we probably didn't have a chance in hell. The only way out that I could see was to try to find something in Wu's files that I could trade to Jones for protection. Cleo stared at me for a second, and then nodded.

Wu must have guessed my plans.

"Not even Jones can hide you," he said.

"We're not through yet, Wu," I said. "Mikey knew what you were doing here and you had him killed, but I'm a tougher target. Do the Feds know about your 'artwork'? Maybe they won't be so keen on your blanket pardon if they know what you're doing with it."

"The President will maintain a degree of plausible deniability," Wu replied. "But they care more about a steady supply of augmentable embryos than what happened to a few tunnel sluts. They know the raw material for their embryos has to come from somewhere."

Deuce's pulse rifle barked with a sizzling crack.

Wu's expression changed from smug to surprised as he stared down at the hole in the center of his chest. His eyes glazed over and he fell face-down on the deck.

Deuce looked me in the eye, daring me to say something. "For Mikey and Amber," he said, and lowered the rifle. He rolled Wu over with a foot. "Pardon revoked."

"What's happening?" Rabbit asked over the link.

"Not now..."

"But we've got company. A police cruiser on a parallel course. It's the *Federales*. They're hailing us."

CHAPTER TWENTY-TWO

I stared down at Wu. Even dead, he was trouble. I'd been a step behind since that first day at the casino, and now I had another handful of bodies to explain. My back was on fire, my head throbbed with each heartbeat and the last thing I needed was another visit with a Federal magistrate. Especially since it was clear that the illegal embryo program went all the way to the top of the system. I'd never see the outside of a jail cell—assuming I'd live that long.

My first impulse was to run for it. We could get back to the *Profit* and hightail it away at maximum speed. We didn't have the firepower to outgun the *Federales*, but *Profit* had the legs to outrun almost any ship in existence. If we could reach the Belt, they'd never catch us.

I almost called Sylvia to tell her to get ready to run, but found I couldn't. Someone had to step up and end this. Mikey had died trying to do right by Amber Walenska. Metternich was dead because Jones and Wu saw through his mad dream, to the seat of real power. The Feds were no better than Jones and his gang. They'd found a willing accomplice in Wu and bought him off with a nod and a wink at his perverted art form. I'd put my toe in this swamp when I took Wu's contract. It was time to dive in headfirst and sink or swim.

"What do I tell them, Zack?" Rabbit asked.

"Patch them through to my link. Did you wipe the ship's AI?

"Not yet. Do you want me to do it now?"

"No." I breathed a small sigh of relief. "We'll need to convince the Feds Wu's files are genuine. I need you to arrange a little show and tell; Wu's deal with Jones, the Federal contract to produce embryos, the blanket pardon, and Wu's art collection; all of it."

"Sure, Zack. You want to talk to the Feds now?"

"Patch them through." Half a second later, the comm light blinked in the lower corner of my right visual field. "This is Zachariah Mbele," I said. "Captain of the free trading vessel *Profit*. We are in freefall space and conducting legitimate business. By what authority are we being detained?"

"Cut the crap, Zack," Hank's voice sounded tired. "What the hell are you doing aboard Kwai Chang Wu's private yacht?"

"Hank? How did you find me?"

"I planted a tracker in that empty box we searched on your ship, day before yesterday. Figured you were meeting Wu when you lifted a few hours back. Now tell Wu to answer his hail and heave to."

I looked down at Wu's body. "Sorry Hank. Wu's not able to talk right now."

"Why not?"

"Is this a secure channel?" I asked.

"Yes. Why?"

"You the only one listening?"

"No, damn it," Hank said. "What the hell is going on, Zack."

"Give me a secure channel, just you and me, and I'll tell

you."

"You're in no position to bargain here."

I sighed. "No, maybe not. I'm asking you to trust me. There's stuff you need to see and hear."

There was a long pause. I could almost see Hank rubbing his scalp as he considered what to do. "Everybody off the comm," he said. "Private conversation here." He paused again. "Ok, your move. Talk to me."

"Wu's dead. So is Talafofo. Jones sold me out to Wu. I welshed on the deal I made with him back at the Golden Moon and he wanted my hide, literally."

"Your body count is getting out of hand," Hank complained. "Talafofo I could pass, but you can't kill the son of the second richest man in the solar system and expect me to look the other way. Open your docking port. We're coming aboard. And make sure Deuce behaves himself. I've got to take you in, Zack."

"Hold on, Hank. I said there was stuff you needed to see. Wu was into some bad shit. Stuff you won't believe unless you see for yourself. Some of it involves the government. I need you to come over here alone and see this. If you still want to take me in after that, I'll keep Deuce under control."

"I won't insult you by asking if you mean to keep me as a hostage. You know BPS policy on that anyway. But what makes you think I can bend the rules for you? My God, Zack! We're talking about the Kwai family here."

"Don't you think I know that? You're my last chance, Hank. It's all I can do to keep from firing up my drive and making a run for the Belt. Please, just take a look at what we found here."

I don't know if it was what I said, or the very real tone of desperation in my voice, but something got through to him. After a few moments, he let out an exasperated sigh. "All right, if it's that damned important to you. But don't even think about doing a runner. We've got half a dozen guns trained on you."

"Don't worry Hank. I won't make you shoot me."

He just grunted and signed off. I turned to Deuce and Cleo. Rabbit rolled in from the command center and stopped beside Cleo. "Hank will be here in a minute," I said. "Whatever happens, this is down to me, understand? You three just came along for the ride."

"Bullshit, LT," said Deuce. "I ain't backing down. Wu deserved to die."

Cleo glared at me. "You're going to throw it all away, aren't you?" she said. "Never mind that we all knew what we were getting into. This is all Zack Mbele's show. You never thought to ask us.

"Well let me tell you something. None of us are going to let you get away with that. Rabbit and Deuce both insisted on coming to get you. If I'd refused they'd have tied me up, taken the ship, and come anyway. I could have had the ship free and clear, been my own woman. But, no! You had to go and get yourself kidnapped and force the rest of us to come get you. And now you think you're going to flush it all over a dead girl and a bunch of illegal embryos? Forget it! We're here and we stand together, and that's it."

Hank stepped through the docking port as Cleo wound down. "Am I interrupting something?"

Cleo gave him a hard stare. Hank held up his hands in mock surrender, then caught sight of Wu's body—and Deuce's pulse rifle.

"Your handiwork again, Zack?" he asked.

"I killed him," growled Deuce, lifting the pulse rifle.

I put a hand on his arm. "Down, boy." I winced as the movement sent another wave of pain up my shoulder. "I made a deal with Hank. Told him you'd behave yourself."

"Funny thing about your ship, Zack," Hank said as he glanced around. "The tracker works fine, but our Nav and Targeting AI can't see you; insists there's only one ship here. Had to aim our guns at the signal from the tracker I stuck on the cargo box in your hold." He looked to Rabbit.

"You the magician? Is that why those goons tortured you?"

Rabbit shrugged but didn't answer.

Hank turned to me. "What did you want to show me?" he asked, keeping a wary eye on Deuce.

I turned and lifted the back of the loose shirt Cleo had draped over my wounds.

He exhaled sharply. "Wu did this?" he asked.

I let the shirt fall—a mistake. It felt like sandpaper on my torn flesh—and turned to face him. "He was just getting started when Cleo and the boys showed up. I was about to be his latest art project."

"Art?" Hank raised an eyebrow.

"Rabbit," I said, "start the show and tell."

Rabbit rolled to his the left, and activated the holoprojector he'd brought in from Wu's 'art room.' Amber's picture from Mikey's file filled the matrix. Hank gasped as it was replaced by Wu's study in mutilation. Image after image flicked through the matrix. Cleo turned away and retched. Even Deuce blanched, gripping the pulse rifle so hard his knuckles turned white. Hank stood rigidly, watching.

The pictures of mutilated women were followed by the contracts between Wu and Jones, between Wu and the Feds and finally the blanket pardon. The holoprojector flicked off. No one spoke.

I broke the silence, speaking to Hank. "Wu wanted me to steal a cargo container from the *Grant*. It was Jones' share of the embryos. Wu was behind on production and didn't have enough for both Jones and the Feds. He planned to tell Jones the container was stolen and then give the embryos to the Feds. I think he ultimately planned to pay Jones off, but just didn't have enough product to go around.

"Somehow Jones got wind of the double-cross. While Deuce and I were snatching the container, Jones kidnapped Cleo and used her to force us to give him the embryos."

"I'm surprised anyone could get the drop on Cleo," Hank said wryly.

"Jones has hired himself an assassin, a guy named Adam Recker," I went on. "He could take down almost anyone."

"And what's so special about these embryos?" Hank asked. "Why would the government give Wu a secret contract to make them on Ceres, rather than at Ulan Bator?"

"What do you know about the experiments on prisoners in the Bear?"

Hank looked uncomfortable. "Look Zack, we've been through this before. I watched out for the cell block. I didn't have the clearance to know what happened in the 'tank rooms. They just left guys like me to pick up the pieces after the prisoners came back."

"But you never asked, did you, Hank?" I said. "You kept your head down and did your job, and never asked. I'll tell you what went on in those rooms. Metternich put thousands of us into the biotanks, trying to juice up our nervous systems with nanofibers. Most died in agony. But a few, like me, came out with a stable bond between their own nerves and the nanos.

"He found out that there was a specific combination of genes that allowed a stable bond. Those embryos are the fruits of all those deaths. They're created from the girls in Wu's picture gallery, girls chosen for Wu by Colin Jones because they had the right combination of genes. Wu bred them like cattle, and then carved them up when he had enough of their eggs for breeding. Metternich's price for the genetic code was a share of the embryos. He wanted to bring back the Revolution. But Wu and Jones had their own ideas."

"Metternich?" Hank frowned. "Metternich's dead. You said so yourself."

"He is now," I said, pointing to the container that had served as my prison. "His body's in that container. Since the Reunification, he's been hiding out with Jones as his chief of security."

"You're telling me that Metternich is Henry Middleton?"

Hank rubbed his scalp for a moment. "Shit! It actually makes sense. Jones' security has tightened up in the last few years, and nobody believed Middleton had the juice to be responsible. He'd always been a small-time operator before hooking up with Jones." Hank paused. "Did you kill him, too?"

"No. Jones had Recker do it as soon as Metternich verified that the embryos were the real thing. I suppose he wanted me dead too, but Recker couldn't pass on the chance to make a few yuan. He sold me to Wu. Recker's the tall guy from Rabbit's place. He also killed Mike Finney."

"What's Finney's connection to Jones and Metternich?"

"None that I know of," I said. "Mikey and a burned out juicer named Tobias Harding found out about Wu's artwork while Mike was looking for Amber Walenska. I don't know what Mike's interest was in Amber. She was from the Belt, so I suspect he knew her family. Maybe he was doing them a favor, trying to find the girl.

"Anyway, Wu wanted them dead and Recker took the contract as a side job. He's a freelancer, follows the money. He killed Mikey at Rabbit's place and got Harding in a pod-flop in Lower Conrad."

Hank exhaled through pursed lips and rubbed his scalp. "Look, Zack, I understand how you feel about Wu. Hell, I'd want him dead myself. You could even say it was self-defense. But that's a question for the law. A proper trial in a proper court, not gundeck justice." He looked down at the body on the floor. "Damn! We've been trying to get Wu for the better part of two years. Why couldn't you have told me what was going on? We could have set up a sting when he made the trade for the container."

"Wouldn't have made any difference, Hank. Didn't you see the pardon? 'Any and all past or future criminal acts' it said. No matter what kind of case you put together, he'd get off and you'd be walking a beat in Freetown." I flashed the pardon up on the matrix and pointed at the signature.

"Look at it, Hank. This goes all the way to the President. They're willing to give Wu a pass on anything, as long as they get those embryos. Gundeck justice is the only kind that Amber and the others are going to get."

"What do you want me to do about it?" Hank demanded. "I'm a Lieutenant in the BPS, not a politician."

"Step up, like you did in Bruneault. Like you did after the Reunification. Take the embryos to someone in the government who can use them to stop all this."

"With Wu dead, there's no one to corroborate the contracts. Without the embryos, it won't go anywhere." Hank shook his head. "Sorry, Zack, but I can't sit on this. I have to report Wu's death, at least."

"So report it," I said. "But leave us out of it. You followed the tracker signal here and found Wu and his buddies dead. Rabbit can erase any trace of us on this ship. We'll take these three," I pointed to Wu's surviving men, "somewhere where they can't call for help for a while. The *Profit* was never here. Your own AI will swear to it."

"So you disappear, and I'm left holding this bag of shit?"

"For a little while. Meanwhile, I call Jones. By now Recker has told him I'm dead. That should get him to take my call. Then I show him the contracts with Wu and the names of all the girls he shipped from the Belt to Wu's lab. That should get him to meet with me." I held up a hand as Hank started to interrupt. "I get him to meet me at a place I feel safe. I offer a trade—the contracts and names for safe passage to the Belt and enough money to disappear. I'll keep the tracker on the *Profit* so you can keep an eye on me. Jones makes the trade. You swoop down and pick him up."

"And the embryos? They're still out there. What's to stop another one of Metternich's boys from taking up the mantle and carrying on?" Hank asked.

"That was never Jones' plan. He used Metternich to get the embryos. Why? I don't know. My guess is, he plans to use them to blackmail the Feds into guaranteeing him a safe haven in the Belt. Maybe give him more control over Tharsis. If you have Jones, he'll make a deal. If it's a choice between the embryos and his own skin, he'll talk."

Hank rubbed his scalp again. "Putting Jones away, even for a little while would be a big win for the BPS," he said, thinking out loud.

"It wouldn't hurt your career, either," Cleo added, speaking up for the first time. "Listen to him, Hank. Zack's right. Someone has to expose this, if only to do right by those girls."

"I don't see the President standing up for Wu now that he's dead," I said. "He'll want to make the whole thing go away. Jones may do more time than you think."

"And if anyone's going down for killing Wu," said Deuce. "It's gonna be me."

Maybe it was the prospect of trying to arrest Deuce, or maybe Cleo's plea for the dead girls did it. In the end, Hank agreed. Rabbit wiped Wu's AI; not only was there no record of the *Profit*, there was nothing left except the base personality program.

Hank took copies of all the files, and we undocked from Wu's ship, leaving the BPS to clean up. Hank planted a tracker under the skin of my forearm. I let Hank think he was in control, but my nanos accessed the tracker immediately, and could turn it off any time. In truth, I didn't know what I was doing. I was just trying to stay alive.

Once we were undocked, and Rabbit and I were in the cockpit, I consulted Sylvia. "What's our best time to Tycho?"

"Four hours at nine-point-five G, Zack," she replied. "Faster if you want to push the inertial dampers."

"Do whatever it takes to get us there in two hours."

"Okay, Boss, but don't blame me if we burn out an induction coil."

"Just do it," I said. "Rabbit, if I want to send a message and make it seem like it's coming from Wu's ship, can you set it up?"

"Sure, Zack. I have the comm codes. Anything we send tagged with them will look like it came from Wu."

"Good. Get me through to Colin Jones."

Rabbit paled. "Jones? You don't want to talk to him. We're in the clear. Let's head for the Belt."

"Can't do that, Rabbit. There's nowhere we can run that either the Feds or the Dragons can't find us. Now get me Jones, and make it look like I'm still on Wu's ship."

"Okay ..." he said doubtfully. "I'll set up a false location through Sylvia's com link, but with Wu's recognition code. Then I'll insert a fake backdrop behind you; make it look like you're in Wu's command center. Of course that'll take—"

"Just do it. I don't need to know how."

He nodded and set to work.

"Ready, Zack," he said a minute later. "Just touch the comm screen and the call will go through."

I straightened up, squared my shoulders and touched the screen. A second later, it lit up with the image of a very pretty young woman in a plain dark-green business suit.

"Cymru Investments," she said, sweeping her eye over me. "How may I help you?"

"Mr. Jones, please," I said.

"I'm sorry; he's unavailable at the present time. If you'll leave a locus and—"

"Listen, sweetie," I said, being deliberately crude. "You tell your boss that Zack Mbele is calling, and he has exactly thirty seconds to get on the line before I call the Feds. Get the name right: Mbele—and tell him Recker made a big mistake. He'll understand."

She looked doubtful, but put me on hold. A swirling red and green logo filled the screen. Exactly twenty-five seconds later it was replaced by Colin Jones' frowning face.

"Damn, Zack!" he said. "You're a hard man to kill."

"Nice to see you again, too, Colin," I said. "Wu's dead. So's his best gun, Vincent. Recker sold me to Wu instead of killing me himself. Big mistake."

"Where the hell are you?" he asked.

"On Wu's ship. I don't have much time. Kwai Hong ships are probably on their way right now. Things got messy, and I'm sure the AI sent a distress call. Likely bring the Feds in, too."

"Then you're in a world of hurt, Mate," he laughed. "Why are you calling me?"

"Because I have a bunch of pictures of once-pretty girls that Wu used as seed stock for those embryos—and then turned into human sushi."

His eyes narrowed warily. "And why should I care about that?"

"Because you supplied the girls. Recruited them from the Belt, or from your brothels in Tharsis, set them up with phony contracts as 'entertainers' and sent them off to Wu. He kept copies of the contracts. And you knew damned well what was really going on."

The sudden shift of his eyes and slight hunch of his shoulders told me I was right.

"What do you want?" I had to admire his control. His tone was mild and neutral, as if he were asking the price of a pair of shoes.

"Safe passage to the Belt and enough money so I don't have to worry about hauling freight anymore." I grinned. "Three quarters of a million would be a good start. Who knows, Colin? I might even end up working for you."

"How do I know the Feds won't come knocking once they search Wu's ship? Won't they find the same things on its AI?"

"No fear, Colin," I said. "Eddie the Rabbit is with me. You know, the guy you sent Recker to torture because he tried to welsh on you? He's good enough to wipe the AI clean. I'll have the only copies of those files. I'll trade them for cash and a Dragon IFF code for the *Profit*."

"Send them on, then. I'll transfer the money wherever you say and upload the code to your AI."

I shook my head. "No deal. We meet in person. I take the money in cash and we test the IFF code together."

He thought for a moment. "Where do we meet? Tharsis?"

"No. And not at Cymru either. Someplace public, but out of the way. I'm radioactive right now. The Feds will be looking for me."

He laughed harshly. "What's the matter, Zack? Scared?"

"You bet. You're a snake, Colin—poisonous and deadly—but you're my only option outside a federal prison or an 'unfortunate accident during arrest.'"

"How about that dive next to the spaceport?" he suggested. "The Booby or some such."

I smiled. "The Blue Booby. Yeah, that'll do. It'll take me about six hours to get there. Say we meet at 03:00, Lunar Time."

"I'll see you then." He reached out and broke the connection.

"Sylvia," I said. "Send a tight-beam laser to Hank. Tell him about the meeting. Tell him to keep his boys well back and wait for my signal. The Dragons are smart; any whiff of cops will queer the whole deal."

"On it, Boss."

"Rabbit, did you take the scrambler from Wu's ship, or can you build me a new one quickly?"

His face lit up. "Sure, Zack. Piece of cake. I'll just take a broadband comm unit and—"

I held up my hand. "Rabbit," I said, as gently as I could, "I don't need the details. No one cares how you work it, as long as it works."

He grinned. "Oh, it'll work all right." He turned and rolled along the catwalk toward the salon.

I eased myself out of the command couch and stood, holding the bulkhead to steady my wobbling legs. "Fire up the autodoc, Sylvia. I need a little repair work."

"Yes, Zack," she said, her voice soft and loving. "Let me take care of you."

CHAPTER TWENTY-THREE

The autodoc finished with me just as Sylvia set the *Profit* down in her berth at Tycho spaceport. With the heavy doses of protein, anti-inflammatories and blood substitute that had been pumped into me, I felt better than I had in days. I flexed my back, feeling some tightness in the new skin there, but no pain.

Deuce and Cleo were waiting for me in the salon. Rabbit rolled in from the cockpit a few seconds later.

"What's the plan, LT?" asked Deuce.

"We've got a four-hour jump on Jones," I said. "I figure he'll try to be early to the meeting, but not much more than a half hour or so. He won't want to attract attention by fielding a lot of muscle for very long. The authorities might get curious and crash the party. We need to beat him to the Booby and meet him on our terms."

"You think he'll try to double-cross you again?" asked Cleo.

"I'm counting on it."

She frowned. "Then why are we doing it this way?

Wouldn't it be better to hole up here, tell the cops about the meeting and let them handle Jones?"

"Unless they catch him with the files, there won't be anything to hold over him. I need to make him involve himself in a conspiracy to hide evidence before Hank can put the squeeze on him." I shrugged. "Besides, this is personal now. He tried to kill me. He stood by while Wu killed Amber and the other girls, and he sent Recker to torture and kill Rabbit."

"A vendetta? This is too important for settling scores."

"No!" I said, a bit too loudly. I took a breath and continued. "No, Cleo, it's not. Once this is over, the only thing we have to give us any juice on the street is reputation. People know we get the job done, no matter what, and we don't get pushed around. Jones knows it. That's why he'll try to kill me. Otherwise he loses face on the street."

She sighed that exasperated sigh of hers, but didn't argue.

Rabbit cleared his throat tentatively. "Um, Zack? What do you want me to do?"

"I want you on communications and jamming. I don't want Jones or any of his people to be able to call for reinforcements once the meeting starts, but we need to be able to signal Hank when the time comes."

"No problem. I can handle that."

"Good." I turned to Deuce. "You're on weapons. I want as much firepower as we can carry."

Deuce grinned. "On it, LT."

I looked at Cleo. She was still angry, but nodded. "I know. I'm with Deuce, and I watch the back door once things go down. I've been here before. I know what to do."

"I know you do. Everyone get a little rest. We'll leave in an hour."

The others filed from the salon to make their preparations. I sat for a few moments, trying to settle my nerves. As long as Jones was alive, there would be no safety for us. It didn't matter what kind of case Hank might put together; Jones would be just as dangerous in prison as he was walking the Promenade. I knew what I'd have to do.

Sylvia interrupted my thoughts with a chime on my link. "What is it, Sylvia?"

"I'm not sure, Boss," she said. "There's a message for you from a public net link. The only thing it says is 'Tharsis seventeen' and then a com locus. Do you know what it means?"

My mouth went dry. Only one person besides Deuce knew the significance of those words. 'Tharsis seventeen' was the code designation of the insurgent cells Deuce and I had recruited during the run up to the Revolution. There was one only other person who knew that code: the man who'd given it to us.

I activated the com locus with my link.

"Colonel?"

"Yes, Zachariah." His voice was unmistakable; his tone light, almost teasing. "Things are not always what they seem. I have my own resources outside of Jones' organization."

"The inspection booth," I whispered, seeing again the Colonel step into the booth and someone in a p-suit with an opaque visor step out a few minutes later. I hadn't actually seen his face after that, and his voice could have been relayed over any radio link.

"Yes, Zachariah, the booth. Leaders throughout history have used doubles in situations they deemed overly mundane or dangerous."

"Who was the man Recker killed?" I asked.

"A loyal Martian. His name would mean nothing to you. It will be remembered by his friends. And you; are you well? When I learned that Adam had turned you over to Wu, I feared for your safety."

"Sure you did," I said, bitterly. "Your double was supposed to kill me after he confirmed the embryos were delivered."

"Nothing personal, Zachariah," he said. "If I couldn't be

228

sure of your loyalty, I had to be sure of your silence."

I swallowed the fear that rose in the back of my throat. "So what now, Colonel?" I asked. "What do you have in store for me?"

"You've done well, Zachariah. The loss of the embryos and the resources of the Dragons are setbacks, but worth it to have Wu out of the picture. If you are here, then I can safely assume he is dead, correct?" I didn't answer him.

"No matter," he went on. "He was a vile creature, and my hold on him was tenuous once he obtained that pardon. The secret of integrating the genetic code with the proper nano-protein is mine alone, as the Federal authorities will soon discover, to their great distress." He paused. "But that isn't what you're asking, is it?"

"No, it isn't."

"Have no fear, Zachariah," he said pleasantly. "You may still prove valuable to me. And even if you discuss this conversation with your friend Lt. Boucher, my association with Jones is over. I am already beyond the reach of the BPS. Insuring your silence is no longer necessary."

"What will you do now, Colonel?" I asked.

"Goodbye, Zachariah," he said. "Stay well."

"Colonel, wait—"

But he was gone. I felt a chill in the pit of my stomach.

* * *

An hour later, we loaded Rabbit's chair on the back of the scooter. Deuce had rigged it with a pressure bubble. He'd also emptied the weapons locker. He carried his pulse rifle with a dozen extra power packs, two 9mm pneumatics and an honest-to-god crossbow. Cleo opted for her stun batons, a long-barreled Smith and Wesson needler, and a bandolier of extra magazines, all black: cyanide tipped. Even Rabbit was packing a Huang pneumatic and several boxes of ammunition for the other weapons. I eyed Deuce's crossbow.

"What?" he asked. "I got a good deal on it at the Freetown street market."

I shrugged and climbed into the Scooter. Deuce closed the pressure bubble around us, checked the seals and depressurized the ship's cargo bay.

The ride across the yard to the commercial spaceport lock took only a few minutes. Deuce parked the scooter in a public stall near the lock, and we loaded the extra gear onto Rabbit's chair. We walked the half-kilometer to the alley.

The Booby was still crowded when we arrived at a little after one. Loud music spilled out onto the alley, and several drunken tunnel-riggers clustered by the door. They scurried off after a hard look from Deuce.

Few of the bar patrons noticed that we were armed to the teeth, and those who did slid unobtrusively toward the exit. Vassa looked up from behind the bar and frowned. Deuce walked up to him and grabbed him by the back of the neck. I couldn't hear over the music from the show stage, but words were exchanged and Deuce flashed a weapon. Vassa nodded his head vigorously and pointed toward a door near the stage.

Deuce released him and turned back to me. "Jones reserved the room behind the stage for a private meeting. Called Vassa about an hour ago and set it up. Told him to send us back there when we got here."

"Is he in there already?" I asked.

Deuce shook his head.

"Vassa says he hasn't shown yet. Back door is locked, so I don't think he snuck in ahead of us."

"Good. You and Cleo work the room. Look for any hint of Dragons in the crowd." Deuce nodded. I looked to Rabbit. "Rabbit, I need eyes outside that back door."

"No problem, Zack. Give me ten minutes and I'll have full vision plus infrared and motion sensors." He rolled off toward the back room.

I made my own circuit of the bar, but saw nothing unexpected; just the usual mixture of working people, grifters, pimps and hustlers. Rabbit returned and gave me a thumbs-up. I signaled Deuce to watch the front, and gestured for Cleo to follow me and Rabbit to the back room.

The space was large enough for private meetings or dining, though the dirt on the floor told me it hadn't been used for either in a long time. In the back wall, offset from the entrance, a thick door led to the outside. A round table with six chairs occupied the center of the room, and there was a serving counter or bar set along the wall to the right. Behind the bar was a small alcove for food preparation, now dusty from lack of use. Rabbit had set up a tiny monitor screen behind it, out of sight from both doors.

"I've got visual on the back of the building, the front door and the show stage," he said. "And I can switch between visible spectrum and infrared on any of the outer pick-ups. There's a motion sensor on the back door as well. I can feed all of it directly to your link if you want it."

"Good job. Keep an eye on the screen for me."

"When do you think they'll come?" Cleo made a quick survey of the room, getting a feel for its dimensions.

I checked the time. "Soon. Jones will want to put his goons in position at least a half hour before he expects us." I called Deuce on the link. "Look sharp, Deuce. Everything Jake out there?"

"Golden. Got me a cozy spot where I can watch the door and keep an eye on Vassa in case he turns stupid and tries to warn Jones."

"Rabbit's got the front and rear covered," I said. "He'll give you a heads-up when Jones shows."

Deuce grunted in reply and signed off.

I pulled out one of the chairs and sat facing the door to the main room. Cleo turned out the lights and settled behind the small bar to wait. The only light was a faint glow from Rabbit's monitor, filtering around the corner from his alcove.

I used the nanos to shift my vision into infrared. The outlines of the doors, the table and chairs leapt out. I could see Cleo, crouched behind the bar. I shifted my chair so the light from the door wouldn't illuminate me the moment it opened.

Rabbit spoke a few minutes later. "Showtime, Zack. I've got four men at the back door. They're armed, and look like they're taking firing positions about ten meters away. Four more in the alley out front, and Jones is heading for the front door with that tall freak."

"Okay," I said, settling the chair near the wall. "Keep an eye on the guys out back. Send the feed from the interior cameras to me so I can keep track of Jones."

My eye camera flickered and stabilized into an image of Jones and Recker, walking through the crowd at the front of the bar. Recker carried a large black duffel bag over his left shoulder. It looked full. Jones walked calmly toward us. Vassa stared straight ahead. In the shadows across from him, I could just make out a bulky form that had to be Deuce.

Jones and Recker passed Vassa without looking at him, and headed our way. Vassa glanced around nervously—realizing, perhaps, what Jones would do to him when he found us waiting in the room. Vassa edged left as Jones reached the end of the bar and turned toward the show stage. He called out, but his voice must have been drowned out by the music, because he raised an arm and waved at Jones. He stepped toward the end of the bar, then froze as a steel crossbow bolt slammed into his chest.

Vassa staggered, then crumpled out of sight behind the bar. Deuce crossed to the bar quickly and vaulted over the top, crouching out of sight for a few seconds. He stood up, picked up a rag and casually wiped down the bar top. No one looked at him twice.

The camera lost Jones and Recker as they passed the stage. Half a second later, the door swung open and a shaft of neon light fell across the table in front of me. I tensed, but remained in the shadows.

Jones stepped inside, followed by Recker. "Toss the bag over there and see if you can find the lights," said Jones.

The duffel hit the floor with a thud. Recker stepped past Jones, feeling along the wall until he found the panel. The lights came up and he froze as Cleo shoved a needler into his face. I heard a faint whine through my implant; Rabbit's scrambler kicking in.

"Hello, Colin," I said, aiming my Huang pneumatic at him. "Don't move. And, Recker, Cleo's really pissed at you, so I wouldn't give her an excuse to kill you."

Jones made a small move toward the door, but froze again when I shook my head. "Don't try it, Colin. You're not fast enough. Now kick that door shut, slow and easy, and step over to the table."

Cleo eased back a step, out of Recker's reach. "Hands behind your neck, you son of a bitch. Turn around and kneel, ankles together."

Jones glanced at Cleo, but moved to the table as Recker slowly went to his knees.

"Sit down, Colin," I said. "Let's talk."

"Sure, Zack," he said. "No need for guns. We're just here to do business. I brought your money. Seven hundred fifty thousand, all in small used notes. Enough to keep you comfortable for a long time."

"Rabbit," I called. "Check the bag."

Jones pulled out a chair and sat down as Rabbit rolled forward.

"Looks good, Zack," said Rabbit, peering into the duffel. "Of course, unless I count it, I can't be sure of the amount. But it's full of money all right."

"OK. Get back behind the counter and keep an eye on the guys outside." Jones shifted in his chair. "Yeah, Colin,

I know about the boys out back. But hey, I'm sure they're just making sure we're not disturbed, right?"

Jones shrugged. "So I'm careful. You would be too with that much cash." He held up a small disc. "The IFF codes are on here." He tossed the disc to Rabbit. "Now, give me Wu's files and we'll all go home."

"All in good time," I said. I took a data-stick from my pocket and laid it on the table. "First, a few answers. I figured most of it out from the files on this stick, but I want to hear it from you, Colin. Why kill Metternich? You went to a lot of time and trouble to get him off Mars. Why kill him as soon as you had the embryos?"

Jones shrugged again. "He had the goods on Wu. Once I found out what Wu was doing to the girls, Metternich was a liability." He smiled wryly. "Besides, I was sick of his speeches."

"How did you find out?"

"Finney and Harding. Finney was looking for some skirt from the Belt, and turned up Wu's secret art gallery. He got his hands on a data-worm and managed to slice Wu's private network somehow." I could hear Rabbit's sharp gasp at the mention of the data-worm. Jones took no notice. "Finney wouldn't talk. But his buddy Harding, he was stupid enough to call Wu and try to shake him down for ten thousand yuan. Wu laughed him off.

"Then Wu called Recker and took out another contract. Recker took the files Harding had on him and made sure he wouldn't talk about it to anyone else. Once we knew where to look, it wasn't hard to put the pieces together." Jones reached for the stick on the table. He stopped when I twitched my gun at him.

"How did you convince Recker to kill Metternich?" I asked.

"Money," he said with a thin smile. He glanced at Recker. "Ask him yourself. He'd had enough of Metternich's rants, too."

"That so, Recker?" I asked, eyeing him over Jones shoulder. "You sold out the Colonel for cash?"

He glared at me but said nothing.

Jones continued. "So, the man's a professional. Better a man who has a price than a wide-eyed fanatic."

"Just one more thing," I said. "What do you want with the embryos? You were never a true believer like the Colonel. What good are they to anyone but the Feds?"'

"There are people in Ulan Bator who are no friends of the current administration," said Jones. "People who are willing to pay for those embryos."

"Money again, Colin?" I asked. "You'd risk a military takeover of your Belt operations, maybe even Tharsis, for money?"

"We're talking a lot of money, Mate. Enough to buy several small countries. And the political clout to keep the *Federales* out of the Belt forever."

"If your new friends let you keep it," I said.

He grinned. "Let me worry about that. Are we through here?" He reached for the data stick; this time I let him take it.

"Sure, Colin," I said. "We're through here. The files are there. You want to check them? Rabbit can plug the stick into a projector and you can verify them."

"I trust you, Zack. You'd be stupid to try to cross me now."

"Sure you do, Colin." I nodded, still holding the pneumatic on him. "Because this is the way you planned it. You'd sit there and smile and agree to everything, tell me what I want to hear and let me think I had the money. But that would only last until I walked out that door. That's what those boys are for, isn't it, Colin?"

The smile faded from his face and he looked past my shoulder toward the back door.

I raised the gun, pointing it at his forehead. "But that's all changed now because I got here first. Tell me I'm wrong,

Colin. Tell me what's going to happen to the first one to walk out that door."

Jones ground his teeth. A puzzled look crossed his face and he bit down hard.

"Don't bother trying to call your boys. Rabbit's got us covered with a link scrambler." I pressed the barrel against his skull. "So what's it going to be, Colin? Do I kill you right now, or do you take your chances with the boys outside?"

For the first time since I'd known him, real fear flashed in Colin's eyes. "What do you want?" he whispered hoarsely.

"Where are they, Colin—the embryos? I know they're still here on the moon. You haven't had time to move them, and if you'd wanted them on Mars, the delivery would've been at Tharsis."

"Why do you want to know that? They're no good to you."

"Call it curiosity," I said. "You have three seconds. You want me to count like they do in the realies?"

He licked his lips. "No, wait. They're right next door; in the warehouse where the cargo loader is parked."

I pulled the gun away from his head and stepped back. "You just bought yourself a little more time." I gestured toward the back door. "Out. Now. Before I change my mind."

"Wait a minute, Zack. You can't do this."

"No? Did you think twice about sending Recker after Rabbit? Or Metternich? Or me?" I fired a round into the door. The loud ringing clang echoed through the room. "What about now, Colin? What will the boys outside think is going on in here?" I fired again and he started backing toward the door.

"Don't do this, Zack. I can take good care of you. All of your crew, too. There's more money in this than any of us have ever imagined."

"Blood money, Colin. Not for me." I fired into the table top. "Three seconds, Colin."

"Wait!"

I fired again. "Two seconds."

"Zack, stop it." Cleo shouted.

"One second." I aimed the gun at his head. "Or don't you think I have it in me?"

Jones ran to the door and threw it open.

"Don't shoot! It's Jones! Don't—" His shout was cut off by bursts of pulse rifle fire. He staggered back into the room and fell onto the table, blank eyes staring at the ceiling.

I edged up to the door frame and kicked the door closed, locking it.

Cleo stared at me in shock, giving Recker the opening he'd been waiting for. He dove forward and scissored his legs, sweeping Cleo off her feet. Quick as lightning, he spun onto his back and smashed his heel down on her temple. Stunned by the blow, she dropped the needler.

I swung the pneumatic after him, pumping a round into the table top as Recker rolled under it. He grabbed the needler with one hand and wrapped his other arm around Cleo's neck, pulling her on top of his body. He pressed the needler to her throat.

"Stop right there, Mbele," he said.

I held the pneumatic with both hands, aiming at his head.

"Think about it, Mbele," he said. "What was it you once said to me? 'You might get a shot off, might even kill me,' but darling Cleo here will take a needle. Do you want me dead bad enough to kill her too?"

I actually thought about that for a second. Then I stepped back and raised my hands, pointing the gun at the ceiling.

"Put the gun on the floor, slide it toward me and then put your hands on your head."

I did as he said. He kept the needler pressed to Cleo's throat as he got his legs under him. He stood, hauling her to her feet. She shook her head to clear it.

"Now, Cleo and I are going to walk out of here, through the front door if you please." He stepped backwards, taking Cleo with him. "Hold still, darling. There's a black mag in

237

this gun and I wouldn't want to pull the trigger by mistake."

"You're a son of a bitch, Adam," Cleo snarled. "You'd better kill me now, because I'm coming after you."

He smiled. "I'll be looking forward to it," he said into her ear. He kept the needler pressed into her neck as he reached behind his back to open the door.

Rabbit rolled from his alcove holding his pneumatic and shouted, "Duck, Cleo!" He fired twice as Cleo dropped to the floor.

But Rabbit was a lousy shot. Recker dodged to the left and Rabbit's slugs smashed into the door beside his head. Cleo rolled away under the table as Recker turned the needler on Rabbit.

With all the nano enhanced speed and strength I could muster, I dove across the table, grabbed Recker's gun hand, and shoved it upward. Needles stitched a line across the wall a centimeter over Rabbit's head. We crashed into the door. I slammed Recker's hand against the wall, pinning it, wrestling for the needler with both hands. He grabbed at my neck with his free hand, trying for a choke hold, but I tucked my chin and continued to smash his hand against the wall until the gun clattered to the floor.

He twisted his hip into me and brought a knee up into my groin. Pain shot through me. I managed to keep my feet, but he wrenched away and landed a solid punch to my right kidney. I staggered into the wall and he jumped away.

We faced each other, Recker moving catlike toward the back door. Cleo popped up from below the table and barred his way, her stun batons crackling.

"Cleo, don't," I shouted.

Recker's fist lashed out faster than thought, rocking Cleo's head back. Two more blows followed to her chest and abdomen before she could counter, slamming her into the wall. It distracted him just enough.

I flew at him in a flat dive, driving both fists into his face. He spun sideways and I connected with empty air. Cleo slumped against the wall, eyes glazing over.

Fire surged up my spine and flowed into my arms and legs. Time seemed to stop. I could see Cleo's hair flying in slow motion, each strand standing out. Recker seemed to stand still, his eyes half closed in an involuntary blink, a bead of sweat standing out on his forehead.

I tucked into a ball and rolled, turning over in midair. I hit the wall with my feet, pushed off and dropped to the floor. I swept one of Cleo's batons from the floor and crouched facing Recker. He spun on his heel, aiming a roundhouse kick at my head.

I snapped my head back, feeling his shoe tip brush my nose. I swung the baton, but he danced back out of range and pulled a short-bladed palm knife from the heel of his shoe.

I shifted my gaze from his eyes to the knife. The broad three-centimeter blade protruded between the second and third fingers of his clenched fist. He'd aim for my face, trying to gouge an eye or slice my forehead and blind me. We danced and feinted around each other, our movements blurred by the speed of the nanos.

Though I expected it, his thrust nearly caught my right eye. I dodged back and he slashed at my groin. I countered with the baton, but he spun away and aimed a high cut at my neck. I blocked it with my left and the blade sliced into my forearm. Blood spurted across his hand as I forced the blade aside. The knife caught on the baton's handle, twisting it out of my hand. It skittered across the tabletop in a shower of blue sparks.

Recker grinned, thrusting the knife at my abdomen. I grabbed his wrist and turned the blade aside. He hooked a knee behind my leg and shoved me off balance. The back of my head slammed into the wall, but I managed to keep a grip on his knife hand.

Blood ran down my arm and soaked our hands. I could feel my grip slipping as the wet slickness flowed between my fingers. Recker felt it, too and grinned savagely as he pushed harder. The blade crept closer until the point touched my belly, just below my breastbone.

My flesh rebelled at the contact. I didn't survive two years in the Bear to be knifed in the back room of a sleazy bar. My grip on his hand tightened, and I turned the knife to my left as I planted a foot on the wall and spun my body to the side. The blade scraped across my lower ribcage and plunged into the wall.

Using Recker's momentum, I slammed his head into the wall as well. I stepped behind him and caught his neck in a choke hold. My arm was slick with blood. I struggled to hold on as he twisted and bucked.

"Zack!" Rabbit shouted. He tossed Cleo's needler at me. I caught it as Recker broke my grip on his neck. I pressed the needler into his back and fired twice. He stiffened and gasped, then sank to the floor.

I sagged against the table. Rabbit rolled back into his alcove and spoke urgently into his link. Cleo struggled to her feet and leaned against the wall. "Are you okay?" I asked.

"Yeah," she gasped, holding her chest. "Hurts to breathe, but I think I'll live."

A second later, Deuce burst through the front door, pulse rifle leveled. I held up a hand and he stood down.

"Conejo said you needed help." He looked down at Recker. "Guess not."

"What's going on out front, Deuce?" I asked, retrieving my Huang from the table.

"A couple of Dragons are working the room, trying to look casual, but they're setting up to cover the door here. We'll have to shoot our way out if we go through the bar."

I turned. "Rabbit, it's time to get a line to Hank."

"Okay, Zack. On your link in five seconds."

I used the time to check my arm. The bleeding had already stopped.

Hank's voice came over the link. "Zack. What's going on? My troops reported shooting a few minutes ago."

"Everything's golden here, Hank. Jones is dead. His own boys shot him."

"Dead? Damn it, Zack, you weren't supposed to kill anyone! What about the embryos?"

"I know where they are. I also have all of Wu's files and video of my session as one of his projects. Between that and the embryos themselves, you should have enough for the magistrate."

"What's your status?"

"We're holed up in the back room of the Booby, behind the show stage. Better send some troops. Deuce has made at least two gunmen covering the door. Back was covered by four pulse rifles; don't know if they're still there. Be careful, Hank. I don't want to add you to my body count."

He made a rude reply and signed off. In the distance, I could hear the whoop-whoop of a cop siren.

I could feel the whine from the scrambler ease as Rabbit shut it off. Cleo stood and retrieved her needler.

As I watched her move, it occurred to me that I didn't care why she chose to stay, only that she did.

"So much for loyalty, eh, Colonel?" I whispered, smiling grimly.

"Zack?" asked Rabbit." Who were you talking to?"

"No one," I said," Just ghosts." I shivered slightly. Cleo walked over and bent down to open the duffel bag. I pointed the pneumatic at her.

"Get away from the money, Cleo," I said.

"What? Zack what are you doing?"

"Move away from the bag," I ordered. "Do it now."

She stood, frowning. "This isn't funny, Zack. Put that gun down right now."

I raised the pneumatic. "I only want to know one thing. How long were you working for Wu? Was it just for this one job, or does it go back before that?"

She folded her arms. "What the hell are you talking about?"

"You were working with Wu all along. Now answer me. What did he offer you?"

"You're crazy, Zack. Why would you think I'd work for that slimeball?"

I heard the words, but with the nanos I could see the tells. Her pupils dilated, the left side of her mouth turned down and there was a tiny quaver in her voice when she said my name. She was lying.

"Enough lying," I shouted. "You were the one who found out about the rigged tables. But you couldn't be there when I made my play. Some casino employee might have recognized you and blown your story, so you had a 'date.'"

"You're reading too much into—"

"Shut up!" I shouted again. "You set me up to be nabbed by Vincent and Wu. Vincent knew your name the day he delivered the container. I never introduced you, but he knew exactly who you were. And afterwards, you came to my bed and tried to persuade me not to go after Wu."

She glared at me, but kept silent.

"When you found out about Mikey, the first thing you asked was what he had to do with Wu. You knew Wu was looking for Mikey."

Deuce paled. "Cleo?" he said.

I pressed on. "At Mike and Mariko's, the guy you skewered was one of Wu's casino guards. He recognized you. He might have talked, so he had to die. Tell me I'm wrong, Cleo."

"Tell him, Cleo," said Deuce.

Her shoulders slumped. "Deuce...I didn't know Mikey would get hurt."

"What did you think Wu wanted with him?" I demanded. "You could have warned Deuce, or me."

"I could have saved him, Cleo." Deuce's voice was an anguished whisper.

Cleo hung her head. "I didn't know, Deuce. I thought

Adam was working with the authorities. I thought we'd take Wu down before anything could happen to Mikey."

I stepped forward, pressing the gun to her head. "What did he offer you? What was your price to sell us out?"

"It wasn't like that, Zack. Wu just wanted to get you to do a job. I told him you wouldn't do it, but he said he had leverage. He just wanted a meeting. Then Adam approached me and said he'd take Wu down. That there was a big reward in it from TransAstral."

"What was your price, Cleo?" I snarled, the gun now shaking in my hand.

She flinched away from the pneumatic. "The ship!" she shouted. "He guaranteed me ownership of the *Profit*. Once you told me what the job was, I figured it wouldn't matter. If you succeeded, we'd have the ship. If not, I'd end up owning it outright. Either way we'd be safe."

"We? You mean you. I'd be out and you'd own everything."

"No, Zack," she said, shaking her head. "I did it for both of us, to give us a chance to build something. If Wu stuck to the deal, *Profit* would have been all yours. I voided the divorce decree and signed my half over to you three days ago."

"Why should I believe that?" I demanded

"It's true. Have Eddie check."

"She's right, Zack," said Rabbit a second later. "Petition of change was filed the day after you saved me from the Dragons."

"Why?" I repeated.

"You know why," she said quietly. "You know."

I gripped the gun tighter. "Tell me."

She shook her head.

"Say it!" I shouted. "If it's worth saving anything we ever had, say it!"

"Because I love you, damn you!" she cried. She fell to her knees next to the duffel, her shoulders and her voice shaking as she cried. "I still love you."

I lowered the pneumatic. It had taken a gun to her head to make her say it, and the prospect of a share in seven hundred fifty thousand yuan didn't hurt—but there it was, finally. For the first time since I'd married her, she said it.

I knelt on the floor and pulled her to my chest, stroking her hair. I glanced up at Deuce. "You okay?"

He nodded. "Yeah. I'll see you at home." And after a second, "You too, Cleo."

He walked over and hefted the duffel bag to his shoulder. "Wouldn't do to have the cops find this here," he said. "Not a bad bit of profit for a few days work, eh?" He turned to Rabbit. "Conejo, are those goons still out back?"

"No, Deuce. They took off right after they shot Jones. There's a BPS fire team working their way around from the front. They'll be out back in about thirty seconds."

"Then let's go, shipmate. No need for all of us to be stuck here when the cops show up."

Rabbit rolled forward, grinning. "Did you mean that, Deuce? Shipmate, I mean?"

"Shut up," said Deuce. "Don't make me regret this."

The whoop of the siren stopped. Through the door, I could see Hank striding across the barroom with a phalanx of uniforms.

I looked at Cleo. She dried her eyes, watching Deuce and Rabbit make their way out the back door. Her gaze never left the duffel.

"Are you ready to talk to the cops?" I asked.

"Yes," she said, taking my arm. I helped her to her feet. "Let's go talk to Hank."

She touched my cheek and gave me her most dazzling smile. I fell into those magical green eyes. And the bright line between ecstasy and despair gleamed brightly behind me as I crossed it once again.

I shook my head. That's just the way it is when you love a woman like Cleopatra Lee.

About the Author

Bruce Davis is a Mesa AZ based general and trauma surgeon. He finished medical school at the University of Illinois College of Medicine in Chicago way back in the 1970's and did his surgical residency at Bethesda Naval Hospital. After 14 years on active duty that included overseas duty with the Seabees, time on large gray boats and a tour with the Marines during the First Gulf War, he went into private practice near Phoenix. He is part of that dying breed of dinosaurs, the solo general surgeon. He also is a writer of science fiction and fantasy novels. His independently published works include the YA novel *Queen Mab Courtesy*, and his military science fiction novel *That Which Is Human*. His nonfiction memoir, *Dancing in the Operating Room*, is a glimpse into the life and training of a Trauma Surgeon. *Glowgems for Profit* and *Thieves Profit* are parts of a continuing series of stand-alone novels about Zach Mbele, former Republic of Mars commando and captain of the fast freighter, Profit. They and his latest work, *Platinum Magic*, his first foray into the world of fantasy, are published by Brick Cave Media. *Platinum Magic* represents the start of an exciting new series set in a surprising modern world, like our own, only different.

Made in the USA
Columbia, SC
05 December 2024

47452112R00139